The UNFORGETTABLE Tales of ADELINE BIGSBY

WHISPERS IN THE FOREST
BOOK 1

ELIZABETH MOWERY

Wild & Free
—PUBLISHING—

To Kalyn Elizabeth High, who was the bravest girl I've ever known. This one is
for you.

Chapter One

Waves crashed against the shore, foaming as they rolled up the beach. The chilly water soaked everything in its path, including Adeline Bigsby's bare feet. She couldn't feel her toes as they sunk into the wet sand.

It was early April in Sunset Beach, North Carolina, and although it was cool in the evenings, Adeline loved that time of year because the swarms of tourists wouldn't arrive for another month. She could enjoy the beach without the flocks of people who overcrowded her small town every year.

Adeline lived a few miles inland and took every opportunity to come to the beach. It wasn't uncommon to catch her jogging down the shoreline or swimming in the ocean.

She had an adventurous spirit and was very active, which was one reason she got along so well with her father, who walked by her side. They had just finished a three-mile run and were heading back to their car before the sun set.

With socks and running shoes in hand, Adeline and Dad stared out at the horizon, inhaling the salty breeze. They were the only ones on the beach watching the sun dip below the waterline. Pink and orange dominated the sky as though a painter had created it just for them. Adeline was sore and a little cold in her running tights and T-shirt, but there was no place she would rather be.

"Are you up for running again tomorrow morning?" Dad asked, his dimples deepening as he smiled down at her.

"You are out of your mind if you think I'm going to wake up early on a Saturday," Adeline said with a laugh.

"Come on. It will be nice to knock out our workout in the morning."

Adeline had always been an athlete and now, as a freshman in high school, Dad had trained her to become an even better one. He was always pushing her to run farther, lift heavier weights, and eat a healthy diet. She could already see a big difference, and so could everyone else on her varsity volleyball team.

"I'd rather sleep."

"And that is why I am faster than you," he said, knocking into her with his shoulder.

Adeline giggled, shivering as a cold wave lapped at her ankles. The sun dipped lower, and she wished the moment could last a little while longer.

"Want to race?" Dad asked, flashing a mischievous expression.

Adeline pushed her long, wavy ponytail over her shoulder and looked toward the car. It was maybe a football field away from where they stood. Despite the weariness in her legs, she smirked. "Sure, but I get a head start."

"I'll give you five seconds."

"Deal."

Adeline stepped away from the sea and slipped into her socks and sneakers as Dad did the same. Tiny grains of sand stuck between her wet toes as she laced up her shoes. There was a slim chance she could win, but it wouldn't stop her from trying.

Once Dad was ready, he stood and gave her a smile. "First one to the car wins. On your mark...get set...*go!*"

Adeline shot off like a cannon, flinging sand in the air as she battled against her aching body. The wind was loud in her ears and bit at her skin, but she didn't slow down.

Pumping her arms, she grinned when she heard Dad's deep laughter behind her.

"Here I come!"

Adeline picked up the pace, locking her gaze on the flapping North Carolina flag that marked the beginning of the boardwalk. She rushed by the sand dunes, her lungs burning as she pushed herself to go faster.

Dad blew past her as she stepped onto the walkway. His shoes knocked against the worn planks as he booked it to the empty parking lot. He didn't slow until he smacked his palm on the hood of their beat-up Jeep Wrangler.

"Victory!" Dad threw both arms high in the air and did a goofy victory dance.

Adeline couldn't help but giggle as she slowed her pace and tried to catch her breath. Her fair skin prickled with heat as she crossed the old boardwalk and stepped into the sandy parking lot. "I almost beat you."

"Not a chance, Addie."

Dad reached into the pocket of his sweatpants and pulled out the keys to the car. Adeline zeroed in on them. She'd had her permit for a while now and wanted to practice driving every chance she could. She was turning sixteen in September, which meant she could get her license if she passed the driver's test. It was still several months away, but she wanted to be prepared.

"Can I drive?" she asked, giving Dad her best puppy-dog face.

The jingling of the car keys was music to Adeline's ears as Dad placed them in her hand. She bolted to the driver's side and unlocked the door. Once inside, she adjusted the seat and mirrors to her liking. Although the light-blue Jeep Wrangler was extremely old and starting to rust, it was perfect for the beach. Sand covered the floor, and the worn seats were proof of their many adventures over the years. The top was always down and since the car could die on them at any moment, they only drove it short distances.

Adeline trembled with excitement as she jammed the keys into the ignition and cranked it. The car engine sprang to life, letting out a loud, heart-rending cry as Dad plopped into the torn passenger seat.

"Let's get home before your mother sends out a search party for us," Dad said.

Adeline laughed. She would never forget the time Mom called the cops when they'd been at a community picnic in the park. She had assumed someone had kidnapped Adeline, only to find out that her oldest daughter had been playing in the nearby woods with friends.

Adeline buckled in and put the car in drive. She placed both hands on the steering wheel before gently pressing the gas pedal. Butterflies fluttered inside her stomach as the Jeep puttered its way through the sandy parking lot surrounded by palm trees and brush.

Tiny stars appeared in the velvety sky as she turned onto the main road. She took a quick right onto another paved street that would lead them home. The breeze blew through the aged car, chilling the sweat on her skin. She pushed a lock of auburn hair out of her eyes. There was something magical about breathing in the fresh, salty air. It revitalized her soul.

The lampposts raced by them, providing small glimpses of light as they made their way home. The road was dark, but Adeline wasn't worried; she had driven that stretch hundreds of times and knew it like the back of her hand. The beach house she'd grown up in wasn't too far away.

Between the breeze, the radio, and Dad harmonizing with the country song, Adeline felt relaxed and at peace as she drove with her favorite person.

Until a deer darted into the middle of the street.

Adeline slammed on the brakes and swerved to avoid the frightened animal. The Jeep's tires squealed as it went off the road.

They missed the deer, but Adeline couldn't avoid the sturdy oak tree.

Metal crunching. A loud bang. Pain slammed into Adeline's face as the airbag slammed into her.

Then the air went still, silent aside from the slight hissing coming from the engine.

Adeline didn't move for a few long moments as the airbag slowly deflated. Finally, she lifted her head. It was pounding, but she didn't feel seriously injured.

She rubbed her forehead with shaking fingers, tears blurring her vision as she looked through the cracked windshield. Clouds of smoke poured from the crumbled hood. The Jeep was totaled.

"Dad." Her voice trembled. "Are you all right?"

No response.

Something was wrong.

Adeline turned her aching head toward the passenger seat, and all the air left her lungs.

Her father's airbag hadn't deployed.

His forehead was planted against the dashboard, and he wasn't moving. A steady stream of blood rolled down his blank face.

A scream erupted from Adeline as she scrambled to unbuckle her seatbelt. Once released from its tight grip, she grabbed Dad's shirt and shook him.

"Dad! Wake up!"

But it was too late.

He was already gone.

Chapter Two

Six Months Later

Rain fell like bullets from the black sky, smashing into the windshield of the old Bronco. Adeline stared out into the darkness, watching the outline of the forest roll by. She was tired of sitting in the crammed vehicle with Mom and Rebecca, Adeline's younger sister. They had been driving nonstop for five hours.

"Are we almost there?" Rebecca asked from the back seat.

"Not too much farther," Mom said, keeping her gaze on the road.

Adeline rolled her eyes. Even the sound of Mom's voice annoyed her.

Two weeks ago, Mom had ruined her sixteenth birthday by breaking the news that they were moving. School had already begun, but it didn't stop Mom from forcing her two daughters to pack up everything they owned and head west to Black Mountain, North Carolina.

Mom was certain the small town outside of Asheville was the perfect place for them to start over since they had family there. Though Adeline had a close relationship with her relatives, she had no desire to live in the mountains. She wanted to go home.

"This is our road," Mom said as she turned right.

The headlights flashed against a small green marker with the words *Pivotal Point Road* stamped across it.

Dense trees stacked the sides of the paved road. It was strange that there were no houses. Adeline wasn't used to seeing so many trees. Where would the deserted road lead them?

The long, empty road confirmed that there were no neighbors. Growing up in a suburban neighborhood, Adeline had enjoyed having her friends around. Clearly, she wouldn't be making friends with the neighborhood kids because there were none.

The only sign of civilization was a gated driveway surrounded by trees. The expensive iron gate swirled to create the letter *M*, and Adeline assumed an extravagant house hid beyond the gate and the trees. Whoever lived there obviously wanted privacy and likely wouldn't be interested in making new friends.

The smooth road turned to gravel, and towering trees shadowed them as the Bronco bounced along the uneven driveway. Holding back tears, Adeline held herself together as Mom stopped in front of an aged house.

"We're here," Mom said in a hushed voice.

The headlights gave them a preview of their new life, and there was nothing nice about it. The house was much smaller than their previous home, with chipping paint and crooked shutters that showed its neglect.

"You cannot be serious." Adeline's mouth hung open in disgust. "That's the house you bought?"

"Watch your tone, young lady."

Adeline smashed her lips together, trapping in the wrath that matched the thunderstorm outside. She had never struggled with anger in the past, but she was a different girl now that Dad was gone—and Mom was her usual target.

The rain continued to pour from above, so they each grabbed a few things before darting through the storm. Adeline double-checked to make sure she had her cellphone in her backpack before jumping out of the passenger's side.

Splashing through the puddles, Adeline raced up the long flight of wobbly steps and waited underneath the covered porch for Mom to open the front door. She was protected from the downpour, but the icy wind cut through her jacket, chilling her to the bone. The October weather felt more like winter.

Why would anyone want to live here?

Mom slid the key into the old lock and pushed on the door. It whined as it gradually opened like a haunted house that had no desire for visitors. She flipped the light switch, awakening the ancient structure from its long slumber.

Adeline rushed inside behind Rebecca. The musky smell instantly annoyed her. So did the dusty old light fixture that was missing half its bulbs.

Mom placed her bag down, shook off the rain from her brown curls, and forced a smile as she looked around the vacant living area. "I know it needs some work, but it will feel like home in no time."

Adeline scanned the ugly wooden panels lining the living room walls and the old brick fireplace that hadn't felt the warmth of a fire in years.

That house would never feel like home.

Everything about it was awful, and the attached kitchen was even worse. She could see the obnoxious apple wallpaper from where she stood, along with worn appliances that needed to be thrown out.

"This place is a dump," Adeline said.

Mom pinched the bridge of her nose. "Would you *please* keep your opinions to yourself, Addie?"

Hearing the nickname her father used to call her triggered something, and she scowled at her mother. She wouldn't let *anyone* call her by her nickname after he died, not even her family or close friends. "Do *not* call me that."

"That used to be the only name you would go by."

"Not anymore."

Tossing her damp backpack on the hardwood floor, Adeline tugged off her wet jacket and threw it on top of her bag before stomping down the tight hallway. Her sneakers squeaked against the floorboards as she entered the first room and flipped on the light. She cringed at the crimson red walls that screamed for attention. Her future bedroom was half the size of her old room, and the repulsive color only added to her frustration as she stormed out. "This house sucks."

It didn't take Adeline long to explore the other bedrooms; they were just as unpleasant as the rest of the house. Nothing homey about them. The house was the best Mom could afford, but Adeline still hated it.

Stepping into the hall bathroom, Adeline examined the tiny room, equipped with only the essentials. The walls were covered in flower wallpaper and there was no window, which made the space seem even more cramped.

Adeline turned to the old-fashioned mirror above the sink and felt a wave of sadness. She didn't recognize the miserable girl staring back at her. The joy that used to be on her pretty face had vanished, drained away with the sparkle of life that once radiated from her deep blue eyes. All she could see in her reflection was pain and anger.

Everything in her life had fallen apart. In that moment, she wished she had died in the accident with Dad instead of facing life without him.

Adeline sniffled and wiped her eyes with her sleeve. She knew she needed to be thankful for what she had, but she always drifted back to what had been taken from her. She didn't want to start over in a new place. She wanted to go back to her old life with Dad. Back when she was happy.

Tears broke through, but Adeline forced them back down. She hated crying, especially with her family around. She saw it as weakness, and weak was the last thing she wanted to be.

Taking a deep breath, she walked down the hallway to the living room. There was a big air mattress in the middle of the bare floor. Mom blew it up for them to sleep on, and Rebecca was already getting herself settled on it.

The mattress bounced a little as Rebecca removed her glasses before tucking her skinny frame under the sheets. Pulling them up to her chin, she closed her weary eyes and rolled over to face the wall.

Adeline couldn't wait to join her. It was well past midnight, and she wasn't only physically exhausted, but mentally drained, too.

The hinges on the kitchen cabinets creaked, and Adeline watched as Mom inspected each one with a sour look on her face. She clearly hated the house just as much as Adeline did, but she would never admit it.

Catching her daughter's stare, Mom closed the dusty cabinet and straightened. Her brown curls bounced above her shoulders as she approached Adeline. She wanted to look strong, but the dark circles under her eyes gave away how fragile she was. So did her skinny physique. She had always been petite, but she'd lost weight since Dad's death and was having a hard time gaining it back.

"You should get some sleep," Mom said quietly. "We have a long day tomorrow."

"I cannot believe you sold our beach house for this piece of crap."

Mom sighed and rubbed her eyes. "Can we please not do this now?"

"I'm *not* living here!"

"I know you're upset with me." Mom folded her arms over her chest. "But you'll thank me for this one day."

"For what?" Adeline shouted, flaring her arms in the air. "Ruining my life?"

"I am trying to make things easier for all of us."

"By forcing us to move here? This is all your fault!"

"You think I wanted to leave our lovely home for this?" Mom's eyes prickled with tears as she gestured to their surroundings. "We are here because of *you*, Adeline! You killed your father!"

Adeline gasped, and Mom's hand immediately shot to her mouth. Tears blurred her vision as Rebecca bolted upright, staring at Mom with wide eyes. Although Adeline had suspected Mom felt that way, she *never* expected her to say it out loud.

Mom slowly peeled her hand away. "I didn't mean that."

"Yes, you did." Tears dripped down Adeline's cheeks.

"Adeline, I'm so sorry."

Mom reached for her, but Adeline was already running down the hall. She disappeared into the tiny bathroom and slammed the door. The entire house shook as she pressed her back against the door and slid down to the cold, hard tiles.

She covered her face with her hands, muffling her cries as she rocked back and forth. Her chest ached as she released her sorrow, devastated by the unfair hand life had dealt her. She would never forgive herself for what happened.

As she curled onto her side and cried herself to sleep, Mom's words echoed in her mind.

You killed your father.

Chapter Three

A QUICK KNOCK ON the door jolted Adeline out of her nightmare. Her heart pounded as she raised her head off the tiles and sat up. She hadn't meant to spend the night on the bathroom floor, but exhaustion had gotten the best of her.

"The movers are here," Rebecca's soft voice said through the door.

Adeline groaned as she climbed to her feet, massaging her stiff neck. She would never do that again. Opening the door, she was glad it was only her little sister and not Mom.

"I brought your bag." Rebecca offered a strained smile and held out the black backpack. "I figured you would want to change."

"Thanks," Adeline said, retrieving her pack.

There was pain in Rebecca's pale blue eyes as she tucked her straight brown hair behind her ears and looked at the floor. They were only a year apart and had never had a close relationship because of their different interests, but Adeline had always appreciated her sister's kindness.

"I'll be out in a minute." She shut herself back into the bathroom.

Adeline stretched her knotted shoulders before forcing her slim legs into her favorite jeans. She threw on a cozy sweatshirt and went to work on her bedhead. Her long auburn hair was a curly mess, but after combing her fingers through it a few times, it looked somewhat presentable.

She laced up her well-loved sneakers and pulled on her fleece jacket. Her cellphone came out of the backpack next, and it had plenty of battery life to last the entire day. She took a minute to check her text messages before stuffing the phone in her pocket and heading out the door.

Hurt and anger ignited in Adeline when she saw Mom directing the movers where to place boxes and furniture. She would get herself in trouble if she stayed inside, so she made a beeline to the kitchen. The frigid air stung her face as she slid the glass door open.

Before she could exit, Rebecca rushed after her. "May I join you?"

"If you want to." Adeline stepped out into the cold.

Rebecca followed, but right when her boots hit the rickety porch, Mom spotted them from the living room.

"Don't go too far, girls!" Mom shouted. "Aunt Peggy will be here any minute!"

Adeline glared at Mom before slamming the door. With her chin held high, she zipped her fleece jacket up as far as it would go. It was just as cold and windy as the night before, but she would much rather be outside in the cold than stuck in the house with Mom.

The bright sun warmed her cheeks as she breathed in the fresh air. The porch was spacious, wrapping around the entire house, but it was weathered with age and desperately needed a fresh coat of paint.

The uneven boards groaned as Adeline joined Rebecca at the railing. They were at least twelve feet from ground level and had a great view of their small, grassy yard. It was square and plain, but that wasn't what drew their attention.

Colorful trees surrounded the yard, and rolling mountains towered above the tree line, touching the sky. Miles of forest grew in every direction, making it look like the endless trees would swallow their small house up. Fall colors dominated the view and looked fantastic against the healthy evergreen branches mixed in with them.

Adeline hated to admit it, but it was a stunning sight.

Apart from one serious eyesore that was hard to ignore.

A tall chain-link fence stood between the back section of their backyard and the forest. It only blocked off a small section that surrounded the property, which made it look strange and out of place. At each end of their property, the fence took a sharp diagonal turn into the woods instead of going straight back like most property lines.

It was in horrible condition, like it had been there for decades with no maintenance. Overgrown branches poked through the openings in various places, along with tears in the broken wires that were covered in rust. "No trespassing" signs hung all over it—some rusted and hanging by a single nail, while others appeared to be brand new.

"That's an odd place to put a fence," Adeline said.

"Mom told me someone from town owns that section of the forest," Rebecca said, adjusting her thin glasses. "I guess they don't want anyone in there."

"Clearly." Adeline stared a little harder at the fence. "But why is there a gate that leads to our backyard?"

Both girls inspected the worn entrance that was securely locked. A rusted chain looped around the entryway with a heavy-duty padlock latched onto it.

No one could open it without the key...or some bolt cutters.

"I don't know." Rebecca shrugged.

"This place is so weird."

Stepping away from the shabby railing, Adeline headed down the steep steps that led into the backyard. It was just as worn as the deck, but it was sturdier than it looked. She made it to ground level with no issues. So did Rebecca.

Another cold gust of wind sent Adeline's auburn waves in all directions as she scanned the basic, flat yard. The shed in the back corner looked just as old as the fence it was backed up against. It did not look interesting, but Adeline figured it would kill some time.

Dew sprinkled Adeline's shoes as she moved through the grass with Rebecca following her like a shadow.

"What time did you get up?" Adeline asked over her shoulder.

"Maybe an hour ago." Rebecca quickened her pace until she was walking beside her. "I didn't sleep well last night."

"Me neither. I don't recommend sleeping on the bathroom floor."

Rebecca hunched her shoulders. "I'm sorry about what Mom said."

Adeline fought back tears. She didn't want to think about that.

"And just so you know, I don't blame you for what happened to Dad."

Tears filled Adeline's eyes, but she wiped them away. She didn't believe Rebecca, but she appreciated the kind gesture. "Thanks."

Adeline quickened her steps until she reached the shed. It was in worse condition than she thought, with a busted window and a roof that was sinking in. It could crumble at any moment, but that didn't stop Adeline from pushing on the ajar door.

It opened with a noisy squeal as the sunlight revealed emptiness. A few dead leaves had found their way inside, along with spiderwebs that coated the ceiling, but that was all.

Adeline's skin crawled as she stepped back. She hated spiders.

The girls abandoned the old shed and didn't bother closing the door as they ventured back toward the house.

"I'm going to go warm up." Rebecca's teeth chattered. "I'm freezing."

Adeline shivered, but quickly decided that she would much rather freeze to death than face Mom. "I'm going to stay out here."

Rebecca ran up the steps while Adeline went underneath the deck to check out a black door that was connected to the house. There was a small window toward the top that had collected filth for years.

Adeline wasn't short by any means—being five foot six—but she had to stand on her tiptoes to peek through the dirty window. She used her sleeve to clean the grime off the glass before pressing her face against it.

The dark, empty room was an unfinished basement with dusty shelves and a corroded hot-water tank. Adeline wiggled the doorknob, but it was locked. Although she was curious about exploring the creepy room, she wasn't about to ask Mom for the key to open it.

Adeline's ears perked up when she heard gravel popping underneath the pressure of an arriving vehicle. She couldn't see the driveway, so she walked to the front of the house where the movers still carried boxes and furniture up the wobbly set of stairs.

Aunt Peggy's old Honda Civic was in the driveway, and Adeline deflated. She was Dad's older sister and was the one who had suggested they move to Black

Mountain. She had even gotten Mom a teaching job at the elementary school in town and helped her find an inexpensive place to live.

Adeline loved her aunt, but she hadn't seen her since Dad's funeral and wasn't sure she was ready to do so now.

Stepping out of her vehicle, Aunt Peggy glanced around the property with a cheerful expression. She was slightly overweight but carried it well as the breeze brushed through her short brunette hair. She didn't see her niece at first, but when she did, her face fell. Tears formed in her blue eyes as she approached Adeline and wrapped her in a hug. She didn't say a word as Adeline's tears soaked into her fleece jacket.

After a lengthy moment, Aunt Peggy released her. "I'm so glad you're here."

Sniffling, Adeline wiped her cheeks and stared at her worn shoes. Guilt and shame gnawed at her once again.

Aunt Peggy gently grasped Adeline's chin, tilting it until their eyes met. Her blue irises were identical to Dad's, and Adeline had to look away.

"I know all of this is new, sweet Adeline," she said, kindness lacing her words, "but you'll like it here."

Adeline nodded, though she didn't agree. "Where's Uncle Pete and Carol?"

"Pete is at work, but Carol should be here in about thirty minutes." Aunt Peggy smiled. "She was getting out of the shower when I left the house."

Adeline was extremely close with her cousin, Carol. They were the same age and always had a good time when they were together. That was the only perk of moving there. Adeline was still furious about her new living situation, but transitioning to a new school would be a little easier with her cousin around.

"Hi, Peggy." Mom tried to sound chipper as she greeted her from the porch. "Thank you for coming."

Aunt Peggy gave a friendly wave. "Good morning, Victoria."

Before Aunt Peggy climbed the stairs, she pulled Adeline into another warm hug, pressing her mouth to her ear. "If you need *anything*, call me."

Adeline held back a sob and dug her fingers into Aunt Peggy's jacket. She hadn't been held in a long time and hadn't realized how much she needed it.

Aunt Peggy released Adeline with a genuine smile before moving herself up the old steps and pulling Mom into a hug. Adeline was tempted to follow, but she wandered into the backyard instead. She wanted to hide away for a while, so she found a spot underneath the covering of the porch and sat with her back against the house.

Adeline glanced at her phone. It was eight o'clock. She would keep herself occupied outside until Carol arrived.

She pulled her knees to her chest and watched the trees dance behind the tall chain-link fence. They swayed with the breeze, slapping their leafy branches against the barrier like they were trying to break free. Had someone placed the ancient fence there to keep intruders out or keep something locked inside? And why was there a gate in her yard?

No logical explanation came to mind. Adeline watched the trees for a few minutes, then couldn't take it anymore. She had to investigate. She had deprived her adventurous spirit for the past six months, and it was dying to come out.

And there was no stopping it once she jumped to her feet.

Chapter Four

Adeline was dying to know the forest's secrets as she marched toward the rusted gate. She could easily step into the woods around her property that was not sectioned off by the fence, but something within her burned to explore the parts that were off limits.

The closer she got to the chain-link fence, the more she realized how tall it was. She could climb over it, but feared she would tear her clothing or injure herself on the sharp, jagged edges at the top. She also didn't want Mom to catch her trespassing on someone else's property.

As she sized up the fence that soared above her head, something odd snagged her attention. There was a strange ripple in the air along the fence line, like heat distortion that comes off asphalt on a hot summer day.

What is that?

Sticking her fingers through the openings in the wires, a warm sensation slightly distorted the way her fingers looked, like she was looking at a mirage.

Her brows pinched together as she pulled back her hand. Her pale skin looked the same as always, and she could no longer feel the warmth of the bizarre haze she had touched. She didn't know what to think as she moved to the locked gate.

Most people would probably honor the "no trespassing" signs hanging like ornaments on the fence, but Adeline wanted to explore the forest and nothing would stop her.

She shot a quick glance over her shoulder before grabbing the padlock and giving it a good, hard shake. The gate rattled, but it didn't budge.

"Find the key," a faint voice whispered in the wind.

Goosebumps rippled through Adeline as she jumped away from the fence. She turned in a slow circle, but she was alone.

Weird.

Her heart raced. Could she find the key? She doubted it. But then again, maybe it was nearby.

A ping of excitement sparked in Adeline as she began the hunt. She flipped over every stick, leaf, and rock along the fence line but came up empty.

When she reached the rundown shed, she got down on her hands and knees and thoroughly inspected the outside. No key.

Huffing, Adeline stood and wiped her filthy hands on her jeans as a strong breeze knocked into her. Her muscles tensed from the bitter cold, and she gave up the search.

Screech.

Adeline jerked her head back, eyeing the shed door. It whined in the wind, swaying back and forth slightly.

"Find the key," the mysterious voice said again.

Adeline froze, her heart pattering against her ribs as she scanned the backyard. No one was there.

Combing a hand through her long hair, Adeline's gaze narrowed on the entrance to the shed. Someone or something wanted her to find the key, and the last place for her to look was inside the shed.

Adeline winced as she crouched and snuck through the entrance. The shed was high enough for her to stand up straight, but there were cobwebs above her head. She saw nothing along the decaying walls and warped floorboards. A waste of time.

Adeline scooted backwards to exit the dreadful structure, but stopped when something caught her eye.

Sunlight shimmered through the broken window, highlighting a corner of the shed near Adeline. The small pile of leaves looked as if someone had purposely tucked them there to hide something.

Adeline swatted the pile of leaves away, revealing nothing but a rotten board that had once been a part of the floor. Looking closer at the decaying corner, she found a small hole large enough to fit a hand. She didn't give herself time to think about what could be in there as she stuffed her hand into the opening. Fear churned in her gut as she ran her fingertips along the bottom, roaming over the dead leaves and grime that lived there.

Her stomach lurched when she touched something cold.

Adeline grabbed the small object and yanked her hand from the gap in the floor before bolting outside. She stepped into the bright sunlight, breathless, and opened her palm.

She had found a key!

Sprinting to the gate, Adeline clutched the icy lock. Her hands shook as she stuck the key in and turned it.

Click.

A devilish smile spread across her face as she unfastened the padlock and checked the time on her phone: 8:10.

Twenty minutes until Carol gets here. I have time.

Adeline tucked her phone away and removed the heavy chains that were a little too noisy for her liking. Once they were out of her way, she turned to make sure no one was looking before pushing on the gate and stepping through.

The gate wailed like it was trying to tattle on Adeline, but it didn't stop her from intruding.

Leaving the key in the padlock, Adeline shut herself inside and rushed down the worn path. The trees concealed her in a matter of seconds, and her house disappeared from view. The wind blew once more, but in place of the biting chill, there was warmth.

Why is it warmer here?

She expected it to be colder without the sun shining down on her. She wasn't warm by any means, but she wasn't freezing anymore. Tossing the thought from her mind, Adeline crunched through the dead leaves and pine needles.

Why is the ground dry? It poured down rain last night.

There was no evidence that it had rained at all. Everything was dry. So much so that a forest fire could blaze through it.

It was bizarre, but the loveliness of the nature trail distracted her too much to dwell on it. Yellow, red, and orange leaves spread like fireworks. They were even more stunning now that she was standing underneath their magnificence, appearing to be more vibrant than before.

She had seen fall-colored leaves in the past, but nothing that matched the striking colors that surrounded her. Even the birds added to the profound beauty as they darted through the trees, chirping as they skirted along the branches.

The single path split into three, worn and well-used, and Adeline stopped.

Adeline tapped her chin. Each path went in a different direction, and there were so many trees that she couldn't see where they would take her.

Since she was running short on time, she headed down the middle path. It was a little tighter compared to the other two, but spacious enough for her to walk comfortably without any branches knocking into her.

The bright leaves twirled to the ground, painting the path with their beauty. A tiny smile tugged at her lips as she meandered down the trail through the oak and maple trees that stood among the evergreens.

It didn't take her long to reach a stream trickling over the path. The slow-moving water was only ankle deep, but it was too wide to jump across.

There was a row of steppingstones someone had built across it. They were mostly flat and a little uneven, but they would allow her to cross the stream without getting wet.

Pressing her lips together, Adeline put her foot on the closest rock, testing its sturdiness. It didn't wobble, and she put her full weight on it before moving to the next one. She made it to the other side without making a splash, only to find a fork in the road.

Adeline paused for a moment, listening to the calm water trickle over the rocks behind her. There was a chance of her getting lost, but she was past the point of caring. Anything to get away from that house. She straightened her posture and went left.

The further she walked beneath the canopy of color, the more the forest expanded. It was much larger than she had first assumed. There was no telling how many acres it was.

Adeline hesitated at another split in the trail. She wanted to keep exploring, but logic told her to turn around. Carol would arrive soon, and she didn't want Mom to notice her absence.

Releasing a heavy sigh, Adeline pivoted and started back toward her new life. She dragged her feet as a thick cloud of sadness loomed over her. She no longer admired the gorgeous fall colors as her thoughts went to Dad.

Tears pooled in her eyes as she imagined him walking by her side. She could see his picture-perfect smile as he admired the colorful forest and could hear his deep laughter that always brought her joy.

"I'm so sorry, Dad," she whispered to the quiet forest.

Swiping away her tears, Adeline refused to let herself cry. There was no point in getting worked up over something she couldn't change. Dad was gone, and he was never coming back.

"Addie," a gentle voice echoed through the trees.

Adeline stiffened. She didn't recognize the tender male voice. The only man in town that knew her nickname was Uncle Pete...but he was at work.

Silence struck the forest, and all that could be heard was the pounding of her chest.

She scanned the trees, knees threatening to buckle.

No one appeared.

"I am losing my mind." Adeline rubbed her forehead.

Before Adeline could continue onward, she heard the quiet voice say her nickname again.

"Addie."

A cold sweat broke across her skin, and she took off. Her sneakers slammed into the solid ground as she sprinted toward the house. She ran full speed across the stream, soaking her shoes and the bottom of her jeans.

Her sides were burning, and her lungs were on fire. She regretted not having worked out in six months as her muscles begged for mercy, but she had to get away.

Glancing over her shoulder, Adeline didn't see anyone chasing after her. She darted her gaze ahead and gasped.

WHACK!

Adeline slammed into a tree, knocking her backward into a pile of dead leaves. A sharp pain exploded in her head, and everything went black.

Chapter Five

"Are you all right?" a lightly accented voice asked.

Adeline fought to open her eyes as pain thumped in her head. She peeled one eye open, then the other, and saw an old man standing over her.

"Who are you?" Adeline sat up, scooting away from the man who appeared to be in his mid-seventies.

Thin wrinkles lining the old man's face deepened as he let out a chuckle. "My name is Henry Snow." He removed his newsboy cap and did a quick bow. "And who might you be, young lady?"

His accent was pleasant, but Adeline didn't know what to think as she eyed his white hair and strange attire. He was well-dressed in black trousers, a vest, and a gray tweed coat. He looked like he had stepped out of a 1930s photograph.

"I-I'm Adeline."

"Pleasure to meet you, Miss Adeline," Henry said, extending his aged hand. "Allow me to help."

Everything about the old man was odd. She could easily picture him in a bustling city or on a movie set in Hollywood, not in the middle of the forest in North Carolina.

"I promise I won't bite." Henry's white mustache wiggled as he grinned.

Adeline gave him another long, hard stare before hesitantly accepting his outstretched hand. His skin was soft, but his grip was tight as a knot as he hoisted her to her feet. He was a lot stronger than his frail figure appeared.

As Adeline steadied herself, she got a front-row view of his golden-brown eyes. They were the most captivating color she had ever seen, like honey glistening in the sun.

"That was quite the collision you had with that tree."

His comment jarred Adeline's memory as she plucked the dead leaves from her clothing. She was sure Henry hadn't called out her name because the male voice didn't have an accent. Plus, there was no way he knew her nickname.

But then again, maybe she had just made it all up in her head.

Unease settled at the bottom of her stomach and intensified when she remembered she was trespassing. She feared he was the one who owned the property and felt heat rise to her cheeks.

"I better get going," Adeline said, lowering her head.

"Are you wanting to leave because you feel guilty about trespassing?" Henry asked, stroking his white beard. "Or are you afraid your mother will notice you're gone?"

Adeline paled. "How did you know that?"

"You'll come to find that I am unlike anyone you have ever met." A slight grin tugged at his lips. "And there is no need to worry, because you are not in trouble, nor will you be with your mother when you decide to go back."

Adeline's eyes widened. *Who is this old man?*

"I am on my way back to my cabin to have some breakfast. Would you like to join me?"

Adeline studied him suspiciously, but the mention of food made her stomach growl. She hadn't eaten anything since the day before.

Despite her hunger, she questioned if she could trust him.

She had watched enough late-night news to know there were tons of crazy people in the world. But as she lost herself in his gentle, honey-colored eyes, a wave of peace rolled over her.

"You must be hungry." Henry clasped his arms behind his back. "And I have been told a time or two that I am quite the chef."

Adeline's stomach rumbled again, like it was agreeing with Henry Snow. But the fear of getting in trouble outweighed her curiosity.

"I can't," she said, picking at her nails. "I've already been gone too long."

"No problem at all, Miss Adeline. It was a pleasure to meet you, and I hope to see you again." Henry gave her a polite bow before whistling to himself and moving down the path that went deeper into the woods.

Frowning, Adeline went in the opposite direction. Henry's catchy tune faded as she dug into her coat for her phone to check the time. It was completely dead. It hadn't been fully charged when she left the house, but it shouldn't have died that fast.

Gritting her teeth, Adeline smashed the power button repeatedly, but it wouldn't turn on.

"Unbelievable!"

Adeline stuffed her cellphone away. Her mind spun with the idea of having to get a new phone, but it quickly subsided when the man's whistling stopped. She turned to get one last look, but he was gone.

Why was she so fascinated with Henry Snow? Was it his accent? Or maybe his friendly personality?

Whatever the reason, Adeline couldn't shake the itch to follow him. It consumed her thoughts. After a couple of minutes of wrestling with the idea, Adeline took off after him, no longer caring about the consequences she may face later.

"Mr. Snow!" Adeline yelled. "Wait for me!"

The path curved, and the thin old man was waiting for her.

"I've changed my mind." Adeline was out of breath as she slowed her pace. "I want to go with you."

"Fantastic!" Henry clasped his hands together.

Turning on his heels, Henry continued his journey with Adeline walking by his side. Again, she noticed a sense of peace as she steadied her heavy breathing. The peace she had once known had vanished months ago, but it hovered over her like a cloud as they strolled through the radiant forest.

"So tell me, why were you all alone in this grand forest?" Henry asked.

Adeline gave a simple shrug. "I was just walking around."

"Ah...I see. This forest does have a special effect on some people," he said, watching a cardinal dart in front of them. "Did you find what you were looking for?"

"I wasn't looking for anything in particular," she said. "I just needed to get away for a little while."

"No one comes into *this* forest without seeking something," he said. "But don't worry, you will find it."

Adeline made a face as she looked around. The forest was beautiful, but it looked like all the other woods in the North Carolina mountains. She didn't question it and continued to walk with him. They went left and right way too many times for her to count.

It made no sense to her why an elderly man would want to live so far away from civilization. Did he have to hike into town every time he needed supplies? What if he got injured and needed medical assistance?

Worry started to rise in Adeline as she thought about her trip back to her house. She couldn't do it on her own; hopefully Henry could guide her. As far as she could tell, he seemed well acquainted with the layout of the forest.

As Adeline glanced over at Henry, her worries eased a little until they faded entirely. She couldn't put her finger on it, but there was something about the old man that made her feel comfortable and safe, like she had known him her entire life.

Catching her eye, Henry's lips twitched. "What do you think about your new home?"

"How did you know that?" She stepped away from him. "Have you been spying on my family?"

"Of course not, Miss Adeline."

"Then how do you know that?"

"As I said earlier, I am unlike anyone you have ever met." Henry lifted his chin, exuding confidence. "I was also close friends with the wonderful man who used to live there."

Adeline took another step away from him. Was he being honest, or had he been silently watching her through the trees?

One look into his warm, brown eyes destroyed her suspicion. He was being honest with her. She felt it in her bones, though she had no way of explaining how she knew that.

"Why did he move?" Adeline asked as they walked again.

"He didn't move," Henry said sorrowfully. "He passed away."

Adeline's gut knotted. "I'm sorry. How did he die?"

"He was an older gentleman, and when he got sick, he was forced to move into a nursing home. He died shortly after."

Dad came to Adeline's mind, and her throat tightened. She felt an internal pull to tell Henry about him, but she quickly dismissed it. She was used to bottling up her pain and didn't want to talk about the accident, especially with a stranger.

So, she kept her agony and grief to herself and continued to travel with her new companion.

Chapter Six

"Here we are," Henry said with excitement. "Welcome to my home."

The trail opened to a spacious, grassy area with a charming, one-story log cabin. It was bigger than a typical cabin and was in the center of the most spectacular landscape Adeline had ever seen.

"You live here?" Adeline asked, shading her eyes from the sun.

"I sure do," Henry said. "Follow me."

Adeline inhaled the sweet aroma of the gardenias as she soaked in the view. Every color imaginable was in the massive flowerbeds filled with trimmed shrubs and fully bloomed flowers in too many varieties to count.

She knew little about plants, but the cold weather should have killed most everything by now, including the grass. The yard looked almost too perfect to be real, and so did the monstrous red oak trees with their bright green leaves. Their healthy branches swayed as she walked under them.

Adeline didn't bother asking Henry how everything thrived in the frigid air as she climbed the steps to the wrap-around porch. The wind chimes played a soft melody as the sturdy rocking chairs and the porch swing moved with the tune. It was a nice setup.

"Let's get warmed up, Miss Adeline." Henry unlocked the front door and stepped inside.

Adeline sucked in a deep breath before entering the cabin. She was hit with the pleasant warmth of a fire and the rich smell of burning birch wood.

Henry's cabin was one of the coziest she had ever seen. The kitchen, living room, and dining area were open to each other, but the space didn't feel over-crowded at all.

Adeline paused at the door, infatuated with the stone fireplace that was the centerpiece of the entire space. The warm flames made the cozy sitting area glow, but that wasn't what held her interest. The burning logs were neatly stacked and looked like they had just been placed inside the fireplace.

That's strange. How did the fire not burn out while he was gone?

"What do you think?" Henry asked as he hung up his tweed jacket and news-boy cap on the coatrack.

"It's really nice," Adeline said, pulling her eyes away from the flames.

"Allow me to take your coat." Henry held out his wrinkly hand.

Wiggling out of her jacket, Adeline handed it to Henry while doing another scan of the room. For a moment, she had forgotten she was in the woods behind her new property.

"Please sit down, my dear." Henry motioned to the barstools at the kitchen island. "I will prepare our breakfast."

Adeline ran her hand across the back of the smooth leather couch as she made her way into the kitchen and slid onto the barstool. Frying pans clattered atop the burners. While they heated, Henry retrieved a carton of eggs and a pack of thick bacon from the refrigerator.

Henry hummed his way back to the oven as Adeline waited. Her mouth watered as the bacon sizzled. She couldn't remember the last time Mom had cooked breakfast.

The intoxicating aroma of the bacon filled the cabin as Henry moved around the kitchen like he was doing a dance he had practiced his whole life. He even made setting the table look graceful, placing the utensils, plates, and glasses in a perfect arrangement.

Henry winked at Adeline as he flipped the sizzling bacon. He did a quick stirring of the eggs before grabbing two plates and piling them high. Steam drifted from the delicious breakfast as Henry placed it on the island and took the seat next to Adeline.

"Eat up," Henry said, placing his napkin on his lap.

Adeline bit into a piece of crispy bacon and was hit with an explosion of salty goodness.

"Whoa!" Adeline said. "What did you put in this bacon? Magic?"

"Something like that." The corner of his mouth lifted.

Adeline took another quick bite. "You weren't kidding when you said you could cook."

"Just wait until you try the eggs," he said as he poured Adeline and himself a glass of orange juice.

Adeline stabbed the pile of scrambled eggs with her fork. Steam rolled from the fluffy eggs as she blew on them and took a small bite.

"Wow." Adeline melted into her seat. "I didn't realize eggs could taste this good."

Henry chuckled. "Aren't you glad you joined me for breakfast?"

"Yes!"

Adeline valued each bite like it was a gourmet meal. She licked her fingers after she had eaten the last piece of bacon. It took all her self-control not to lick the plate.

"Someone was hungry," Henry said, popping his last piece of bacon into his mouth.

Adeline nodded, taking a sip of the orange juice. Not only was it cold, but it also had the perfect balance of sweetness and acidity, like it was freshly squeezed. "That was good."

"I'm glad you enjoyed it."

Henry gently folded his napkin onto his empty plate. Adeline couldn't pull her eyes away from him. Deep wrinkles lined his face, and there were a few age spots here and there. His age showed on his face, but his straight posture presented a greater confidence and strength.

Adeline found herself wanting to know everything about him. "How long have you lived here?"

"Many years," Henry said, swiveling his chair toward her. "We built this splendid cabin a very long time ago and have been here ever since."

"We?" she asked, looking around to see if there was evidence of a second person. "Other people live here?"

"Why, yes," he said, relaxing into his chair. "I live here with my two best friends."

"Where does everyone sleep?"

Henry directed to a wide hallway that led away from the living room. "This cabin is a lot larger than it looks. There are six bedrooms and five bathrooms down that hall."

"Really?" Adeline blinked. From the outside, the cabin hadn't looked that big. "I would have never guessed that this place could hold so many people."

"Looks can be deceiving," he said. "Not all things are as they appear to be." There was a hint of mischief in his light brown eyes as he raised his glass of orange juice and took a sip.

"Where are your friends?"

"They're out on an adventure and won't be back until later this evening." Henry stood and started to clean.

Adeline's imagination ran wild. What were his friends like? Were they old and happy like him?

Once the island was clear, Henry told Adeline stories about his life in the forest with his friends. His tales were animated and funny, especially when he described the harmless, but funny pranks they would play on each other like a bunch of kids.

Adeline was nearly in tears when he finished telling her about the time he wrapped rubber bands around the kitchen sink sprayer, soaking his roommate. Never had she heard a simple story told in such a theatrical way. His storytelling was just as excellent as his cooking.

He reminded her of Dad, who always told funny stories at dinner. Nowadays, dinners were not the same. Mom had never valued humor, and Rebecca wasn't much of a talker, especially after Dad passed away.

But being around Henry was like hanging out with a friend she had known her whole life. His joy was contagious. He was the breath of fresh air she had needed, and she didn't want to leave.

Having a blast with her new friend, Adeline completely lost track of time.

"Oh, no." She sat up, interrupting Henry's story. "I need to leave."

Her palms started to sweat as she searched for a clock, but she couldn't find one. Even the stove and microwave didn't show the time.

"Do you know what time it is?" She hoped Mom hadn't called the cops.

"Sure don't." Henry shrugged.

"Will you check your phone and see? Mine died."

"I don't have a phone, Miss Adeline. Nor do I have a clock."

"You don't have a clock or a cellphone?"

"Nope." His accent rang out happily. "I have no need for either."

There was no hiding the surprise that flashed across her face. She had never met anyone without a clock or a phone. What if he needed to get in touch with someone? And how would he ever be on time if he didn't have a clock?

"Okay...well, I need to go, Mr. Snow." Adeline jumped out of her seat and went to the coatrack.

"Call me Henry." He rose from the barstool. "And allow me to take you back; I wouldn't want you to get lost in those woods."

The corner of her lips lifted as she shoved her arms into the sleeves of her warm jacket and followed Henry out the front door.

Chapter Seven

ADELINE TRIED TO IGNORE the rising pressure in her chest, but it gripped her tighter as she neared her property. She hadn't said a word to Henry and had spent the whole walk back thinking of an excuse for why she had gone beyond the fence. Nothing came to mind that would curb Mom's wrath.

The gate came into view, and Adeline drew in a slow breath. As much as she didn't want to face Mom, it was inevitable.

Henry stopped before reaching the fence and gave Adeline a sweet smile. "This is where I must leave you. You are always welcome to come back to my cabin whenever you like."

"How will I find it?" she asked, tucking her hands into her pockets. "I don't want to get lost."

"Follow the stars."

"The stars?" She frowned. "But there are no stars out during the day. And even if I traveled at night and could see them, it isn't like I would know how to follow them to your place."

"Follow the stars, Adeline, and you'll find me."

Henry tipped his hat to her and walked back the way he came. She was clueless to what he was talking about as he disappeared behind a cluster of trees.

But she had other things to worry about.

Adeline approached the gate and skimmed the backyard before opening it. The rusted gate screeched as she closed and locked it, slipping the key into her pocket.

Her stomach was in knots as she glanced toward the entrance to her property. There were no police vehicles, but the moving truck was still there. She thought for sure they would be done by now.

Hugging herself, Adeline hurried through the cold toward the house.

Bing!

Adeline stopped, fumbling for her phone. It was no longer dead.

What the heck?

Adeline read the text message from her childhood neighbor, who wished her the best. They had once been very close, spending most of their free time riding horses, but after the accident, Adeline had shoved her away like everyone else.

Adeline sent her a quick thank you before glancing at the time.

It's still 8:10?

Scratching her head, Adeline checked again. That couldn't be right. It had been 8:10 when she had first stepped through the gate. She must have been gone for at least an hour or two.

Adeline pocketed her phone and scuttled to the deck stairs. Right as she climbed the first step, she heard gravel crunching. Someone had just arrived.

Maybe Uncle Pete got off work early.

Redirecting herself, Adeline rounded the house and slowed her pace. Carol was pulling into the driveway. She had assumed Carol was already inside with her family and was surprised to see that she was late.

Carol jumped out of her Toyota Corolla and adjusted her baggy sweatpants. The wind blew her damp, light brown hair away from her face as she hustled toward the house. A grin appeared when she saw Adeline coming from the backyard. Carol raced to her, crushing Adeline into a hug. "You made it! I was afraid you were going to run away or something."

"I thought about it." Adeline pulled out of the hug.

"I'm glad you didn't," Carol said, displaying her straight teeth. "I know this town is small, but it doesn't suck that bad."

"That bad?" Adeline stifled a grin.

"It'll grow on you." Carol wrapped an arm around Adeline's shoulders, leading her toward the front steps.

"If you say so. What took you so long?"

"What do you mean? I got here as fast as I could." Carol pointed to her wet hair.

"Your mom got here at least an hour ago and told me you would be here shortly after."

"Very funny. I just saw my mom, like, ten minutes ago when I got out of the shower," Carol said, following Adeline up the rickety steps. "I threw on some sweats and was out the door a few minutes after she left."

Adeline froze, her hands latched onto the railing. *That can't be right.*

"Hurry up." Carol lightly pushed on Adeline to get her moving. "It's freezing out here."

Adeline raced up the steps and into the house, her mind muddled by the apparent time glitch. There were a few boxes stacked against the wall and some furniture here and there, but the movers had made little progress since Adeline had left.

A lump formed in her throat when she spotted Mom talking to one of the movers. She was glad Carol was with her. Hopefully it would ease some of Mom's anger. But to her surprise, Mom didn't seem upset when she looked her way. Her weary expression warmed a little as she came to greet Carol.

"So great to see you, honey." Mom pulled Carol into a gentle hug.

While Carol hugged Mom, Adeline slipped past them when she saw Rebecca walking down the hall with a box. Adeline rushed after her and slipped into the dark green bedroom. The color made the room look small, but Rebecca didn't seem to mind as she placed the box on top of a bigger box.

Rebecca jumped when she saw Adeline staring at her. "You scared me!"

"Sorry." Adeline glanced behind her before looking back at her little sister. "Did Mom notice I was gone?"

"Gone?" A flash of confusion swept across Rebecca's face. "I was just outside with you."

"No, you weren't. I've been gone for a long time."

"I saw you ten minutes ago," Rebecca said, dropping her voice to a whisper, "and so did Aunt Peggy and Mom."

"Ten minutes!"

Rebecca's face fell from the sudden outburst. "You're acting weird," she said, pulling the flaps of the box open.

Adeline couldn't figure out why Rebecca was lying; she always told the truth. It made no sense, so she left the room to find Aunt Peggy. She would be honest with her.

"Have you seen Rebecca?" Carol stopped Adeline in the hallway.

"Yeah, she's in her room," Adeline said, pointing to the open door.

"Thanks."

Carol disappeared into Rebecca's bedroom as Adeline headed into the living room. She maneuvered around the furniture and boxes and found Aunt Peggy standing on the kitchen counter. She was humming to herself as she cleaned the dirty cabinets with a steaming rag.

"Aunt Peggy." Adeline approached her from behind. "When was the last time you saw me?"

Aunt Peggy gave Adeline the same look Rebecca did. "What do you mean, sweetie?"

"Like...what time did you see me today?"

"Oh, maybe ten minutes ago," Aunt Peggy said as she went back to cleaning.

Adeline grasped the counter for support. She had been gone much longer than ten minutes; she was sure of it.

"Why do you ask?" Aunt Peggy asked, bending to dunk the rag into a bucket of water.

"No reason."

Am I losing my mind?

Everything she'd experienced in the forest had felt real, but what if she had just dreamed it or made it up? She stuck her hand in her jacket pocket and wrapped her fingers around the key. She had been gone a long time, but no one seemed to have noticed.

It was as if time had stopped while she'd been in the forest.

"Hey," Mom said as she came into the kitchen. Adeline waited for her to yell, waited for the berating. Instead, Mom's lips quivered. "I'm sorry about what I said yesterday. I was tired and didn't mean it."

Adeline played with the hem of her sweatshirt, avoiding Mom's gaze. She didn't believe a word Mom said, but at least she wasn't getting scolded.

"Will you forgive me?"

Adeline pulled her eyes from the floor and looked Mom in the eye. All she could see was pain; pain she had caused her. Guilt gnawed at her, and she quickly averted her gaze. "Yeah."

"Thank you." Mom's voice cracked as she pulled Adeline into a weak embrace. "We will get through this together."

Breathing in Mom's flowery perfume, Adeline remained still. Life without Dad was suffocating. It was impossible to imagine they could ever move on without him.

"I'm going to unpack the boxes in the living room if you want to work on the kitchen with Aunt Peggy," Mom said with a tired smile.

"Okay."

Adeline would rather watch paint dry than unpack, but she didn't put up a fight and moved to the round dining table. Brown boxes covered the worn surface and the tile floor below; the task ahead of her wouldn't be easy.

She fell into a rhythm of carefully pulling the paper away from the dishes and bowls. Beyond the mess, her eyes drifted past the rusted gate to the forest.

Something odd had happened in that forest. And she wanted answers.

"I'll help you," Aunt Peggy said, climbing off the counter. "I got all the top cabinets clean, so we can start putting dishes in there."

Adeline nodded, ripping open a box with her hands. Her thoughts were consumed by the forest as she pulled out a stack of mixing bowls that hadn't been used in months. It was pointless to keep them; Mom rarely cooked.

Adeline dug into the same box and remembered her aunt had lived in Black Mountain for years. "Aunt Peggy," she said, heaving a blender out of the box. "Do you know anything about this property?"

"I do," Aunt Peggy said, grabbing the paper Adeline had thrown around the floor and stuffing it into a trash bag. "Mr. Wilder used to live here. Everyone in town knew him."

"Mr. Wilder?" Her eyebrows arched. "Who is that?"

"Just an older gentleman who lived here all of his life."

Her hands trembled as she reached into the box once more, recalling what Henry Snow had told her about the last owner of her new home.

"What happened to him?" Adeline asked.

"He passed away."

Aunt Peggy confirmed exactly what Henry Snow had said. Despite battling with thoughts that she was mentally unstable, she was confident that what she had experienced was real. She wasn't losing her mind.

"Do you know why that part of the forest is fenced off?" Adeline pointed outside.

Aunt Peggy looked out the sliding glass door. "Oh yes. Mr. Wilder owned that section of the woods. All the other acres around here are owned by the McThorn family, the richest people around. They own a real estate company in town, and most of the buildings here. Even the nice cabin up the road."

Adeline remembered seeing the gated driveway with the letter M engraved on the iron bars. It had to be the cabin Aunt Peggy was referring to; it was the only other driveway on the long, forgotten road she now lived on.

"But my mom bought Mr. Wilder's property, so why didn't it include that forest?"

"Because that plot of land is legally protected and can never be sold, unlike this old house. It can only be passed down to the Wilder family," Aunt Peggy said. "And after Mr. Wilder died, the land went to his grandson, since he is his only living relative."

"Why?" Adeline asked.

"I guess the original owner wanted to keep it in his family," Aunt Peggy said, jamming another wad of paper into the trash bag. "It doesn't make much sense since the lot is only about five acres, which is incomparable to the hundreds of acres that surround it owned by the McThorns. They have tried to purchase it many times over the years, but they can't because the legal documents have been set in stone."

How did Henry Snow and his cabin fit into the equation? Adeline was also positive that the forest she'd explored was much bigger than five acres. If she had to guess, she would say it was well over a hundred acres.

Something strange was going on, and Adeline was determined to get to the bottom of it. She would be stuck unpacking boxes for the rest of the day, which meant the only time she could sneak away would be early the next morning.

With a plan already in mind, Adeline couldn't wait to talk to Henry.

If she could find him again.

Chapter Eight

Sheer determination woke Adeline up early the next morning. It was her second morning in Black Mountain, and she was set on finding Henry Snow's cabin again.

She rolled out of bed and crept toward the window. Her muscles strained as she yanked up the dusty blinds, pleased to see that the sun was rising without a cloud in sight. She wouldn't tell anyone where she was going. Not that it mattered; time seemed to freeze once she passed through the gate.

Adeline dressed in a hurry and shoved the key into her pocket before grabbing her charged phone off the bedside table. It was dark as she tiptoed down the hallway, cringing with each step as the floorboards creaked. Her plan would be ruined if Mom saw her.

She plucked her winter jacket off the coatrack next to the front door and stuffed her feet into her sneakers. By the time she zipped up her puffy jacket, she was ready to go.

Adeline held her breath while turning the deadbolt and slowly opening the front door. It let out a loud, angry squeak. Her shoulders braced as she waited to see if anyone stirred.

The house remained silent.

The biting wind whistled past Adeline as she gently shut the door. Tempted as she was to go back inside to get away from the miserable weather, she was determined to find Henry again.

Adeline snuck around the porch to the back of the house and dashed down the steps. She headed straight toward the old gate, tucking her hands deep into her coat pockets. She should have worn gloves.

The cold bit at her fingers as she placed the key in the padlock and gave it a quick turn. It unlocked and screamed in defiance as the gate opened. She closed it behind her, leaving the key in the lock. She couldn't risk losing it somewhere in the woods.

The temperature was a tad bit warmer, just like the previous day, as Adeline started down the path. Once her house was out of view, her shoulders relaxed as she walked down the worn trail, enjoying the beautiful trees and pleasant fall weather. A rabbit scurried by as she climbed over a mossy rock, avoiding the low brush around it. She had no idea where she was going, but figured she would eventually find her way.

Boy, was she wrong.

When she came to the first split in the path, she stopped. She had already traveled down the middle one but was unsure whether she should go down it again. Henry had told her to follow the stars, but there were no stars that early in the morning. So, she chose the path leading to the right.

The crisp air settled in her lungs as she walked. She felt different here. After spending time with Henry the day before, it was like her soul was waking up.

After Dad's death, her sense of adventure and wonder had vanished. She rarely went outside and kept to her bedroom, doing nothing but watching movies and playing on her phone. Now she couldn't imagine being stuck in the house all day—especially the one she lived in now.

The path led her deeper into the woods and close to a breathtaking maple tree. The early morning sun illuminated the red leaves, casting a reddish glow on the ground. She pulled her phone out to take a few pictures, but it was dead. Completely dead.

Not again!

Adeline pushed the power button over and over, but nothing happened. Her phone had been fully charged right before she left the house, so why did the battery die so quickly?

Adeline sighed and shoved the useless phone back into her pocket, giving the beautiful tree one last look before continuing her search for Henry's cabin.

SNAP!

The tiny hairs on the back of her neck rose as she stood rooted to the ground. Someone or something had stepped on a twig, forcing it to break. It had sounded close. Fear crept up her back as she remembered the voice she'd heard the day before. What if she was being followed?

She wanted to run, but her legs wouldn't work. Her feet stayed glued to the path, ignoring her commands to move.

CRACK!

Heart hammering, she turned toward the noise. The quiet forest revealed nothing.

Just when she gained enough courage to make a run for it, a squirrel hopped onto the path. Its fluffy tail flapped as it gave her a quick glance before hustling through the pine needles and climbing up a tree.

Adeline released a nervous laugh. *Just a squirrel.*

Shaking off her nerves, she continued her quest to find the cabin.

There's nothing to worry about, she told herself repeatedly, but her heart had yet to settle.

The sun inched higher in the sky, and irritation quickly replaced Adeline's fear. She couldn't find the cabin. It felt like the paths were leading her in circles.

"I'm leaving," she grumbled. "This is impossible."

Spinning around, Adeline stomped down the path. She had no clue where she was, but hopefully she could navigate herself back to her property.

Adeline stumbled in her haste, souring her mood even more. The underbrush was thick in that part of the forest.

Then it happened again. Surely, she wasn't that clumsy—

Wham!

Adeline fell face first onto the path, sending pine needles and dead leaves scattering in her wake. Something, a very thin something, wrapped around her ankle. She flipped around and sat up. A thin green vine had coiled itself around her ankle like a snake.

Adrenaline coursed through her as she pulled and tugged on the vine. Finally, she ripped it off and threw it far away from her. The rest of the vine slithered into the ferns.

With shaky limbs, she stood up. Every part of her was screaming to flee, to get away from there, but something caught her eye. There, on a nearby tree, was a light sparkle.

Adeline moved closer and discovered a small silver star, the size of a dime, pinned to the tree. It blended in so well with the gray bark that it was almost impossible to see.

Looking at the star straight on, it was dull and barely noticeable. But when the sunlight hit it just right, it glimmered like it had just fallen out of the sky. Adeline ran her fingers across the small star. It was cold to the touch and wouldn't move as she tried to pry it out.

She gasped, forgetting about the strange vine. That had to be what Henry Snow had meant. He hadn't been talking about the stars in the sky, but the ones pinned to the trees.

Adeline's pulse quickened as she searched for another star. She moved through the undergrowth, breathless, stepping over rocks and inspecting each tree as she went.

She found another shimmering star in the bark of a poplar tree back on the path. Once she knew what she was looking for, it was easy to find the dime-sized stars that navigated her way. The trail of stars led her, finally, to a line of trees colored in red, orange, and deep yellow.

She rushed along the path, stopping at the last star, and smiled as she saw smoke curling out of the cabin's chimney like it was inviting her to come inside.

"I found it."

Chapter Nine

THE DAZZLING SUN BROKE through the clouds, highlighting the cabin and the flowerbeds placed throughout the yard that looked as if it had just been mowed. Monarch butterflies and fat bumble bees pollinated the area as the smell of spring wafted toward Adeline.

She stepped from the forest, excited to see Henry again. The lights were on inside, but there was no way of knowing who was there.

She paused. What if she had come back too soon? What if she was intruding on Henry's day? Or worse, what if he wasn't home? Then what?

Adeline battled with her thoughts, ideas of what may or may not happen if she knocked on the front door. None of them ended well, and she nearly retreated into the woods.

But as she stared at the welcoming cabin, watching the smoke twirl into the sky, it reminded her of all the weird things that had happened the day before. Things she couldn't explain. Things she needed answers to; she wouldn't get them if she went back to the house.

Determination for answers outweighed her nagging fear as Adeline trudged through the grass, dodging the abundant flowerbeds and trees until she was on the porch. She stood before the door, dread building.

She exhaled. *I can do this.*

Biting her inner cheek, Adeline knocked on the door. She withdrew her hand, pinning it by her side as she waited. Her body tensed when she heard faint footsteps inside the cabin.

Someone was approaching.

The front door swung open, and Henry Snow poked his jolly face outside. His white hair was perfectly combed to the side, and he looked just as elegant as he had the day before in a white button-up shirt tucked into a pair of black slacks.

"Hello there, Miss Adeline," Henry said, opening the door wide. "I see you found me after all."

Seeing his delight melted her worries away. "I found the stars that were on the trees."

"Well done!" Henry's accent happily rang out. "I knew you would find your way."

"Why didn't you just tell me you put little star pins on the trees?"

"Now, where is the fun in that?" Henry's lips twisted in amusement. "I knew you would eventually find them. Come in. I just finished making pancakes."

Henry ushered Adeline inside and helped her out of her winter jacket as the warmth of the cabin tickled her cold cheeks. She could smell the sweet aroma of the pancakes over the birch fire.

"Please sit down, Adeline." Henry stepped into the kitchen, gesturing a hand toward the barstools.

The logs inside the stone fireplace crackled and popped, casting soft shadows against the leather sofas as Adeline headed to the kitchen. When she reached the island, it had already been set for two people. Her stomach dropped. Was he expecting someone else? Maybe she shouldn't be there.

"Actually, I forgot that I have to help my mom with something today," she said, taking a step back. It wasn't a good lie, but it was the first thing that popped into her head. "I better go."

Henry smiled as he poured fresh-squeezed orange juice into two glasses. When they reached the rim, he looked at her. "I set the table for us, my dear girl," he said with a hint of humor. "No need to lie."

Color rushed into her cheeks as she avoided his gaze. "How did you know I was coming?"

"Lucky guess," he said, releasing a soft chuckle. "Now, please sit down and make yourself at home."

Henry attended to the pancakes that were ready to be served. Their light, warm aroma stirred Adeline's senses as she took a seat. She watched Henry stack the fluffy pancakes on a large serving platter. She thought for sure the tower of pancakes would topple over as he placed them on the island.

"Let's eat." Steam swirled off the hot breakfast as Henry slid into the seat beside Adeline. "Please help yourself."

Adeline tucked her hair behind her ears before stabbing a small stack of pancakes with her fork and setting them on her plate. She drenched them in butter and maple syrup before cutting them into pieces and taking her first bite.

A collision of sweet, sugary bliss plowed into her taste buds as Adeline closed her eyes, savoring the flavor. They were the best pancakes she had ever eaten. The taste kept getting better and better. She wasn't sure how Henry could make ordinary meals taste that good, but it thrilled her.

"Do you like it?" Henry asked.

"Yes," she said, stuffing another piece into her mouth.

"Wonderful!"

They both ate, enjoying the sound of the fire. The kitchen window showed a view of the forest, the trees and their colored branches swinging lazily in the breeze. It was an incredible sight. The longer she stared, the more certain she was that the color was more vibrant than the trees at her house. It was like they had been splashed with paint.

There were plenty of leftovers when they finished eating. Adeline wanted to eat more, but her stomach wouldn't allow it.

"Thank you for breakfast," Adeline said, placing her napkin beside her sticky plate.

"You're so welcome."

Adeline wasn't used to someone being so nice to her and didn't know how to act as she stared at her hands in her lap. After her father's death, everyone had treated her differently, and she feared Henry would too if he found out about the accident. She wasn't planning on telling anyone in Black Mountain about it. That was a secret she would take to the grave.

"Mr. Snow…"

"Call me Henry," he said cheerfully. "Mr. Snow makes me feel old."

"Henry." She flashed a quick smile. "Strange things happened yesterday, and I was wondering if you could help me understand them."

"Of course," he said, flattening the hairs of his mustache.

"When I got back to…the old house yesterday, it was as if I'd never left," she said, tossing her natural waves over her shoulder. "No one had any idea I'd been gone, even though I was away for a long time."

Henry turned in his seat until he was square with Adeline. "What do you think happened?"

"I don't know what to think, that's why I asked you."

"Well," he said, stroking his trimmed white beard, "it sounds to me like time stood still."

"That's impossible. There's no way that can happen."

"But it did." Henry grinned.

Adeline sat in silence, contemplating Henry's words. He acted like time standing still was as casual as talking about the weather. But he was right. Time did seem to freeze when she was in the forest.

"How?"

"You are no longer in your world, Adeline."

"W-what?"

"You have discovered one of the best-kept secrets of all time," Henry said, eyes sparkling in the kitchen's light. "Once you stepped into the gated forest, you entered a different realm."

"That can't be true." Adeline slumped back into her seat. "My aunt told me this section of the forest was owned by a man named Mr. Wilder, and it's only five acres of woods."

"That is true. He did own it. But that small piece of land is a supernatural portal to this realm," Henry said. "Mr. Wilder's ancestors figured that out decades ago. That's why they fenced it off and protected it, so that no one would find out about this secret. Over the years, there have been a few daredevils who climbed over that old fence and entered this world, but unfortunately, it didn't end well for them because they weren't prepared."

"This is crazy." Adeline raked a shaky hand through her auburn hair.

"It may sound crazy, but I can assure you it's real."

"So I'm no longer in Black Mountain?"

"That is correct."

Adeline stood and started pacing. "Is that why my cellphone has been acting weird?" She pulled her dead cellphone from her back pocket and held it out to him.

Henry nodded. "It will shut off anytime you step into the forest that is owned by the Wilder family and will not turn back on until you are back in your world."

"Let me get this straight," Adeline said, tucking her lifeless phone away. "The gate behind my house is some kind of entrance to this world, and anytime I go into it, time stops until I come back?"

"Yes," Henry said with a nod. "You could stay here for months, and no one would ever know you were gone."

Adeline blinked. "I don't understand."

"You don't have to understand, Adeline."

"But I want to!"

"You'll soon find that this place differs greatly from the world you grew up in." Henry's brows flattened. "There are mysterious things here that will bypass the understanding of your natural thinking. You must let go of what you know to be normal and trust what happens, even when you cannot grasp it."

"None of this makes any sense."

"I know it doesn't, but it will one day." Henry slid his thin frame from the barstool. His wrinkles deepened as he smiled, plucking Adeline's thick jacket from the coatrack and handing it to her. "It's only your second day. Give it time, and you'll understand how things work here."

Adeline put on her coat, clueless to where they were going. "Where am I, Henry?"

"You're in my cabin, of course," he said.

"I know that." Adeline gave him a look. "I mean, what is the name of this world?"

Henry slid his arms into his gray tweed jacket before placing his newsboy cap on top of his head. "It doesn't have a name," he said, buttoning up his coat.

"Why not?"

"It just doesn't. But the more you come here, the more you'll learn about the different territories and regions that are spread out across this world."

"There are other places here?"

"Oh yes, this planet is quite large," he said. "You have already been in the forest and my cabin; next, I'll show you the garden."

"The garden?"

"Yes." Henry's face lit with delight. "It's by far my favorite place to explore, and I am certain it will be yours as well."

He strode past the living room and into the dining area, heading toward the back door. Adeline was at his heels, wondering what to expect as she brushed by a long oak table. She tingled all over as he reached for the doorknob.

With one twist, the door opened, and Adeline's hand flew to her mouth.

Chapter Ten

Adeline suppressed a small laugh as she stepped onto the porch, eyes fixated on the garden that went on for ages. She took no notice of the furnishing on the wooden deck. Her interest was solely on the cherry blossoms shading the cobblestone paths that roamed through the stunning flowers and trees that had no end.

Unbelievable.

Marble fountains, along with bird baths and statues, decorated the neatly groomed area. Their number was impossible to count. Gazebos and arbors overgrown with honeysuckles were spread throughout the manicured garden, along with benches resting beneath the shade of the apple and pear trees full of delicious fruits waiting to be picked. The cold weather affected nothing; everything was in full bloom.

It was perfection.

"Go on." Henry gestured to the garden. "I know you want to explore it."

Adeline's eyes went wide. "You're not coming with me?"

"Not this time."

She lifted a hand against the sun, looking out at the garden. It was so vast. "Will I get lost?"

"Sometimes the greatest treasures are discovered by getting lost."

"That doesn't answer my question."

"Have fun." Henry planted himself into a sturdy rocking chair. "I will see you later."

Studying him for a moment, Adeline realized her newest friend enjoyed speaking in riddles. And though she was nervous about going alone, the garden was too beautiful to ignore.

Adeline departed from Henry Snow, drinking in the fresh air as she ventured down the first path she saw. Every square inch seemed to be covered with colorful flowers in full bloom. Chipmunks scurried by as Adeline took her time, soaking in the beauty.

She rounded the corner and entered a tunnel encased in lush greenery. It was short and pleasant, leading to a flowery paradise arranged in the most spectacular way.

Butterflies, big and small, fluttered from one flowerbed to the next. Adeline couldn't stop herself from picking a daffodil as she passed. She sniffed it, enjoying the sweet fragrance, before tossing it into the breeze.

Adeline jumped from path to path, mesmerized by all she saw. She stumbled upon a peaceful pond full of swans and ducks, along with a grapevine that went on for miles. She plucked a grape free and popped it into her mouth. The sweetness of the fruit awakened her taste buds, and she picked another one before carrying on.

Her mind couldn't comprehend who could have created such an enchanting place overloaded with detail and beauty. There had to be thousands of gardeners working day and night to keep up with the vast garden.

But where were they? She hadn't seen gardeners—or anyone, for that matter. It was like the garden took care of itself.

Overwhelmed with the garden that kept getting prettier with each step, Adeline forgot about her pain and misery and became completely submerged in the enchanted world she found herself in.

The further she explored, the more she realized that each section of the garden was unique and beautiful in its own way. No two areas were the same, and each new path opened into several others for her to explore. It would take hours, or even days and weeks, to experience every part of the garden.

Then she saw a narrow path. Nothing was glamorous about it, only a dirt trail surrounded by large evergreens, but something pulled Adeline toward it.

The evergreens lining the path grew close together, making it hard to see through them. Adeline felt safe within their canopy. The only sounds were the pops and cracks of the sticks and pinecones beneath her sneakers as she ventured onward. It was a peaceful stroll, not overly long or short. When it ended, Adeline paused for a moment, using her hand to block the brilliant sunlight.

She was disappointed to see a plain pasture surrounded by a thick barrier of evergreen trees. It was spacious and green, but boring compared to the other parts of the garden.

Movement in the center of the field caught her eye. Someone was standing there.

Adeline hid behind a stout evergreen. She tried to slow her breathing as she stared at the stranger. They held up a bow and pulled the string taut, sending an arrow into a large hay bale.

She thought it was a woman at first, but realized the tall, lean figure was a young man with chestnut-colored hair nearly as long as hers. He wore dark jeans, and his white shirt showed the pop of his back muscles when he pulled back the bowstring with ease.

The breeze rustled his wavy hair as he stood tall and took aim. He was at least fifty yards away from the target, against a line of huge evergreens. Adeline could barely see it from where she stood.

The arrow zipped through the air, nailing the bullseye.

"Whoa," she said.

The young man peered over his shoulder, sending Adeline into a panic. Throwing her hand over her mouth, she could have kicked herself for giving away her location as the stranger did a slow scan of the empty field.

A contagious smile erupted on his face, as if he could see her behind the tree. She glimpsed his full beard before he faced the target again. He reached into the quiver strapped to his back and loaded his bow with another arrow, hitting the bullseye again with little effort.

Who is he? Why is he shooting in the middle of nowhere?

Adeline didn't know what to do. Should she talk to him or go back the way she came?

Though the young man was skilled with a bow, Adeline was sure he wasn't dangerous. She was more worried about introducing herself to a stranger.

Just thinking about it made her sweat, but there was something about him that intrigued her, like the feeling she had when she'd met Henry Snow. She had to find out who he was.

Forcing herself out from her hiding spot, Adeline stepped into the sunny pasture.

Chapter Eleven

Nerves simmered in Adeline's stomach as she moved through the field. Her heart rate doubled as the man casually turned around, his bow relaxed at his side.

"I thought I heard someone." The young man gave her a dazzling smile. "You must be Adeline."

Warmth flooded Adeline as she looked into his emerald green eyes. They stood out against his tan skin. He wasn't overly attractive, having plain features that wouldn't stand out in a crowd, but his green eyes were hypnotizing.

"How do you know my name?" she stammered.

"Henry told me all about you," he said, stepping forward and extending his hand. "I'm Jesse."

Seeing that he wasn't strikingly handsome settled some of Adeline's nerves as she shook his hand, feeling the rough calluses on his palm. He was a lot taller than her and evidently in shape, with a lean frame that illustrated his strength. His friendly smile made her think he wasn't like most guys in their early twenties.

"Do you live in the cabin with Henry?" she asked, withdrawing her hand.

"I do."

From the stories Henry had told her, she'd assumed Henry's friends were around his age. Clearly not. How had they met?

"Would you like to try?" Jesse asked, following her gaze to the longbow that was almost as tall as she was.

Adeline took a step back with a quick shake of her head. She didn't want to embarrass herself. "No, thanks."

"Come on." Jesse held the bow out to her. "It will be fun."

"I've never used a bow before."

"Let's change that," he said, his lips pulling into a smile. "Follow me."

Reluctantly, Adeline trailed behind him as he walked toward the target.

"Let's shoot from here." Jesse stopped when they were about ten yards away from the target nestled amongst the hay. "I'll show you the proper stance and have you mimic it."

With his bow still in hand, Jesse turned his body sideways. His feet were shoulder width apart and firmly planted as he rotated his upper body toward the bale of hay. He retrieved an arrow from his quiver and nocked it against the string. His muscles flexed as he pulled back with ease until his fingers touched the corner of his mouth.

Holding her breath, Adeline watched as he released the arrow. It cut through the air and slammed into the bullseye, sending pieces of hay flying into the air.

"Now you try," Jesse said, handing her the bow.

Adeline gripped the bow and nearly dropped it. Her muscles fought against the bow's weight as she inspected the smooth wood that looked like it had been carved by hand. It was beautifully made, but way too long and heavy for her liking.

"Wrong hand." Jesse laughed, helping her put it in the correct hand.

"But I'm right-handed."

"This bow has to be in your right hand in order to shoot it properly," Jesse said. "And I know it's too big for you, but you'll still be able to use it."

Adeline pressed her lips together as she looked ahead. Pulling the bowstring back with her left hand would be challenging. She doubted she was strong enough, but she decided to give it a try.

Adeline copied his stance and turned her upper body toward the target without moving her legs. Once she was situated, Jesse helped her nock an arrow.

"Now pull the string back toward you," he said.

Adeline's arms shook as she attempted to draw back the string. She gritted her teeth, her muscles burning. When it felt like her elbow was bumping against a brick wall, she let go, relieving the tension in her arms.

The arrow leaped into the air and landed in the grass a few feet in front of her.

Dropping her head, Adeline couldn't stop the heat from rushing to her cheeks.

"That was a good first try!"

Jesse's enthusiasm surprised her, but she shook her head. "That was terrible."

"You have to start somewhere." Jesse handed her another arrow. "And besides, the draw weight for this bowstring is over sixty pounds, which means you're *very* strong. Most people your age wouldn't be able to pull it back at all."

Adeline's brows furrowed. "But I didn't pull it all the way back."

"But you pulled it back some. Let's try again. This time I'll help."

Placing another arrow in the bow, Jesse positioned himself behind Adeline, which caught her off guard. Her mouth went dry as she caught the scent of cologne; it smelled like cedarwood.

Adeline raised the weighty bow, and Jesse leaned down to her level, helping her aim toward the bale of hay. Heat pooled in her stomach when he placed his hand over hers. His callouses rubbed against her knuckles as he helped her get the tight bowstring to the correct position.

Even though Jesse did most of the work, her arms stung from the pressure as she held the bow steady while lining it up with the bullseye.

"Now," Jesse said.

Adeline released her fingers, and the arrow shot out like a bullet. The sharp point nailed the center of the bullseye, knocking pieces of hay from the unlucky target.

Adeline squealed with laughter.

"Good job!" Jesse gave her a high-five. "Want to try again?"

"Nope," she said, extending the bow to him. "I'd rather end on a high note."

"Works for me." He chuckled, taking hold of his bow, and walked toward the haystack to retrieve his arrows.

Adeline followed, plucking an arrow from the hay. "You're really good, by the way."

"Thank you."

"How long have you been doing it?"

"A *very* long time."

A group of robins flew from the evergreen branches, heading toward a tall wooden structure in the distance. Adeline squinted at some kind of ropes course that soared over the tree line.

"What is that?" she asked, pointing.

Jesse used his hand to block the sun. "That's our obstacle course."

"You have an obstacle course?"

"Yeah," he said, placing the last arrow in his quiver. "We have tons of stuff in our training facility."

"Training facility?"

"Yep." He nodded. "It's where I do most of my workouts and drills."

Adeline shaded her eyes from the sunlight. The obstacle course seemed to touch the sky. The thick forest covered most of it, but she could see a tight rope ladder and wooden platforms that could only be accessed by jumping to them. "So, it's like an outdoor gym?"

"It's way better than a gym."

Adeline's adventurous spirit stirred once again. She had always liked obstacle courses, especially the ones at summer camp. "What else is over there?"

"Only one way to find out," he said as his green eyes lit with an inner glow.

Jesse set out in that direction with his bow in hand. Adeline rubbed the back of her neck, wondering if she should go with him. But as he neared the tree line, an engulfing sense of peace settled around her. There was no denying she was drawn to him. Jesse had the same magnetic pull Henry did.

"Are you coming?" Jesse asked as he neared the path through the trees.

Adeline bit her bottom lip as she looked from the obstacle course to him. He smiled widely. Everything about him radiated happiness, and she needed some of that in her life.

"I'm coming!"

Chapter Twelve

Adeline's auburn hair flew behind her as she ran to catch up with Jesse.

"Almost there," he said, smiling as she fell into step beside him.

The small path through the evergreens was exactly like the previous one she had followed, peaceful and covered with pine needles.

"Do you hunt a lot?" she asked, clasping her hands in front of her so she wouldn't bump into him.

"Not really. I mostly use my bow for protection."

"Protection?" Her eyes darted from tree to tree, expecting something to come rushing toward them. "From what?"

"You'll soon find out."

Adeline's stomach clenched. "Is this world dangerous?"

"It can be," he said, nudging her with his elbow. "But you're safe with me."

Her face reddened as she focused ahead.

"You're really going to like the training area," Jesse told her, moving a wild branch out of their way. "It's one of my favorite places."

Adeline forced a smile, but it quickly faded. "Why do you want to hang out with me?"

"Why would I not?" he asked with a slight frown.

"Most guys your age wouldn't want to."

Jesse grinned. "You'll come to find that I am unlike anyone you've ever met."

"That's what Henry said when I first met him."

"It's true."

Adeline waited for him to explain, but he didn't as they continued quietly down the path. She enjoyed being around him and Henry, and that was enough for her.

The path took them to a beautiful area full of flamboyant hibiscuses and butterfly bushes that were taller than she was. Hundreds of butterflies fluttered through the air as Adeline and Jesse stepped onto a cobblestone path and journeyed onward.

Breathing in the honey-like fragrance, Adeline felt like she was in heaven as a few butterflies gently landed on her shoulders. They rested a moment before fluttering away.

Crossing over a stone bridge, Adeline saw two brick pillars covered in jasmine. They were about ten feet apart, an iron arch connecting them at the top like a rainbow. Matching walls extended from them, with white jasmine climbing up the red bricks. Adeline couldn't see what they were hiding; she could only see the top of the obstacle course.

Adeline's mind ran wild as she neared the entrance. It was wide open for anyone to come and go as they pleased. A current of nerves stopped her in her tracks. The training area was more intimidating than she'd imagined.

The outdoor area resembled a military training camp, but that wasn't the part that troubled her. It was the huge weapon rack lining the back wall, stocked with a variety of weapons that looked medieval. There were axes, war hammers, swords, and spears aplenty. With so many weapons to choose from, it looked like they could supply an entire army. There were also wooden dummies with deep gouges carved into them.

"What do you think?" Jesse asked, placing his hands on his hips as he looked around.

"I wasn't expecting this." Adeline backed up a few steps.

"Don't worry, they won't hurt you." Jesse fought back a smile. "Let me show you around."

The area was packed with training equipment, divided into different stations. Jesse showed her some of the metal exercise equipment until they reached a section that was clearly used for archery. A few hay bales were backed up against the brick wall with red targets spray-painted on them. Some had arrows stuck in them, while others looked like they had never been used. A sturdy wooden rack was loaded with recurve bows and quivers full of arrows. They were all different sizes, some even small enough for a child.

"This is where I practice my archery." Jesse motioned to the bales of hay. "Hence the red targets."

Adeline grinned, following Jesse to a huge playground for adults. While it looked fun, nothing about it looked easy. It was high off the ground, and the only way up was to climb a tricky corkscrew climber with impossible twists and turns. A Burma bridge and shuffle bars extended from the climber, ending in a length of monkey bars over a deep pool of mud that had a stench to it. Every part of the structure looked like it was designed to make its challengers fall fifteen feet to the ground.

"This is a great place to work on strength and perseverance," Jesse said, gesturing to the large metal arrangement. "I can't tell you how many times I have fallen over the years."

"That's really high."

"You think that's high?" Jesse snickered. "Wait until we go to the obstacle course."

The obstacle course took up most of the training area. Adeline's stomach plunged when they stood under it. She wasn't usually afraid of heights, but the sheer height of it made her uneasy.

It wasn't a typical obstacle course. Swinging axes, spiked barriers, and uneven platforms would force anyone to lose their balance. Adeline counted twelve levels, and the farther up it went, the more challenging it became. There were no nets to catch anyone if they fell, and there wasn't a rope to attach oneself to, which meant there could be no mistakes.

One fall from the top would mean death.

"You actually go on that?" Adeline swallowed hard.

"Oh yeah, it's a lot of fun once you get used to it," Jesse said, hands on his hips again as he stretched to look up at the highest part of the course. "But we don't let just anyone use it."

"You couldn't pay me to do that," Adeline told him, watching the ax blades glisten in the sunlight.

"One day, you're going to beg me to try it." Jesse smirked as he turned to leave.

"I highly doubt that."

Jesse showed her around another part of the training camp; it was filled with equally complex obstacles.

"Who uses this place?" she asked.

"Mostly me," Jesse said. "Over the years, I've trained people of all ages here, but most of them didn't stick with it."

"I can see why."

As they headed back toward the entrance, Adeline spotted a plain metal building tucked in the corner. It was big enough to be a garage with double doors in the front, but it looked more like a storage unit with no windows.

Adeline pointed. "What's in there?"

Jesse looked, adjusting the quiver around his chest. "Ah, that's our combat simulator."

"Meaning...?"

"I'll show you."

Jesse opened the door for her, and the lights turned on automatically. Adeline relaxed when she saw that the room was empty, the white walls and concrete floor bare.

"What's the point of this room?"

"This is where you can work on strength, speed, stamina, and agility."

"How do you do all that in here?" Adeline asked, thrusting a hand at the space. "It's empty."

"Just wait."

Jesse pressed his palm on a square device made of metal next to the double doors. A red laser appeared, slowly scanning his hand. It beeped once, and a holographic screen popped up on the wall next to it. He tapped something on the keyboard made of light.

With a final beep, the room transformed into a winter wonderland as if Adeline had been dropped into the middle of a snow-covered forest. Birds chirped in the distance as snowflakes fell from the sky, dusting the tree branches.

"Is this some kind of illusion?" she asked, holding out her hand to catch the snowflakes.

"It's better than that." He tossed her a grin. "Touch the snow."

Thinking her hand would go straight through it, Adeline bent down and was stunned when her fingers grazed soft snow. She scooped up a handful, shocked when it froze her bare hand. The texture, the temperature, the color—it all seemed real.

"How is this possible?" She tossed the snow back to the ground and wiped her wet hands on her jacket.

"Anything is possible here," Jesse said, staring out into the snowy forest.

"But why is it in the training area?"

"Because it's used for combat exercises."

"Combat?" Adeline stuffed her cold hands into her jacket. "This place looks more like a dream to me."

"That's because I haven't activated the challenger yet."

"The challenger?"

"Yep. Each program has different challengers," Jesse said as snowflakes sprinkled his thick beard, "but they don't appear until I say the command."

Adeline didn't like the sound of that, but it intrigued her. She rolled her shoulders back. "Show me."

"Are you sure?" Jesse cocked an eyebrow.

"Yes."

"Okay." He extracted an arrow from his quiver. "Stand behind me."

Adeline sucked in a breath of air as she rushed behind Jesse. She shivered as snow melted into her sneakers, soaking her socks.

"Are you ready?" Jesse asked over his shoulder.

"As I'll ever be."

Jesse placed the arrow on the bowstring. "*Ready!*"

The sudden roar of a lion reverberated through the forest, knocking snow from the evergreens. Adeline moved closer to Jesse, frantically searching for the beast as it roared once more.

Then she saw it.

A massive lion charged through the trees, heading straight toward them. It was running full speed, its enormous paws pounding into the snow.

Adeline clutched Jesse's shirt, stifling a scream, but it didn't faze his concentration. He simply raised his bow and aimed his sharp arrow, his attention fully on the raging lion.

A gut-wrenching roar filled the air as the lion jumped at them, but Jesse's arrow slammed into its open mouth. The creature smashed into a nearby tree and fell to the ground. Its eyes rolled to the back of its head as it lay unmoving in the snow before slowly disappearing.

A scream ripped from Adeline's throat, and she took off in the opposite direction. Tree branches slapped across her face as she desperately searched for the door, but she couldn't find the bare white wall she had seen earlier.

"*Off!*" Jesse called from behind her.

The snowy woods faded away like dust to the wind until all that was left was the empty room. Even the temperature changed, warmer now that the snow was gone. But Adeline was still cold, and her wet socks confirmed she had been running through a snowy forest.

Panting, Adeline placed her hand on her chest as she glared at Jesse.

"Are you all right?" Jesse ran up to her, his face clouded with concern.

"That was terrifying!"

"I'm sorry, Adeline. I didn't mean to scare you."

Adeline jammed her shaking fingers through her long hair, trying to calm her erratic breathing. The last thing she'd expected to see in the peaceful forest was a lion.

"Can you get hurt in the simulator?" she asked, voice trembling.

"Oh, yeah," he said. "There have been quite a few people who have programmed it outside of their skill level and gotten injured."

"So, that lion could have killed us?" she asked through gritted teeth.

"Well, technically, it could have," Jesse said with an easy shrug, "but I wouldn't have allowed that to happen."

Adeline's mouth fell open. "I could have died."

"Trust me, that thing had no chance of touching you," he said. "That was one of the lower levels."

"Killing a lion is considered a lower level?" Her eyebrows flew up in shock. "I don't even want to think about what would be at an advanced level."

Jesse laughed as he opened the door, allowing the sunlight to pour into the room. "I won't be showing you those levels today."

The sun warmed her cold cheeks as they exited the building. Adeline was glad to escape from the strange room. The simulator was by far the most advanced technology she had ever used, making her certain that nothing quite like it existed in her world.

"Let's check out some other places in the garden," Jesse said, his bow still in hand.

Adeline gave a quick nod, though she wasn't sure she could handle much more. The extravagant beauty of the garden, along with meeting Jesse and exploring his training facility, had been more than enough for her. But instead of protesting, she followed Jesse into the garden.

Adeline spent all day exploring the magical garden with Jesse. The more they roamed, the more she realized just how massive it was. They had walked for hours, and Jesse told her she hadn't even explored a third of the beautiful landscape.

Exhaustion set in as evening approached, and Adeline was thankful when Jesse offered to take her home. It was clear he knew the forest well. He easily guided her down the multiple paths that were too overwhelming for her to remember. Hopefully, she would learn her way around at some point.

The last path ended, and Adeline frowned at the old, rusted gate. She didn't want to go back, but there was no avoiding it.

"Good luck on your first day of school tomorrow," Jesse said.

"How did you know it was my first day?" Adeline asked, brows stitching together.

"See you around, Adeline." The corner of his lips rose as he turned and faded into the trees.

Kneading her forehead, Adeline didn't bother dissecting his comment as she opened the loud, rusty gate. A lot of things hadn't made sense lately. No use overloading her brain any more than it already was.

The forest was growing dark fast, but the sun was rising for the day as Adeline entered her world. Turning around, she was baffled to see it looked identical to her world. The falling darkness she'd just walked through was nowhere to be seen. Instead, sunlight shone through the trees and the birds tittered about, readying themselves for the day ahead.

Adeline stepped back into the forest. As soon as she passed through the open gate, it was practically nighttime, and the temperature had dropped.

"What the...?" she said aloud, staring at the shadowy forest.

Adeline left the forest once more and had to shield her eyes from the bright morning sun.

"This doesn't make any sense."

Adeline glanced back at the woods; sunshine was filtering through the leaves. There must be something that made the forest match her world, something that shielded it from outsiders.

"So weird." Adeline pulled the key from the lock.

Her mind whirled as she closed the gate and quickly wrapped it with the chain and locked it before heading toward the quiet house. It was still early in the morning, but she was exhausted.

She wasn't looking forward to spending most of the day unpacking the remaining boxes and moving furniture from room to room, but there was no getting out of it. Mom would force her to help.

When she snuck into the dark house, she was relieved to find her family still asleep. She yawned as she crawled into bed, shutting her weary eyes. She wouldn't be able to sleep long, but it was better than nothing.

CHAPTER THIRTEEN

ADELINE HUGGED HER KNEES as she sat on the old gymnasium floor, listening to the physical education teacher explain the rules of dodgeball. It was her first day as a sophomore at her new high school, and she already hated it. Carol was in most of her classes, which made things a little better, but she felt out of place and didn't like the strange looks from other students.

Adeline had survived most of the day; she just had to get through gym class. She normally loved physical exercise, but she was counting the minutes on the clock that hung above the double doors.

One more hour and she would be free to go.

Adeline tuned out the P.E. instructor and scanned the thirty students in her class. She recognized a few of them she had seen throughout the day, but most of them were new, likely from a different grade.

Her heart skipped when she noticed a guy with dark curls. He looked more athletic than the other students standing near him. He was also a head taller than most, and Adeline had to admit, shockingly handsome.

He was sandwiched between two pretty girls who were eating up whatever he was whispering to them. They quieted their giggles as he continued to tease them, flashing a perfect smile. Adeline needed to know his name.

Adeline leaned closer to Carol and whispered, "Who is that?"

Carol followed her gaze and smiled. "That's Jonathan McThorn," she said in her ear. "He's the most popular guy in school."

That last name sounded familiar. "Does his family own the land around my house?"

"Yep. They're stupid rich."

"Is he our age?"

"No." She kept her voice low. "He's a senior."

Adeline was enthralled by Jonathan's stunning appearance. It didn't seem fair to the other guys around him. He put them all to shame.

"Do you see that pretty girl with black hair?" Carol whispered. "The one with the blue shirt."

Adeline quickly found her among a clique of haughty girls, but describing her as pretty was an understatement. She was gorgeous. Her hair was long and straight as a board, and her hourglass figure would make any girl jealous. Arrogance spewed from her big brown eyes, however, and Adeline decided she wanted nothing to do with her. She looked like trouble, and that was the last thing Adeline needed in her life.

"Yeah. Who is she?"

"Jonathan's twin sister, Raven."

Raven McThorn looked bored out of her mind as she inspected her manicured nails. Adeline could now see the resemblance to her brother. Both had a tan complexion that made it seem that she and her twin had Native American in their blood. She was beautiful, but she looked like a typical snob.

Adeline went back to staring at Jonathan. He was the most attractive human she had ever laid eyes on; it was impossible to look away.

Jonathan glanced in Adeline's direction. His eyes caught hers, and she froze. His gray-blue gaze was curious as he watched her, not caring that he stared.

Adeline's face burned as she casually looked back to the gym teacher, but she was sure her bright red cheeks gave her away.

Adeline had never had a boyfriend before, and though she'd had guy friends back at the beach, none of them looked anything like Jonathan McThorn. His looks alone intimidated her, and so did the girls next to him. He was clearly part of the popular crowd and out of Adeline's league.

Gym class flew by as soon as the dodgeball game began. Jonathan McThorn was on Adeline's team, but she couldn't bring herself to look at him. She caught him glancing at her several times, but figured he was just curious about the new girl at school.

After the school bell rang, Adeline parted ways with Carol and headed toward the school buses. She hated riding the bus home, but she didn't have her driver's license, Mom was at work, and Carol had volleyball practice every day after school.

Adeline was old enough, but too afraid to get her license. She hadn't driven since the accident and wasn't planning on ever doing it again. Fear had crippled her since that dreadful day, and she had no plans to address it anytime soon.

Adeline stopped on the walkway and searched for Rebecca as a rush of students pushed past her. Some were heading to their cars, while others headed toward the buses parked along the curb. A wave of insecurity rushed in as she stood alone, looking for her little sister.

"Out of my way!" a harsh voice said, shoving Adeline in the back.

Adeline nearly lost her balance, but quickly regained her footing. Clenching her fists, she spun around, jaw locked tight.

Her anger quickly turned to fear as Raven McThorn stared her down, surrounded by her friends. Adeline swallowed, her throat suddenly dry. She hated conflict, but she wasn't going to let anyone bully her.

"Push me again and see what happens."

The girls gasped and looked at their leader.

"What did you say to me?" Raven sneered, raising her chin in the air.

Adeline's gut twisted. Raven was a head shorter than her but still intimidating, especially with her friends. Standing tall, Adeline crossed her arms, masking her fear. "You heard me."

"Watch it, new girl," Raven said. "You don't want to get on my bad side."

"I'll take my chances." Adeline turned away and hustled toward the buses, her heart beating a million miles a minute. She thought she might throw up.

Good job, Adeline. You just had to piss off the popular girl.

Adeline didn't stop until she reached the bus. Some students were already getting on, but she wanted to wait for her sister.

"Nice car, new girl!" Raven yelled, devolving into unnaturally loud laughter with her friends as she headed to the parking lot. "I love the color."

Adeline's cheeks flushed red, and tears stung her eyes as she raced onto the bus. She plopped down into an empty seat, trying her best to calm down. Once her emotions were under control, she glanced out the window, watching the students driving away in their cars.

That should be me.

Adeline spotted Raven McThorn driving a brand-new BMW. The solid red paint job sparkled in the sun as it passed the bus. She tried to push away the jealousy she felt. Her family could never afford a vehicle like that, and even if they could...she would never drive it.

Rebecca slid into the worn seat beside Adeline. "How was your day?"

"It sucked," Adeline said tightly, refusing to turn away from the window.

"Mine wasn't much better." Rebecca placed her backpack on her lap and sank lower in the seat.

Adeline didn't bother asking Rebecca for details as the bus pulled away from the curb. Sadness consumed her as she kept her eyes glued to the activity outside her window. It was the place she often went; a place she was used to.

She missed Dad and the beach town she'd grown up in. She missed her friends and playing sports. She missed her teammates and being a part of a team.

As her thoughts spiraled deeper and darker, Henry Snow and Jesse came to mind. The terrible thoughts came to a halt and went directly to her new friends and the forest beyond the gate.

Just thinking about them made a smile break across her face. They were the best thing that had happened to her since Dad died.

Adeline still didn't like Black Mountain, but she was grateful to have found them and couldn't wait to go back to the forest.

Chapter Fourteen

Adeline sighed loudly, tossing her bookbag on the kitchen table. Another long day at school, and she was glad it was over. It was the middle of her second week in Black Mountain, and though Carol wasn't a part of the popular crowd, she was a social butterfly and seemed to be friends with everyone. Adeline had met so many people that she couldn't keep track of names, just faces. Despite Carol's efforts, Adeline wasn't interested in making friends.

"I'm starving," Carol said, dropping into a kitchen chair.

Rebecca placed her bookbag along the wall. "I think we have some chips and salsa."

Carol had given them a ride home since her practice had been canceled and planned to spend the afternoon with them. Rebecca grabbed a bag of chips and two bowls from the cabinet while Adeline headed to the fridge for the salsa before joining Carol at the table.

Carol did most of the talking, like always, and since she had been with Adeline all day, she zeroed in on Rebecca. Rebecca didn't talk much, but she was comfortable with her cousin.

Tuning Carol out, Adeline watched the trees move in the wind. Just looking at it stirred something in her spirit. It had been over a week since she had gone into the forest, and she was dying to go back.

There were no words to explain how the other realm made her feel, but there was something enchanting about it that made her want more. She needed to learn more about it almost as much as she needed to breathe.

"Hello?" Carol waved a hand in Adeline's face. "Earth to Adeline."

Adeline blinked and looked at her cousin. "What?"

"I asked you a question."

"Oh, sorry." Adeline grabbed a chip and dipped it into the bowl of salsa. "What did you say?"

"I was wondering if you've had any other altercations with Raven McThorn," Carol said, digging her hand into the bag of chips. "I saw the way she was looking at you during gym today."

Thankfully, Raven had left Adeline alone, but she continued to give her nasty stares, and so did her friends. Adeline acted like she didn't notice. They were surely gossiping about her, but she couldn't do anything about it.

Adeline wasn't used to having enemies. She had been quite popular at her old school, having been very social before the accident. Much had changed since then. She felt sick to her stomach every time she walked into gym class, but she never showed it. She refused to look weak, especially in front of Raven.

"No, she hasn't said a word to me."

"Probably because you stood up to her," Carol said. "I can guarantee you no one has *ever* done that before."

"Why?" Adeline asked. "She's a bully."

"Her dad is a powerful man, and no one wants to get in his way."

"What does that have to do with Raven?"

"He adores her and will punish anyone who hurts his precious daughter," Carol said before stuffing another chip into her mouth. "Last year there was a girl who transferred from out of state. Raven's boyfriend at the time took a liking to her, and Raven was obviously not okay with it. Well, a few weeks into the school year, the new girl suddenly got expelled and was forced to go to boarding school."

Adeline's stomach flipped. "Why was she expelled?"

"No one knows; it was all very unexpected," Carol said. "But I have a feeling Mr. McThorn pulled some strings and got her kicked out."

"Why would he do that?"

"Because he can."

Adeline shifted uncomfortably in her chair as she crunched on another chip. She didn't like her new school, but she enjoyed being around her cousin and living close to the mysterious forest. If she were to be shipped to a boarding school, her life would be even more chaotic than it already was.

Carol's cellphone vibrated on the table, and her smile evaporated when she saw who was calling. "Crap! I forgot I was supposed to go on a run with Haley this afternoon." She quickly answered the phone and told her friend she was on the way as she snatched up her keys. Then she looked directly at Adeline. "Want to come?"

Adeline had enjoyed running in the past, but she knew she wouldn't be able to keep up with them. "No, thanks."

"Suit yourself," Carol said, heading toward the front door. "I'll see you two tomorrow."

"Bye," they said in unison.

Adeline bit into another chip as Carol exited the house. "How's school going for you?" she asked her sister.

"Okay, I guess," Rebecca said softly. "I think I made a friend today."

"That's good." Adeline smiled. Rebecca had a sweet personality, but her quiet demeanor made it hard for her to make new friends. That was one of the main reasons Rebecca hadn't wanted to move to a new town. "Is it a boy?"

Rebecca's cheeks reddened. "Maybe."

As if on cue, Rebecca's phone dinged.

"Is that him?"

"It's nobody." Rebecca seized her phone and hastily scooted out of her chair.

"I'm sure it's not," Adeline said playfully.

"I, uh...better do my homework," Rebecca said, grabbing her bookbag and heading toward her room.

Adeline grinned, knowing good and well Rebecca wasn't racing to her room to do homework. She wondered who the mystery boy could be.

Adeline cleared the table so Mom wouldn't fuss when she got home from work. She shoved the chips into the tight pantry and placed the bowl in the dishwasher. As she gave the table a quick wipe, she glanced outside and was instantly drawn to the forest that was off limits.

She hesitated. She had a ton of homework she needed to knock out, but it could wait. The forest was calling, and she had to answer.

Chapter Fifteen

Adeline raced to her room. She left her cellphone charging on the night-stand before grabbing the key to the gate. Within minutes, she was on the dirt path, walking under the canopy of colorful leaves.

She left the sun behind in her world. The sky past the gate was covered with dark, low-hanging clouds. It must have just rained. Drops of water fell onto her head and speckled her clothes as she made her way down the trail. Thunder rumbled in the distance, and Adeline wondered if another rainstorm was on the way.

Not wanting to get soaked, Adeline quickly found the first star pin and hustled down the worn path. Fat drops landed around her, splashing off rocks and pattering against the leaves as she searched the trees for another star pin.

The rain came down steadier now, and the thunder sounded closer. Adeline tucked her damp hair behind her ears and stepped onto a new wet trail, searching for the next clue. Her sneakers squished into the mud as she scouted the tree trunks.

"Hello there."

Adeline froze. She didn't recognize the sly male voice.

Fear flared to life when she spotted a young, fit man with short black hair staring at her. He was tall like Jesse, with olive-colored skin and sharp features. He looked to be in his late twenties and could easily pass as a McThorn. His black three-piece suit was an odd choice for wandering in the woods, and it got stranger the longer she looked at it. Thin streaks of gold spread throughout the dark fabric like veins, and they moved like the slow current of a stream. It was the strangest material she had ever seen.

"Who are you?" Adeline asked, eyeing the hilt of a sword strapped to his back.

The man lifted his thin, straight nose but said nothing as he locked eyes with her. They were as black as sin, and she felt a presence of evil pouring out of him like he was the devil himself. "I think the real question is, who are you?"

An icy shiver ran down the length of her spine. His voice alone created a note of terror through her.

"Answer me, girl!"

Shrinking back, Adeline said, "A-Adeline."

"Adeline what?"

"Bigsby."

"Bigsby." He rubbed his clean-shaven chin. "I've never heard of you. What territory are you from?"

"I'm n-not from here," she stuttered.

His black eyes expanded curiously. "You live beyond the barrier?"

Unsure of what barrier he spoke about, Adeline assumed he meant the chain-link fence. She tried to speak but couldn't find her voice. She nodded instead.

"Is that so?" A wicked smile smeared across his handsome face as he glanced around the dreary woods like he was looking for something. Her breathing hitched when his dark eyes focused back on her. She was in trouble. "You need to come with me."

Adeline's heart lurched violently when the man stepped toward her. His leather shoes sank into the wet earth as Adeline moved backward, keeping her eyes on the man. "I better... I need— I should get home."

"I don't think so."

Adeline bolted in the opposite direction, trying to keep her balance as she sprinted on the soft ground. The man tackled her from behind, sending her face-first into the mud. Pain ruptured up her back as she lay underneath her attacker, but he jerked her to her feet and held her arm in a tight, painful grip.

"Let go of me!"

Kicking and twisting, Adeline screamed, but he silenced her with a hard slap across the face. She fell to her knees, but he gripped her arm and forced her to stand once more.

"Scream again and see what I'll do," he hissed into her ear.

Adeline fought for air. Tears streamed down her stinging cheek as her captor tugged her against her will. She was too afraid to call for help or fight back.

Her captor tightened his grip and pulled her along. Her mind raced. Where were they going? What would he do to her?

"Let her go!"

Adeline shrieked, and her captor stopped their march.

Trembling, Adeline lifted her head and saw an overweight middle-aged man with a head full of bushy red hair and a big beard. He was tall, taller than the man who clutched her arm, with a bulging belly beneath his flannel.

"She belongs to me now!" her captor said, pulling her closer.

Crossing his arms, the man with the red hair rolled back his shoulders and squared up with the black-haired man. "I will give you one more chance," the older gentleman said firmly. "Release her at once or face the consequences."

The muscles in her captor's neck tightened as he stared at the unarmed woodsman. Silence hung between them. After a few long seconds, he freed Adeline and took a step back.

Rubbing her throbbing arm, Adeline couldn't stop shaking as she stood in place. She couldn't understand why he'd released her. He was the one with the sword, not the other man. Why obey him?

"Come here, child," the woodsman said, beckoning Adeline to him with a large hand. "I won't hurt you."

There was kindness in his words, and Adeline rushed toward her rescuer, glancing back to make sure the other man wasn't following her.

"This isn't over, Bigsby," the man said before stepping off the path and disappearing into the wet thicket.

Tears fell down Adeline's dirty face as she approached the man who had saved her. She stopped a few feet before reaching him and forced herself to look at him. Her fear faded and peace washed over her. It reminded her of Henry Snow and Jesse.

"Who are you?" she asked, voice shaking.

"You can call me Godfrey."

His kind face ignited into a brilliant smile, and Adeline felt like she had been shot in the chest. Her stomach fluttered with butterflies, and she found it impossible to pull her gaze from his crystal blue eyes that looked as if they had been photoshopped. They were so beautiful and pure they didn't look real.

Adeline smeared away her tears with shaky fingers, her eyes trained on the ground. "Thank you for saving me."

"You're welcome, Adeline."

She stiffened. "Who told you my name?"

"I live at the cabin." Godfrey smiled again, showing a small gap between his two front teeth.

"You live with Jesse and Henry?"

"I do." He nodded.

Relief swept through Adeline. She should have known he lived with them; he carried the same peace they did.

"Would you like me to take you there?"

Adeline nodded, using her sleeve to wipe her running nose.

"It's not too far from here."

Hugging her arms, Adeline fell into step with Godfrey. She breathed in his light cologne that smelled like the ocean breeze. The refreshing scent reminded her of Dad, bringing her some ease as they walked together, listening to the rain.

"Who was that man?" Adeline asked, peering over her shoulder.

"He goes by the name Ralock."

"Ray-lock," Adeline said the strange name quietly. Everything about him made her quiver, even saying his name. She had never felt such horror in all her life and hoped they would never cross paths again. "Do you know where he was taking me?"

"To his territory."

"Why?"

"No need to worry about that right now," Godfrey said with a soft expression. "He didn't take you, and that's all that matters."

Adeline trembled as her mind went to places it shouldn't. But one glance at her overweight companion quickly turned her dark thoughts into curiosity about the man who had saved her. She was glad he was with her. She felt safe with him, just like she had with his friends.

It was getting dark by the time the cabin came into view. Tears of joy appeared as Adeline hustled toward the smoke twirling from the stone chimney, the light rain stinging her cheeks.

Godfrey easily kept pace with her, and they were under the protection of the porch in no time. Her hand shook as she fumbled with the doorknob and quickly let herself in.

The warmth from the fireplace welcomed her, and the tension in her shoulders instantly dissolved. The cabin felt like home.

Henry was chopping vegetables on the kitchen island while Jesse added another log to the fire.

"Look who I found," Godfrey said, presenting Adeline to Henry and Jesse by laying a hand on the top of her head.

"Good heavens, child!" Henry dropped his knife and rushed to her. He engulfed her in a tight hug, and she melted into his thin frame. Tears slipped down her face as he released her and gently placed both hands on her shoulders. "Are you all right?"

Adeline nodded, smearing away her tears. "Godfrey saved me."

Jesse stepped in and drew her into a bear hug. She felt warm all over as tears welled up in her eyes again. They were like family to her, something she hadn't felt since Dad had passed.

Jesse freed her from his embrace. "I'm so glad my dad found you."

"Your dad?" Adeline sniffled as she looked at Godfrey. "He's your dad?"

"Well, yeah." Jesse smiled. "You can't see the resemblance?"

Godfrey and Jesse both chuckled while Adeline peered between them. She would have never guessed they were related. It wasn't just Godfrey's wavy red hair and fair, freckly skin that made him look so different from Jesse; he was much wider too.

Godfrey was heavyset with thick arms and a big belly, while Jesse was lean and fit. The only thing they had in common was their height and their unique eyes. Maybe they were more similar in personality than looks.

"Why don't you freshen up and put on some clean clothes while I finish dinner?" Henry said.

Adeline glanced down at herself and cringed. Her shoes were caked in mud and her entire front was dirty from when Ralock had tackled her to the ground. Color rose to her cheeks. "I didn't bring anything to change into."

"Not a problem at all," he told her. "We have everything you need."

"You have something that would fit me?"

"We have way more than that," Henry said. "Jesse will take you to one of our guest rooms while I finish dinner."

"I sure will," Jesse said. "Come with me, Adeline."

Adeline went with Jesse down the long hallway. Doors lined the walls, but Jesse opened the first one on the right and flicked on the light.

Adeline lit up when she entered the charming bedroom. It was pleasant and welcoming, with a large window that had a view of the garden and a stone fireplace with a mantle full of novels. The loveseat next to the fireplace looked just as cozy as the enormous bed. There was even a connecting bathroom that would make anyone feel at home.

Leaning against the doorframe, Jesse gestured to the maple dresser against the wall. "Everything you need is in there."

Adeline approached the mirrored dresser. One look at her reflection sent her spiraling into insecurity. Mud was smeared across her face and there was a noticeable red mark on her cheek. Her hair was a damp, tangled mess, but she acted like she didn't notice her appearance and opened the top drawer on the left.

It was empty.

Closing it, she searched the rest of the drawers, only to find them empty as well. She spun to face Jesse. "Is this some kind of joke?"

Jesse chuckled as he stepped into the room. "As much as I like jokes, I promise this isn't one."

"There's nothing in these drawers."

"This is no ordinary piece of furniture." Jesse tapped the dresser. "It can produce *any* kind of clothing you want. All you have to do is think about what you would like to wear."

Adeline squinted warily at him. "No way."

"I swear."

"Show me."

"All right." Jesse grinned. "If you could wear anything right now, what would it be?"

"I don't know. Something warm."

"Like what?"

"Maybe sweatpants and a sweatshirt."

"Good choice," Jesse said. "Now open one of the drawers."

Adeline kept her eyes on him. She had already searched the entire dresser.

"Give it another try."

Sighing, Adeline played along and pulled open the top drawer. Her jaw dropped. There was a neatly folded pair of gray sweatpants and a cozy sweatshirt. And they looked to be her size. "That's not possible."

"Isn't it cool?"

Scooping up the soft bundle, Adeline brought it to her face and breathed in the sweet smell of lavender. "This is insane."

"There are many amazing things here that are not in your world. This is one of them." Jesse patted her shoulder before heading to the door. "Holler if you need anything."

Adeline stayed glued in place as Jesse closed the door behind him. She inspected the sturdy dresser once more, but she couldn't find anything unusual about it. It looked like a typical piece of furniture she could purchase in her world, but it clearly wasn't. How had it created clothing out of nowhere?

Adeline shut her eyes and envisioned a pair of wool socks to replace her sopping wet ones. Once she had something in mind, she shut the drawer and jolted it back open again, gasping when she saw the exact pair of socks she had thought of.

"I cannot believe this."

Adeline moved her fingertips along the thick wool. They were just as real as the bundle of clothing in her hand. None of it made any sense.

Shaking her head, Adeline grabbed the socks and headed into the bathroom.

Chapter Sixteen

Adeline felt like a new person after she showered and changed into clean clothes. The outfit from the dresser not only fit her perfectly, but it was the softest thing she had ever worn.

Throwing her damp hair into a messy bun, Adeline exited the bedroom. The table was set when she stepped into the front room and inhaled the smell of a home-cooked meal.

"Perfect timing!" Henry whizzed past her, carrying a hot casserole. He made his way to the dinner table where Jesse and Godfrey sat.

"Come join us." Godfrey waved her over.

Adeline took the seat next to Jesse, who poured her a glass of water. Adeline thanked him with a smile as she eyed the food spread across the entire length of the table. A roast turkey was the centerpiece, surrounded by green beans, mashed potatoes, stuffing, dinner rolls, and much more. She felt like she had just sat down to eat a Thanksgiving meal.

"Is anyone else eating with us?" Adeline asked.

"Nope," Jesse said. "Just us."

"This is a lot of food for only four people," she said.

"I wanted to make something special for you," Henry said, taking the seat opposite her.

"For me? But you didn't know I was coming."

"That's what you think." Henry smirked while placing a napkin on his lap.

Adeline waited for him to elaborate, but he didn't. "So, you made this massive meal for me?"

"Well, of course."

Adeline frowned. She wasn't anyone important, and her life was anything but perfect. However, Henry and his friends didn't seem to care. They treated her like royalty, and she liked that. "Why?"

"Because I wanted to," Henry said. "I knew you could use a good meal."

Henry was right. Since Adeline had moved into the old house, she had eaten nothing but junk. Mom was overwhelmed with her new job, so she ordered takeout every night. But even if Mom whipped up something in the kitchen, it would've been nothing like Henry's cooking.

"Ladies first." Godfrey signaled for Adeline to fill her plate.

Heat warmed Adeline's neck. She hated being the center of attention and didn't want to go first, but all eyes were on her as they patiently waited.

Pushing through her insecurity, Adeline scooped up a spoonful of mashed potatoes and plopped it on her plate. Steam drifted from the hot food as Adeline went to the next dish. She tried to skip a bowl of the vegetables she didn't like, but Henry asked her to at least taste everything he made.

By the time Adeline got a sample of everything, her plate was overflowing. She couldn't eat all of it, but she would try.

Looking around at the others, Adeline saw their plates were as full, though the serving dishes didn't even look like they had put a dent in them. They would have leftovers—lots of leftovers.

"Dig in!" Godfrey raised his glass.

Adeline didn't waste any time and jabbed into a slice of turkey covered with gravy. She gave it a quick blow before taking her first bite. Wow! The incredible taste blew her away.

"This is fantastic, Henry," Godfrey said, biting into his dinner roll.

"I agree," Jesse said.

Adeline's mouth was full, so she just nodded as she stabbed her fork into the warm and gooey pile of mac and cheese.

Everything she tried was unbelievably good. Even the asparagus had been seasoned and cooked to perfection, along with the sweet potato casserole topped with brown sugar. She had never had a meal quite like it and knew she never would again. No one could top Henry's cooking.

It didn't take long for Adeline to feel full. She couldn't finish all the food she had on her plate. She did, however, try everything and enjoyed it all, even the collard greens and black-eyed peas.

"Make sure you save room for dessert." Henry's white whiskers rose as he smiled.

"There's dessert?" Adeline asked.

"Certainly." Henry stood and headed to the kitchen. "We cannot have a meal without something sweet."

Adeline was stuffed, but when Henry placed a homemade cherry pie in front of her, she had to try it.

Henry dished out a slice and placed it on a clean plate before handing it to Adeline. Warm cherries oozed out the sides, sending a sweet-smelling aroma into the air.

Adeline told herself she would only have a tiny bite, but she ended up eating the entire slice. So did the others. She even thought, for a moment, that Godfrey would lick his plate clean.

"I'm stuffed." Godfrey rubbed his large belly.

"Same," Jesse said, leaning back in his seat. "Thank you, Henry. That was awesome."

"You are quite welcome," Henry said, dabbing his mouth with his napkin. "Did you enjoy everything, Adeline?"

Adeline nodded. "I did."

"Wonderful." Henry seemed pleased as he rose from his chair. "Let's get this cleaned up, and then we can enjoy a hot drink by the fire."

"Sounds like a good plan to me." Jesse lifted his plate and headed to the kitchen.

Adeline followed Jesse. Gently placing her plate in the sink, Adeline stepped out of Jesse's way since he was already rinsing the dishes and placing them in the dishwasher. She didn't want to just awkwardly stand there, so she offered to help clean up the leftovers.

"I'll start bringing some of the food over here so we can put them in Tupperware."

"That won't be necessary," Jesse said as he sprayed water on the dirty utensils.

Tilting her head, Adeline moved out of Godfrey and Henry's way so they could place their used silverware and plates in the sink. When she turned to the dining area, her eyes widened. The table was completely bare. It had even been wiped down and cleaned, leaving no indication they had used it at all.

"Where did all the food go?" Adeline asked.

"I put it away," Henry said, placing a kettle on the stovetop.

"There's no way you could've done that." She skimmed over the clean kitchen. "And where are all the dirty bowls and serving dishes?"

Clamping his mouth shut so he wouldn't laugh, Jesse put the last plate in the dishwasher. He wiped his hands dry with a dishtowel and leaned against the counter, an amused look on his face.

"Like I have said before, this world differs greatly from yours," Henry told her.

"So, dishes and food magically disappear here?" Adeline folded her arms across her chest.

"Yes." Henry grinned. "But that should not surprise you, considering your clothes came from an empty dresser."

Jesse laughed. "He's got a valid point."

Adeline glanced down at her sweatpants. She had been so consumed with dinner that she had forgotten about that strange experience.

"The longer you're here, the more you'll understand our ways." Henry raised his chin. "But in the meantime, enjoy yourself."

Rubbing a hand down her face, Adeline leaned against the kitchen island. "I feel like I'm in a dream, and I'm going to wake up to find that none of this is real."

"I can assure you, everything here is indeed real," Henry said.

Adeline smiled. His words brought her comfort. She was falling in love with that mysterious world and would be devastated if she found out it was all in her head.

"I'll help Henry with the drinks so you and Adeline can go relax," Jesse told Godfrey, reaching his long arm into the cabinet.

"Thank you, son." The tiny gap in Godfrey's teeth showed as he directed his smile at Adeline. "Let's go to the living room and enjoy the fire. It's much cozier in there."

"Okay," Adeline said.

Godfrey waddled to the leather couch and dropped into it while Adeline sat on the adjacent couch directly in front of the stone fireplace. She sank into the comfy cushions, mesmerized by the flames.

"Here you are, love." Henry handed Adeline a hot mug.

Adeline cupped the drink that warmed her palms. "What is it?"

"Hot chocolate."

"How did you know I like hot chocolate?"

"Everyone likes chocolate." A chuckle escaped his lips before he returned to the kitchen.

Adeline gave him a quick smile and raised the drink to her mouth, inhaling the sweet smell of milk chocolate.

"So, I heard you had a little run-in with Ralock." Jesse plopped next to Adeline.

Just hearing his name made her shiver. She would never forget those black, lifeless eyes, nor the tangible wickedness that seemed to be stitched to his soul.

"He tried to kidnap me," she said, staring into her drink, "but your dad saved me."

"I sure did." Godfrey straightened in his seat. "There was no way I was going to let that fool take you."

Adeline's lips quirked upward as she caught Godfrey's gaze. His crystal blue eyes radiated kindness that nearly brought her to tears.

There was something about the merry, red-haired man that made her feel loved and accepted in a way she had never felt before. It was strange since she didn't really know him, but she could already tell that they would become very close friends.

"I'm glad you showed up when you did." Adeline looked back down at her drink. "I got really lucky."

"I wouldn't call that luck." Henry handed Godfrey a hot cup of tea before sitting next to him.

"What would you call it, then?" Adeline asked Henry.

"Protection."

"What do you mean?"

"Do you truly believe it was a coincidence that Godfrey was on the same path you were on at the exact time Ralock tried to kidnap you?"

Adeline thought about all the winding paths she had explored in the giant forest. The possibility of Godfrey being exactly where she was when she needed him was next to impossible. So, how did he do it?

"You are our friend, Adeline," Henry said, smiling her way. "And we *always* protect our friends."

Adeline turned to Godfrey, her heart pounding. "You knew Ralock was going to take me?"

"I did." Godfrey dipped his chin.

"How would you know that?" Adeline asked. "Are you some kind of psychic?"

Jesse slammed his hand over his mouth and nearly spit out his coffee. He tried his hardest not to laugh when Adeline shot him a suspicious look. She wasn't trying to be funny, but he clearly thought she was.

"We are not psychics." Godfrey glanced at his son, who struggled to control his rising laughter. "But we know everything that goes on in this realm and outside of it. Nothing is hidden from us."

"How?"

"We just do," Godfrey said plainly. "We know the past, present, and future of everyone and everything."

"Yeah, right." Adeline rolled her eyes. "That's impossible."

"Nothing is impossible, Adeline," Godfrey said, sitting up straight, "especially when you are with us."

Adeline drummed her fingers on her warm mug while staring at Godfrey's kind, freckled face. "So, you claim to know everything?"

"Yes, we do." Godfrey's grin widened.

"Then what's my favorite color?"

"Blue," Godfrey said. "But not just any shade of blue; your favorite is the light blue sky on a cloudless day."

Adeline leaned back into the couch cushions, speechless. Godfrey was spot on with his answer.

"How many siblings do I have?" she asked.

"You have one sister named Rebecca, who is a year younger than you," Henry said without hesitation. "You two are close in age, but have different interests and personalities, which makes it hard for you to connect with her."

How does he know that? Adeline focused on the hungry fire. *I've never told him about Rebecca.*

"My turn." Jesse rotated to face her, careful not to spill his black coffee. "Ask me anything."

Adeline looked off to the side. She thought about asking something about Dad, but quickly changed her mind. She wasn't planning on *ever* mentioning her father to them. After a few silent seconds, a question popped into her mind. One he would have no way of knowing.

"Where was I born?"

"You were born and raised in Sunset Beach, North Carolina," Jesse said, "and lived in a charming home on 305 Barefoot Lane before you moved into the Wilder house in Black Mountain."

Jerking her head back, Adeline stammered, "H-how do you guys know so much about me?"

"We just do," Jesse said with a shrug. "You'll get used to it."

The three men burst into laughter. Before Adeline could stop herself, she was giggling with them. She had no idea why they were laughing, but their joy was contagious.

Happiness surged through Adeline as she shared that moment with her new friends. She didn't understand how they knew her so well, but she decided not to think about it too much. Her mind was already spinning from the bizarre things she had encountered in that realm.

Once the laughter died down, Henry asked, "How are you enjoying your new school?"

"I'm not." Adeline placed her drink on the end table before tucking her legs beneath her.

"That will change once you make some friends."

"I don't plan on making friends."

"Nonsense." Henry cupped his hot tea. "Everyone needs friends."

"I have my cousin, Carol, and that's enough for me."

Henry took another sip of his tea. "Give it time. Everything in your new town will grow on you, even the people."

"Right," she said sarcastically.

Time flew by as Adeline got to know her new friends in the cabin. She had never known a place so tranquil and felt herself beginning to grow sleepy. She planned on heading home soon, but she was too comfortable to leave right away and wanted to rest her eyes for a few moments.

Adeline sank deeper into the soft cushions as she listened to the soothing voices of her friends, along with the crackling fire. Peace wrapped around her like a warm blanket, and before long, she fell asleep.

Chapter Seventeen

The gentle rays from the rising sun crept through the windows of the cabin. It was quiet, and Adeline was sound asleep on the leather couch as the sunlight found its way onto her face.

Her eyes fluttered open, and her hazy mind began to wake as she relaxed beneath a cashmere blanket that engulfed her. It was triple her size, overflowing onto the floor and soft as could be. Adeline stretched, enjoying the warm sun on her face. Then reality hit.

She had fallen asleep in the cabin.

"Oh, no!"

Flinging the blanket away, Adeline jumped to her feet and scrambled to find her dirty sneakers. She ran her hands all along the hardwood floor, forgetting that she had left her shoes in the bathroom the day before.

"Good morning, sunshine."

Anxiety swelled in Adeline as she glanced into the kitchen and saw Jesse smiling at her. He was wearing blue pajama pants and a white shirt, his eyes still heavy with sleep.

"Why didn't you wake me up?" Adeline yelled.

"Whoa." Jesse held up his hands. "There's no need to panic."

"I am way past panicking. My mom is going to kill me!"

Jesse rested against the counter, holding back a laugh. "I think you're forgetting that time in your world stops when you're here."

Adeline massaged her forehead. She still wasn't used to the whole time-freezing thing.

"I mean, if you want to go home right now, I can take you," Jesse said, combing down his bedhead.

Rubbing her sleepy eyes, Adeline sat back down on the couch. She had only lived in Black Mountain for a couple weeks, and she already felt like someone had placed a bomb in her mind and blown up all reason. Even a solid, concrete law and system like time had been completely shot down since she first trespassed into the forbidden forest and followed an old man to his cabin.

"Are you sure time stopped?" she asked.

"Positive." Jesse gave a gentle smile before focusing on the coffeemaker. "No one from your world knows you're here."

"This place is so strange."

The rich aroma of the coffee filtered in from the kitchen as Adeline sank deeper into the couch, trying to calm her racing heart.

"Do you really want to go home?" Jesse poured himself a fresh cup of coffee. "Because we have an exciting day planned for you."

Adeline thought about it for a moment. If she went back to her world, she would have to do her homework and go to bed early for school the next day. Nothing about that sounded appealing.

"What do you have planned?" Adeline straightened her sweatshirt as she stood and walked into the kitchen.

"It's a surprise," Jesse said before taking his first sip.

Heavy footsteps boomed from the hallway.

"Morning, everyone," Godfrey said, his face bright. He looked very comfortable in a silky pajama set that was snug at his belly. The buttons were fastened but looked like they were about to burst at the seams.

"Hi, Godfrey." Adeline waved.

"How did you sleep?"

"Good, I guess," she said. "I didn't mean to fall asleep on the couch."

"We were going to wake you up, but you looked so peaceful." Godfrey touched her cheek as he walked past her to get himself a cup of coffee.

Peaceful wasn't the word Adeline was expecting him to say. She'd had nightmares every night since the accident. They'd followed her to the house in Black Mountain, but last night...

Oh.

She pressed her hand to her mouth. She hadn't had any nightmares the night before.

"Good morning, friends!" Henry waltzed into the kitchen. He looked like he had been up for hours. His short white hair and beard were combed to perfection, and he was fully dressed for the day, like he was about to head to a formal event in navy slacks and a white button-down shirt.

"Where are you going? Adeline asked, sliding onto a barstool.

"I am not going anywhere right now."

"Then why are you dressed like that?" She looked pointedly at his polished leather shoes.

"Because I want to look my best," Henry said, his head held high. He looked very nice, but she didn't know anyone who preferred to wear sophisticated clothing all the time, especially that early in the morning.

"Do you ever wear normal clothes?" Adeline asked.

"Normal?" Henry chuckled while adjusting his collar. "This is normal."

"If you say so."

Adeline rolled her eyes at Jesse, who was making a ruckus as he dug through the pots and pans in a cabinet.

"Who wants blueberry muffins?" Jesse held the muffin tin in the air.

"That sounds wonderful," Henry said.

"It sure does," Godfrey said, taking a long sip of his coffee.

"Coming right up."

Jesse opened the oven door and tossed the empty muffin tin inside.

"I think you're forgetting something," Adeline said.

"I don't think so." Jesse shut the oven door.

Before Adeline could argue, he cracked the door and steam escaped from the opening. Adeline's jaw hung to the floor when Jesse grabbed a pair of oven mitts and removed the hot cooking tin filled with twelve freshly baked blueberry muffins.

"Food magically appears here as well?" Adeline leaped out of her seat to get a better look as Jesse placed the steamy muffins on the stovetop to cool.

"Yep." Jesse removed the oven mitts and tossed them on the counter. "Or you can cook the old-fashioned way, like Henry."

"How does it work?"

"You just think it"—Jesse tapped his temple—"and it appears."

"Just like that strange dresser?"

"Exactly like that."

"So, if I want glazed donuts, I just think about them, and they'll appear in the oven?"

"Yep." Jesse got a baking sheet from the same cabinet and handed it to her. "But you may want to put this inside the oven first."

Adeline was so excited she nearly dropped the baking sheet when she placed it inside the cold oven. Shutting the door, she yanked it back open. A wave of heat followed by a sugary smell collided with her. Six perfectly round donuts sat on the baking sheet.

"It worked!" she squealed, ogling the warm, glazed donuts.

Using the oven mitts, Adeline placed the donuts next to the blueberry muffins. She was far too eager to wait for them to cool and pinched off a small piece. The donut burned the tips of her fingers, but she didn't care as she popped it into her mouth. The sweet dough melted on her tongue.

"This is unreal," she said, tearing off another small section of the donut.

"The refrigerator and microwave do the same thing," Henry said, dishing out plates to his friends. "And the pantry is always stocked with whatever you're craving."

Adeline gave the walk-in pantry a quick glance while chewing the warm donut. The door was closed, but she had a feeling it was spacious and made a mental note to check it out later. "If any kind of food just appears, why do you bother cooking?" she asked Henry.

"Because I enjoy cooking, especially for my friends." Henry smiled, handing her a small plate. "It is one of my favorite things to do."

Placing two donuts on her plate, Adeline sat down at the large island while the others filled their plates and stood around it.

"How do I make a drink appear in the fridge?" Adeline asked as she licked her sticky fingers.

"Same thing," Godfrey said as he went for seconds. "You think it, and it appears."

Adeline rushed to the fridge and imagined a huge glass of apple juice. She couldn't stop her hand from trembling as she grasped the handle and pulled it toward her.

The apple juice was placed, front and center, on a shelf right at her line of sight.

Adeline laughed in disbelief, wrapping her fingers around the cold cup. She took a sip and sighed. The refreshing, cool liquid tasted freshly made.

"This place just keeps getting better and better." She shut the fridge and faced the others. "You guys not only have an unlimited wardrobe, but any kind of food and drink."

"Speaking of wardrobe," Henry said, placing his dirty plate in the dishwasher, "you'll want to change before we head out."

"Where are we going?" she asked, taking a long gulp of her drink.

"A special place in the garden."

"What should I wear?"

"I would suggest something you can easily move in."

Adeline took another sip. "Like jeans and a T-shirt?"

"Something more flexible than that."

"Workout clothes?"

"Precisely!" Henry said, pointing his sun-spotted finger in the air.

The training facility came to Adeline's mind, and a knot formed in her chest. It was the only place she could think of that would require such an outfit, but she had no desire to do any sort of workout there. "I would rather not go to the training area," she said, her voice lowering.

"We're not going there."

The ball in her chest loosened. "Why else would I need to wear workout clothes?"

"You'll just have to wait and see," Henry said. "And it's going to be warm today, so no need for a jacket."

"But it was freezing yesterday." She set her empty glass in the sink.

"It will feel like spring today."

"That doesn't make any sense."

"The weather here differs greatly from what you are used to. Now"—he clapped his hands—"hop to it."

"Okay." She spun on her heel and headed down the hall. "I'll be right back."

Adeline closed the bedroom door behind her. She cringed at her messy hair in the mirror and quickly pulled it free from her hair tie. Using her fingers to massage her tender scalp, she tried to think of a practical outfit while wondering what in the world her new friends had planned for her.

Chapter Eighteen

Adeline stood in front of the mirror, tucking a loose strand of hair back into her high ponytail. She wasn't sure where her friends were taking her, but she thought a pair of leggings and a tank top would do.

Once her hair was presentable, she left the cozy bedroom and went to find her friends. Her long, wavy ponytail bounced with every step down the hallway and into the common area. Henry, Godfrey, and Jesse were dressed and ready to go.

"Perfect outfit!" Henry clapped his hands together.

Adeline scrunched her nose. Henry still wore his trousers and pristine button-down, while Jesse looked as if he were about to work outside in a loose-fitting T-shirt and cargo pants. In place of his bow and quiver, he had a leather sheath hooked onto his belt that held a long blade.

Then there was Godfrey. He wore the most outrageous outfit of all—a colorful Hawaiian shirt and swim trunks. He looked like he was going to the beach, right down to his tie-dye flip flops.

"Let's go!" Godfrey said, heading toward the back door. His flip-flops slapped the hardwood floor, making Adeline grin.

Once outside, Adeline inhaled the fragrance of the garden as the warm sun shined above. It felt like a spring day, just like Henry said it would.

The journey into the garden was just as exciting as it had been the first time. The trail bloomed with life shaded by ancient oak trees with Spanish moss dangling from their branches. They enjoyed the peace and quiet as they strolled alongside a slow stream until the path curved, taking them down a stairway that led to a section of grass in the shape of a rectangle with holly bushes acting as walls. They were planted so tightly together that Adeline couldn't tell where one ended and the other began.

There were a few benches placed against the holly, but in the center of the grassy area there was a lovely marble fountain. It wasn't the size of a normal fountain found in most gardens, but large enough to be a swimming pool.

Adeline gawked at the water that sparkled in the sunlight. It was peaceful and beautiful, the water clear as crystal.

"I can't see the bottom." Adeline gripped the edge of the fountain, leaning over the water. "Do you know how deep it is?"

Jesse's lips curved upward as he unbuckled his sheath, dropping it in the grass. He pulled his shirt over his head and tossed it to the side.

"You're not jumping in there, are you?" Adeline asked.

A mischievous grin appeared as Jesse kicked off his work boots and tugged off his socks. He took a few steps back before taking off toward the fountain and jumping over the edge. In mid-air, he grabbed hold of his tucked legs and plummeted into the water. A splash surged into the air, and Jesse popped to the surface, howling with laughter. Godfrey and Henry joined in as Jesse slicked back his long hair.

"I cannot believe you did that!" Adeline said with a giggle.

"Get in, Adeline." Jesse splashed her. "The water feels great."

"You can't be serious." Adeline wiped the water from her face.

"Don't make me come get you."

A small laugh escaped Adeline as Jesse dove underwater and did flips. She wished she had known to bring a bathing suit. She toed off her sneakers and removed her socks, hearing another splash.

Adeline spotted white hair. Henry had jumped in as well, still fully dressed in his trousers and button-down shirt. He didn't seem to mind as he floated on his back, basking in the sun. "What a wonderful day for a swim."

Adeline stood, shocked. Elderly men of his age wouldn't do such a thing in her world, but nothing about Henry was typical.

"Are you going swimming too?" Adeline asked Godfrey, who had already kicked off his flip-flops.

"Of course." His wide mouth spread into a smile. "I don't want to miss out on all the fun."

Adeline faced the fountain, but right before she took off, Godfrey took hold of her arm.

"Before you go, I need to give you something."

Flashing him a blank stare, Adeline held out her hand. But he gripped her shoulders and lowered himself until they were level.

Adeline swallowed nervously, staring into his electric blue eyes. Her heart rate spiked as Godfrey blew his breath softly into her face. It was ice cold as she inhaled it, but quickly changed into a blazing heat like she was sucking in fire. Her whole body tingled and vibrated as she gasped for air.

"What did you do to me?" Adeline's hand went to her throat as she backed away from him. "My throat—my lungs are on fire!"

"You'll see."

Godfrey let out a hefty laugh, his belly jiggling as he leaped into the pool. Henry and Jesse stormed Godfrey when he reached the surface and tried to pull him under like a bunch of kids goofing around, but Godfrey easily stayed afloat and started dunking them.

No one seemed concerned that Adeline was burning from within. Her chest was still hot and fluttering like crazy as her friends played around in the water. Slowly, the burning subsided to a comfortable warmth.

What is happening to me?

Her breathing calmed, but the warm sensation swirling in her belly didn't let up.

"Jump in, Adeline." Jesse waved her in. "The water is perfect."

"Coming." Adeline released a slow breath before running and jumping into the fountain. She broke through the surface, treading water and pushing her wet ponytail off her shoulder. "This is amazing."

"It sure is!" Jesse floated next to her. "Just wait until you see what's below us."

"Below us?" She glanced downward.

"Well, sure, this isn't just a pretty fountain," Jesse said, wading in the water. "There are tunnels beneath us."

"Tunnels?"

"Yep. Want to check them out?"

Excitement flickered in her gut. "Yeah, but we wouldn't be able to go very far without scuba gear."

Biting back a smile, Jesse looked at Henry and Godfrey before addressing Adeline. "We will be fine."

"But the water is *way* too deep to explore," she said, "and I don't know about you, but I can't hold my breath very long."

"My dad already gave you everything you need," Jesse said as water dripped from his beard. "Now come on."

Before Adeline could voice another complaint, Jesse dove under the water. Clenching her lips together, Adeline gave Henry and Godfrey a look, but they kept smiling at her.

"Go on." Godfrey playfully splashed water at her.

"This is a waste of time," she said with a whine.

"You don't know that."

"We don't even have goggles to see!"

Godfrey smiled gently as his red hair floated atop the water. "Jesse is waiting for you."

Rolling her eyes, Adeline spotted Jesse under the water, motioning for her to follow. He had already been down there for a while, and she didn't want him to lose any more air. She took a deep breath and closed her eyes before submerging herself.

The warm water lapped over her head as she sank. When she opened her eyes, she was surprised she could see everything so clearly. It was like she was already wearing a pair of goggles.

Jesse floated below her, bubbles rolling out of his nose as he displayed his shiny white teeth.

Adeline returned the smile, giving off her own bubbles. After a drawn-out moment, she started to return to the surface for air. But as she swam upward, she realized her lungs weren't burning. She felt perfectly fine.

Her ponytail swayed in the water as she stopped and blew out a heavy breath of air. Bubbles rose to the surface, but the need for air wasn't there.

How is this possible?

"I told you that my dad gave you everything you needed." Jesse's voice entered Adeline's mind like he just spoke to her directly.

Did Jesse just talk to me?

She thought she had imagined it until she heard his voice once more. *"I sure did."*

Her eyes expanded. *"You can hear my thoughts?"*

"Yep, and you can hear mine. That is...the ones I want you to." Jesse's laughter rang inside her head like he was laughing in her ear.

"But how?"

"It is one of the gifts my dad just gave you. I know it's really weird, but you'll get used to it." Jesse dove downward, his waist-long hair waving behind him as he kicked his feet to go faster. *"This way, Adeline."*

This is so weird.

Adeline had no idea how all this was happening, but she swam after him, watching his cargo pants flap against his bare feet as he continued downward.

The deeper they went, the cooler the water became. And though Adeline preferred it to be a little warmer, it was still comfortable to swim in. She was just glad she didn't feel any pressure in her ears and could easily breathe.

"Are the tunnels close by?" she asked.

"They are."

Adeline glimpsed the bottom. Right before they reached the bare marble floor, Jesse turned toward a small circular opening in the wall. It wasn't big, but Jesse easily fit inside.

She bit her lip, practically drawing blood as she hurried to catch up. The tunnel was dark, and she quickly lost sight of him. Light at the end of the tunnel encouraged her to swim faster.

Adeline swam as fast as she could through the passageway until she burst through the opening. She slackened when she saw Jesse, but her attention was quickly drawn to the old man floating next to him. It was Henry!

"How did he get here before us?"

"I have my ways." Henry's accent entered her mind.

"I can hear you as well?" Adeline's eyes grew.

"Yes," Henry said. *"You can hear all three of us now."*

Adeline cracked a smile as she took in the new circular-shaped area. Sunlight shone above, illuminating the three tunnel openings along the stone wall. Each had a large, round opening with a different word on top engraved in the stone. The first tunnel spelled *COURAGE.* The one next to it was *STRENGTH,* and the last tunnel said *PERSEVERANCE.*

"What is this place?" Adeline asked.

"These are the tunnels of lost promises," Henry told her.

"Lost promises?" she asked, her tank top whirling as she spun to face Henry. *"What does that mean?"*

"Do you see the words written above each tunnel?" Henry pointed to the one closest to him.

Adeline nodded.

"Those are the promises given to whomever dares to go inside the tunnel."

Shifting her head, Adeline studied the word *STRENGTH* for a moment.

"How can strength be a prize?" she asked. *"It's not something you can hold or keep."*

"You mustn't forget that things are very different here."

"No kidding," Adeline said, staring into the gloomy tunnel. *"So, all I have to do is swim inside the tunnel and I get the so-called promise?"*

"It is a little trickier than that." Henry's voice turned serious. *"If you truly desire one of these promises, you'll have to fight for it."*

"Fight for it?" Heaviness settled in her stomach. She hoped he wasn't being literal.

"Yes, each tunnel has obstacles that will do anything in their power to stop you from completing the various trials."

Adeline's stomach soured, imagining the sketchy obstacle course Jesse had shown her. If anything like that was inside the tunnels...she wasn't interested. *"What kind of obstacles?"*

"It depends on which tunnel you choose," Henry said, his short white hair gently moving with the current. *"They are all different."*

None of the tunnels sounded enjoyable, and the blackness beyond the entrances didn't ease her increasing fear. But she figured she might as well attempt to get a promise, especially if her friends tagged along.

"Let's try the courage tunnel."

"We're not going with you, Adeline." Jesse floated beside her. *"You'll have to go alone."*

"Alone!" Adeline's face dropped. *"Are you serious?"*

Jesse moved his head up and down.

"You're crazy if you think I'm going into that creepy tunnel by myself."

"Are you sure?" Jesse asked, his expression solemn. *"This is an opportunity of a lifetime."*

"Positive." She crossed her arms. *"I'm not going without you."*

"Very well, but you'll never become courageous if you don't do things that scare you."

Jesse's words punched Adeline in the gut. It was like they were alive within her, begging her to be brave. *"What if I die?"*

"You won't die in there," Jesse said. *"But you'll leave that tunnel with more courage than ever before."*

Adeline bit the inside of her cheek, examining the dark tunnels.

"Don't you want more courage in your life?" Jesse asked.

"Yeah, but I don't want to go in there," Adeline said, signaling to the tunnel. *"It's completely black."*

"It won't stay that way."

Adeline's body shook, though she wasn't cold. She had always been good at acting courageous when she wasn't. Deep down, she wanted to be brave, but now that she was looking it in the face, she wasn't sure she could do it. *"I'm scared."*

"It's normal to feel that way," Jesse said, swiping a long piece of hair from his face. *"But do it afraid."*

A chill ran down her back as she faced the passageway marked with the word courage. She hated the dark and was petrified to go into the unknown without a clue about what lay ahead, but something inside of her wanted to try. *"Okay, I'll do it."*

"You won't regret it," Jesse said. *"Just so you know, you can quit at any time, but if you do...you won't get to keep the promise."*

Adeline still didn't understand how she could tangibly keep a promise, but she nodded like she did. She kicked her bare feet and pumped her arms, forcing herself to swim away from her friends.

The closer she got to the black tunnel, the sicker she felt. Fear hit her like a slap in the face as unwelcomed thoughts entered her mind, screaming for her to turn around.

Overwhelmed with fright, Adeline stopped when she reached the entrance and looked back at her friends. They were both smiling. Jesse even gave her two thumbs up.

"You got this, Adeline!"

Adeline wanted to cry, but the look in his bright green eyes gave her a sudden boost of confidence. With a kick of her feet, she swam inside the dark tunnel.

She paused, the pressure in her lungs increasing as she stared down the long, narrow passageway. The only light was coming from behind her, and it offered little help.

Her ponytail floated in front of her as if telling her to keep going. She tried to convince herself to swim forward into the darkness, but she was too frightened to move.

I can't do this.

Right as Adeline decided to retreat, something crashed behind her.

Adeline thrashed around in the blackness, heart beating wildly as she bumped into a massive rock that was now blocking her from her friends—from safety. She pushed at it and even drove her shoulder into the solid structure, but nothing happened.

She was trapped.

Chapter Nineteen

The water in the tunnel drained, and Adeline was soon able to stand. The cold stone floor stung the bottom of her feet as she pressed her palms against the rock and gave it a forceful shove.

It didn't budge.

"Let me out!" Adeline banged her fist against the rock.

It only took a few hard hits before her hand throbbed. She was stuck there, and the only way out was through the spooky tunnel.

Pressing her back against the rock, she sank to the floor and fought for air, pulling her knees to her chest.

Whish!

Adeline jumped as the torches along the walls lit themselves. The small flames flickered all the way down the quiet passageway, casting shadows along the rocks.

"Don't be afraid." Henry's voice rose out of nowhere, taking over her thoughts. *"You can do this!"*

Adeline shot to her feet, frantically looking for her sweet old friend. Though she heard him in her mind, it was so loud and clear that it felt like he was next to her.

"Henry! Where are you?"

Her desperate cry bounced down the eerie tunnel, but all she heard was the sound of water dripping onto the stone floor, and her own heavy breathing.

Choking back a sob, Adeline yelled again, "Henry!"

"Don't worry, my dear." Henry internally spoke once more. *"I am going to help you."*

Shivering, Adeline wiped her wet eyes. "I want to leave."

"Be brave, Adeline. You've got this."

"I'm afraid."

"I know you are, but you need to battle through the fear."

Hugging her arms, Adeline shivered as she eyed her only exit. It grew longer and creepier the more she stared at it. She had plenty of room to walk freely, but she felt like the walls were closing in on her.

"What's down the tunnel?" she asked, her voice low.

"The promise."

Goosebumps erupted across Adeline's skin. She would have to face her fears if she wanted that promise.

"I can't do this, Henry."

"Yes, you can," Henry said. *"Just put one foot in front of the other."*

Clenching her jaw, Adeline shuffled forward, following the torches along the walls. Water dripped from her clothes, and her feet burned like she was walking on ice.

The tunnel veered to the right, and Adeline found it hard to breathe as she rounded the corner. There was an opening ahead. She tiptoed to the doorway, peeking inside.

There, in the middle of the small space, was a golden stand with a brilliant sapphire resting on it. The round stone sparkled and glistened like a light was trapped inside it, casting blue hues along the rocky walls.

Adeline rubbed her eyes to make sure she wasn't seeing things, but when she opened them again, the sapphire was still there.

"Wow." Adeline stepped into the room and headed straight to the sapphire.

"That is your promise," Henry said.

"No way." Adeline reached the golden platform, staring down at the priceless gem. "I get to keep it?"

"Only if you don't quit."

Adeline decided she would do whatever she had to do to keep it. Though it was gorgeous to look at, she thought about how much money she could make if she sold it, which only motivated her more. "I could get my family a nicer house with it!"

"Let's not get ahead of ourselves," Henry said with a dry chuckle. *"You haven't even started the first trial."*

"Right." She calmed herself down. "So, what do I need to do?"

"Take the sapphire from the stand to open the door."

"What door?" Adeline observed the bare walls. "There are no doors in here."

"Grab the stone and see what happens."

Adeline plucked the gem with a trembling hand, awakening the golden stand. She sprung back as it rumbled, slamming her backside against the cold, damp wall. The platform sank until it was level with the ground and a solid red door appeared on the rocks ahead. It looked like a typical wooden door that could be found in any household, but the crimson color made her skin crawl.

"The trial begins as soon as you go through that door."

"What's inside?" she asked, her breathing ragged.

"It is for you to discover. But before you begin, you'll need to put the promise in a secure place. The obstacles ahead will try to take it from you."

Adeline exhaled. The sapphire was no bigger than a quarter. It was also light, which would make it easy to conceal.

"Where should I put it?"

"I would suggest your pocket." There was humor in his voice.

"I don't think I have any pockets." Adeline patted her soaked tank top.

Her fingers brushed down her wet spandex leggings, and she felt a tiny zipper along her thigh. She unzipped it, surprised to find that the pocket was bigger than she'd expected. It was perfect for hiding the gem.

"Oh, never mind." She pocketed the sapphire. "I found one."

"Fabulous!" Henry said. *"Now, in order to move from room to room, you'll have to possess the gem; the doors will not open for you if you lose the promise or if it is taken from you."*

"Okay." She squeezed water from her wet top.

"Let's begin."

There was no stopping her endless shivers as she stepped forward, eyes on the blood-colored door. Her numb feet splashed into the tiny puddles until she stood before the doorway.

"Here we go," she said under her breath.

She turned the knob, pulling it toward her. It let out a creak as it opened to a much larger room.

Bright torches lined the walls, and the first thing Adeline saw was another red door on the opposite side. She saw nothing dangerous, so she crept through the doorway and flinched when the door slammed behind her. The boom echoed in the space. She ran her hand along the jagged rocks. The door was gone.

"Don't fret about it, my dear girl," Henry said, warmth lining his voice. *"The door you must go through is across the room."*

Facing the exit, Adeline wrapped her arms around herself. The floor was strange, consisting of fifty or more square tiles. Each one had a simple painting, black the only color used. She spotted a lion and a sword, along with lightning bolts, darts, and much more. They were the only things standing between her and the door, but something about them didn't sit well with her.

"What are these weird squares?" she asked.

"In order to get to the door, step on the tiles," Henry said. *"But whatever picture you step on is what will prevent you from getting there. You must choose wisely."*

Adeline's bottom lip trembled. The exit was way too far for her to jump to. She would have to step on a few of the tiles before making it to the other side of the room. "Which ones do I pick?"

"You must choose."

Adeline examined the floor once more, her eyes jumping from tile to tile as she attempted to figure out the best route. Nothing appealed to her, especially the painted black snake.

She scanned the tiles again and stopped when she found one with large raindrops. It was the least intimidating one she had seen so far. It was also within jumping distance.

Adeline scooted back until she hit the solid rock wall. There was little room between her and the first row of tiles, and she needed as much space as she could get. She inhaled slowly, locking eyes with the raindrop tile. She could reach it.

Before she could talk herself out of it, she ran and leaped into the air. Both feet landed on the target, and the tile sank into the ground.

Dark clouds appeared above her. There was one brief clap of thunder before rain came down in sheets, nearly knocking her to the ground. The droplets felt as hard as hailstones. Adeline half-expected the torches along the wall to go out, but they burned steadily.

The forceful rainfall pelted into her as she shielded her eyes and tried to keep her balance. She frantically searched for the tiles ahead of her, but the powerful rain made it impossible to see.

Panic swelled in her as she tried to find the cockroach tile. She had an idea of where it was and hopped forward.

The heavy rain stopped, and the clouds cleared. She wiped her face clear of the rain and looked down. Her heart dropped. She landed on the wrong tile.

Adeline looked up from the tile and saw a massive bull appear in front of the red door. His hollow eyes latched onto hers, gluing her feet in place.

A loud snort rang from the angry bull as he lowered his horns and charged. His weight didn't affect the tiles he smashed into. He was mere feet away when she jumped to the left, landing on a new tile.

The square sank beneath her cold feet, and hundreds of arrows shot from the ceiling. Their sharp points pierced every tile except the one she stood on. The arrows wobbled in place; their deadly heads buried in the stone tiles before vanishing.

Gasping for air, Adeline whipped around, expecting the bull to charge her again, but it was no longer there. It disappeared just like the rain and the lethal arrows. Adeline dragged her fingers through her wet hair, glaring at the painting of a black arrow underneath her feet.

"This is insane!"

Just the thought of an arrow piercing her put things into perspective. This wasn't a game. This was a risky task, one with severe consequences. Jesse told her she wouldn't die...but he'd said nothing about her not getting injured.

"Keep going." Henry's voice broke through. *"You are halfway there."*

Looking ahead, Henry was right. The red door was close. She would have to pick a couple more tiles to reach it. But the floor was slick, so she would have to be careful not to slip and fall onto multiple tiles.

Adeline chewed her fingernails, scanning her options. The wasp tile was quickly dismissed and so was the square with the bear painted on it. She also rejected the alligator, the gladiator, and the fire ants. All her choices were awful, but she had to pick one and went with the tile that was completely black.

Building up what little confidence she had left, Adeline hopped onto the solid black tile. She landed on it but nearly lost her balance. She flung out both arms to stay put as the tile lowered.

Immediately, the torches went out like someone had blown out the flames, and the room was pitch black. It was so dark that Adeline couldn't see her hand in front of her face.

Fear held her to the floor as she trembled in the darkness. There wasn't a sound to be heard besides the tiny drops of water dripping from her clothing onto the tile beneath her.

"Where do I go, Henry?" She embraced herself, desperately hoping nothing would grab her. "I don't know what's in front of me."

"You need to jump forward, but a little to the left." Henry slid into her thoughts. *"You don't want to hit the one that is directly in front of you."*

"What's directly in front of me?"

"You don't want to know."

Adeline's throat locked tight. What could possibly be ahead of her?

She didn't want to find out and jumped as Henry had directed her. She landed hard on the tile, and it sank into the floor.

Rough grains of sand emerged from the ground, rising at a fast pace. Her ankles were already covered as she waited for the torches to come back to life.

But they didn't.

"Run!" Henry shouted.

Fear clawed at her insides as she blindly ran forward through the rising sand. It engulfed her feet as she slogged through, slowing her down.

Knowing the door was within reach, she held out both hands as she tripped through the sand. Her palms stung as she hit the solid wall, desperately scraping her hands along the rough rocks.

"I can't find the door!" she screamed as the sand reached her shins.

"Keep going to the right!"

Stumbling through the impossible sand, Adeline finally felt the groove of the wooden door. She raced her fingers along the wood until she found the cold doorknob.

"Got it!"

Adeline twisted the knob, and the door flung open. Light pierced through the opening as she was forced into the next room. She blinked rapidly and looked down. The sand was still rising, pouring in from the open door. She thought it would disappear like the rain clouds and the bull, but it didn't.

It kept rolling into the room, knocking into her as she fought to keep her balance. It took a moment for her to plant her feet on the ground. Once she felt steady, she tried to close the door. Her arms and back burned as she pushed with all her might against the sand that gushed through the remaining opening. She was making progress, but it was minimal.

"It won't close, Henry!"

"Keep pushing!"

Grunting, Adeline rammed herself against the door while the sand battled against her. Her weak muscles cried out in pain.

Right before they gave out, the door closed.

Adeline stumbled forward before catching herself. Parking her hands on her hips, she drew in quick, raspy breaths while her heart continued to pound.

She completed the first challenge...but there was still more to go.

Chapter Twenty

Adeline, breathing heavily, brushed the sand from her wet skin and clothing. Her dark leggings had gotten the worst of it, but she still had it all over her and it was making her itch. She scrubbed her hands down her pants and tank top, but the pesky grains stuck to her like glue.

Giving up on the sand, she tightened her soaked ponytail and surveyed her new surroundings. The enclosed space was much larger and lit by torches, but one look around made her wish she was back in the previous room.

She stood rigid, her hands clenched at her sides as she stared at the huge black pit at the center of the space. Within the pit were multiple stacks of long, flat rocks piled on top of each other. They made a staggering path to a wooden platform across the room with another red door.

The slightest bit of weight on those uneven rocks would certainly make them fall into the blackness below.

"Well, isn't this just great?" she murmured.

Tiny grains of sand rubbed between her toes as she inched toward the edge. Her gut plummeted as she peered into the darkness. There was no getting out of there if she fell.

"You cannot hesitate as you run across the rocks." Henry's instruction drifted into her mind. *"They will fall as soon as you land on them."*

"What if I fall?" Adeline asked, her voice faltering.

"I suggest you don't," Henry said. *"It's a long way to the bottom."*

"What did I get myself into?"

Again, she thought about quitting, but quickly threw it from her mind. She wasn't parting ways with the stunning sapphire slightly protruding from her pocket. She had to keep going.

Massaging the back of her neck, Adeline calculated how far apart the unequal rock piles were. She was confident she could jump from one to the other. She just had to move fast without losing her balance.

Every nerve rattled violently as she backed up as far as she could to get a running start. Once she felt the cool wall at her back, she closed her eyes and took a few calming breaths.

"Don't look down and you'll be fine," she muttered.

Her eyes shot open and before she chickened out, she took off running and sprang from the edge. She went sailing into the air, landing on the first pile of stones. The hard impact stung her feet, but she wasted little thought on her bruised heels. The rocks shook, warning her they were about to fall.

Adrenaline took over as she jumped to the next rock pile, and then the next while listening to the sound of crumbling rocks bouncing off the sides of the gaping hole.

After the first three piles, Adeline started moving at a tremendous speed. She leaped across the rock path, getting closer and closer to her destination.

Her confidence soared as she jumped onto the last pile of rocks. She quickly steadied herself, but the rocks beneath her rumbled and swayed.

Without a moment to lose, Adeline launched herself toward the wooden platform, but she didn't jump high enough. Panic set in as the door dropped from her line of sight.

"Grab the ledge!" Henry shouted.

Adeline latched onto one of the wooden beams, holding on as she smashed into the side of the cliff. The hit sent a ripple of pain through her body, but she didn't let go as she dangled over the dark abyss.

Her arms quaked, and her muscles were on fire as she dug her aching fingers into the ledge.

"You can do it!" Henry's voice rumbled. *"Pull yourself up!"*

Screaming through the pain, Adeline lifted herself high enough to hook her ankle onto the edge. Once it was secure, she used the strength of her leg to pull her entire body up and over the ledge and onto the solid platform.

Adeline struggled for air as she crawled to safety and sprawled out onto her back. She stared, dazed, at the flames along the wall, waiting for her heart to stop racing.

"That was terrifying," she said between breaths.

"Excellent job!"

"Thanks." Adeline wiped beads of sweat from her brows. "You didn't tell me this tunnel was going to be so hard."

"You wouldn't have tried it if I did."

Adeline rolled her eyes while straining to breathe. Her body ached, and the irritating sand stuck to her clothes wasn't helping at all. She moved a hand to her pocket, feeling the gemstone hidden beneath the tight spandex.

"You better be worth it," she said, tracing her fingertips over the jewel.

Adeline sat up. The world spun and her muscles throbbed, but she forced herself to her feet. A wave of fatigue rocked her. She was tempted to sit back down, but worried that she wouldn't get back up if she did.

Putting her hands on her knees, Adeline inhaled and exhaled slowly. "I am so out of shape."

She considered exercising again, but quickly dismissed it when Dad came to mind. Guilt twined with sadness reared its ugly head. She forced it away. She couldn't do any kind of physical activity without thinking about him. It was too painful.

Tossing Dad from her thoughts, Adeline sucked in a lungful of air. It took a little while for her breathing to go back to normal, but once it did, she straightened and moved to the red door.

Uneasiness rose as she gave the doorknob a quick turn. The door opened. She released a long, steady breath before stepping through the threshold only to hurl herself back, stricken with horror, when she saw what was in the room.

"You have got to be kidding me!"

Hundreds of black snakes slithered and coiled themselves over one another in a large pit. There were so many that Adeline could barely see the bottom.

"Out of everything in the world, it had to be snakes!"

Chills traveled down her spine as she looked past the snake pit at the red door across the room. It was on the same sturdy wooden platform she was on.

Adeline searched for a way to cross the pit of snakes. Surely, there had to be a rope or something to climb along the rocky walls.

"How am I supposed to get to the door?"

"By running through the snakes," Henry said casually.

"What?" Adeline yelled. "You must be joking."

"It is the only way across the room."

"I'm done." Adeline raised her hands. "There's no way I'm getting in there."

"You have come too far to quit now."

"They'll bite me!"

"They're not venomous."

Adeline's mouth dropped. "You expect me to walk through hundreds of snakes without shoes and allow them to bite me?"

"It is your only option."

"You're insane. I'm not doing it!"

"That is your choice, but you'll have to forfeit the promise if you quit."

"Ugh!" She stomped her foot. "I hate this stupid tunnel."

The snakes entangled with one another, making Adeline's stomach curl. They seemed to taunt her with their hisses. She reconsidered forfeiting. The only thing keeping her from doing so was the brilliant sapphire.

She unzipped her pocket and retrieved the magnificent stone that sparkled in her hand. The solid gem glistened in the firelight, reminding her of its value. Her home life would change drastically if she kept it.

Adeline glanced from the sapphire to the snakes below. "Henry, I can't do it."

"Yes, you can," he said. *"Temporary pain is worth a lifetime of victory."*

"But I'm terrified of snakes."

"Standing there and complaining won't make things any easier," Henry said firmly. *"Now get in that pit and head to the door."*

His tone surprised Adeline, but he was right. She could either quit or go through the snakes. Those were her only two options. Nothing in her wanted to get near the nasty serpents, but she wanted the promise.

"Fine. I'll do it."

Tucking the jewel back into her pocket, Adeline crept to the edge. Her insides squirmed as she contemplated the best way to reach the door. She would carefully walk through them and hope to make it across unnoticed. It was the only logical plan she could come up with.

Right when she was about to dip her vulnerable foot inside, Henry instructed her once again. *"I would suggest running through them; they will not like it when you step on them."*

"Right." Adeline was sweating as she took a few steps back.

Never in all her life did she think she would willingly get into a pit full of snakes. The old Adeline would *never* do such a thing.

But there she was...ready to jump in.

"I cannot believe I am doing this," she said, rubbing her clammy hands down her leggings.

Breathing out one final breath, she took off. Her feet pounded against the hard platform before she leaped into the air. She landed on her feet in the pit, but the snakes were not happy to have an uninvited guest. They immediately retaliated and snapped at her.

"Ouch!" The sharp fangs sank deep into her skin, stinging as if she had kicked a hornet's nest.

"Keep going!"

Pain seared up Adeline's legs as she faltered toward the platform, smashing through the aggressive snakes. They hissed and curled beneath her, trying to trip her with their long, rope-like bodies. Blood oozed from her calves and ankles, trickling over her feet as she staggered forward. Her limbs throbbed, but she kept her eyes ahead, ignoring the ongoing strikes from the snakes.

She was in tears by the time she hauled herself onto the platform.

Kicking off a snake that had latched onto her heel, Adeline wheezed for air while scrambling away from the pit. She smashed her back against the door, staring at the hissing snakes.

They could no longer reach her.

Hot tears streamed down her cheeks as she sucked in rapid breaths. Her legs and feet were throbbing, as was her chest. She sat in her misery and inspected the damage.

There were puncture marks all over her leggings, and she could feel her blood trapped beneath the tight fabric. She was in too much pain to roll them up and see the wounds, so she focused on the ones on her bare feet.

The blood seeping from the bite marks made her nauseous. There were more than a dozen of them, and they stung like she had soaked them in rubbing alcohol.

Hugging her knees, Adeline cried. She doubted she could stand, let alone walk. Even if she could, she wouldn't allow something else to harm her.

"I know it hurts, but I need you to go through the door."

"I am *not* going, Henry!" Adeline let her tears fall. "I don't care about the stupid promise anymore!"

"I need you to trust me. Go into the other room."

"So I can get hurt again?" Adeline hunched her shoulders, allowing another wave of tears to rush down her face. She didn't even bother wiping her eyes as the pain intensified. "Please just get me out of here."

"Adeline Bigsby, get up now!"

Adeline froze in place, fear zapping inside her chest. She had never heard him speak in such a stern way.

Using the door as a crutch, Adeline staggered to her feet.

Pain ripped through her legs as she hung onto the doorknob. Her body swayed, blood pooling at her feet. She was afraid she would pass out.

But she kept going.

Fighting through the pain, Adeline clenched her teeth and forced herself to open the red door.

Chapter Twenty-One

ADELINE HELD BACK A cry as she stumbled into the next room. The gentle glow from the torches revealed a small space without a door in sight. A hot spring bubbled in the middle of the quiet area.

Steam rolled from the clear water. It looked inviting, but Adeline stayed back.

"Put your legs in the water," Henry said.

Adeline didn't move. "Is this some kind of trick?"

"Trust me."

Adeline wavered for a few moments before hobbling to the hot spring. The agony in her legs reawakened, but she pushed through the pain and gradually lowered herself to the edge of the pool.

Wincing, she dipped her toes into the scalding water. She thought about retreating, but she was too exhausted to move. She sat at the edge of the pool and put her legs into the water.

It went up to her shins, searing her wounds. She sat in the pain and watched her blood pollute the pure water. The red liquid swirled around for a moment before dissolving into nothing.

Strange.

Her wounds no longer stung, and the pain seemed to lessen the longer she stayed there.

Adeline dipped her dirty hands into the heated spring. The light scent of roses reached her nose as she washed the grime from her fingers and arms. The fresh water felt good against her skin and slowly eased her tight muscles.

Adeline took her time rolling up her leggings, washing the sand away. The intense heat from the water stung as she rubbed the blood from her legs and feet, trying not to scrub too hard.

As she did so, the throbbing pain in her legs dwindled. She lifted her leg to get a better look at the wounds.

The snake bites were gone.

"No way!" Adeline stroked her smooth skin.

"It's a healing spring," Henry said.

Adeline pulled her other leg from the water and found no bite marks. "This is unbelievable."

"Aren't you glad you didn't quit?"

"Yeah." Adeline lowered her head. "Sorry I doubted you."

"No problem at all," Henry said, his voice cheerful. *"Now, on to the last room."*

Another red door materialized along the rock wall. She looked at it apprehensively, not wanting to leave the warmth of the spring, but she couldn't stay if she wanted the promise.

Adeline rose to her feet and rolled down the wet spandex to her ankles as the coldness in the room hit her exposed skin.

"What's in that room?" she asked, rubbing her hands up and down her arms.

"You'll have to see for yourself."

Adeline exhaled loudly, hoping Henry would hear her frustration. He remained silent.

She crossed the room, the cold floor hastening her pace.

"One more room," she whispered as she opened the final door.

The nasty, hot air made Adeline gag even before she entered the last room. The smell of death was so thick, she expected to see rotting corpses as she closed the door behind her.

Breathing through her mouth, Adeline shoved down the urge to vomit as she looked to see what she had just gotten herself into. Before her was a long, swinging bridge made of wooden planks leading to a platform with the final red door. It was suspended over murky water as black as tar. The odor had to be from whatever was hidden beneath it.

Goosebumps trailed down her arms as the dingy-looking bridge swayed a few feet above the dark water like a haunted attraction. It was the only way to reach the exit. After further inspection, it appeared sturdy enough to cross.

Adeline shuddered as she did another slow scan of the creepy room. She didn't see any danger as the flames flickered along the rocks of the cave. All she had to do was walk across the bridge without falling into the water. It seemed simple enough.

Adeline clutched the flimsy rope railings and stepped onto the first wooden plank. The board felt secure under her feet, but the old bridge rocked. She tightened her grip on the thin, frayed ropes and waited for the bridge to settle. It quickly went still.

Exhaling, Adeline eyed the red door. It wasn't far. She would reach it shortly if she went slow. Though the humid, smelly room wasn't pleasant, it seemed to be the easiest trial so far.

She should have known better.

As she took another step, sudden movement seized her attention. A faint shadow appeared before the red door. She turned deathly pale as she stared at the strange phenomenon, hoping her eyes were playing tricks on her.

The distorted shadow turned into a solid creature. Evil seeped out of the demon's hollow eyes as it cocked its head to the side, sizing Adeline up.

"Give me the crystal!" the dark figure shrieked, pointing its long, knife-like fingers at her.

Terror plowed into Adeline like a freight train on steroids as she gripped the ropes until her knuckles turned white. She couldn't move, couldn't breathe. She couldn't do anything at that moment.

"Get me out of here before I die!" Adeline pleaded in her thoughts.

"The demon cannot swim, so get it in the water," Henry said, ignoring her cry.

"Have you lost your mind?" Adeline said. *"I want to leave now!"*

"This is the final trial. Don't quit."

"How do you expect me to get that thing in the water?" she asked in a panic. *"Its fingers are literally knives!"*

"Get it into the water."

"It will stab me!"

Henry's voice turned gentle. *"Adeline, do you want the promise or not?"*

"Of course I do."

"Then move forward and knock the creature into the water."

Henry made it sound like a simple task, but Adeline couldn't fathom getting any closer to the horrifying demon who guarded the door. Just looking at it made her want to run away.

"Do it afraid," Jesse's voice popped inside her mind.

"I'm way past being afraid!"

"Fear will only leave when you face it, and that creature is a representation of your biggest fear."

Adeline stood frozen in place. *"Will it hurt me?"*

"Temporary pain is worth a lifetime of victory," Jesse repeated what Henry had said earlier.

"That's not what I asked!"

"Do you feel the pain from the snake bites?" Jesse asked.

"No."

"It will be the same with this demon," he said with confidence. *"Now go!"*

Adeline remembered the power of the healing spring. Even if she did get hurt, she could go back. With a plan in mind, she went for it. Her knees knocked together as she forced her fingers to loosen their grip on the ropes.

The demon still guarded the door with its dead eyes on her. Adeline took a baby step forward, and the small movement awakened its wrath. The demon puffed up its chest and screeched, sending chills through Adeline.

"Give the crystal to me," the demon said, showing a set of jagged teeth that were just as sharp as its fingers. "Or I will slice you in half!"

Adeline whimpered as she shook, rooted to the singular plank of wood, but that only infuriated the demon.

It bellowed a gut-ripping scream before charging at her. The feeble bridge bounced and bobbed as soon as the creature stepped on it, almost sending Adeline over the fragile railing. She was too stunned to move as the evil beast ran full speed, bashing into her like a linebacker.

Pain rocked Adeline as she sailed into the air, back slamming onto the solid platform. She wheezed as she struggled to rise. When she locked eyes with the monster now looming over her, her muscles stiffened.

It let out a mocking laugh as it raised its arm, ready to strike. Slamming her eyes shut, she screamed as she shot both hands up to protect her face from the sharp fingers that were already on their way.

A sharp pain ignited along the length of her thigh. She felt the warm blood before she saw it flowing down her leg. Its claws had ripped through her leggings with ease, leaving long gashes.

Her heart stopped. The sapphire had been torn from her pocket, rolling unevenly on the ground. The creature laughed horrifically as it scooped up the shiny stone with its claws and marveled at the prize. It no longer had any interest in Adeline and turned its back to her.

The demon stepped onto the rickety bridge and made its way toward the red door. Adeline trembled on the floor, tears pooling in her eyes.

"Now is your chance!" Henry's voice struck her thoughts, sending a sudden jolt of adrenaline through her.

Adeline sprang to her feet, awakening the pain in her leg. She hobbled forward, testing the torn leg's strength. It hurt, but she wouldn't let that stop her. She took a few more steps before she was sure she could run.

Her weight shook the bridge, but the monster was so infatuated with the stone that it didn't notice.

Adeline crept forward and shoved the demon's back, making it lose its footing. It flung out its arms and fluttered them in the air before plummeting over the railing into the black, polluted water.

The demon sank like a rock, and Adeline shouted for joy. But triumph quickly turned to panic when she realized her crucial mistake. The creature still had her sapphire!

"No!" Adeline screamed at the black water.

"Go get it!" Henry exclaimed.

Without a second thought, Adeline jumped into the sickening water.

Adeline felt like she had jumped into a barrel of molasses as she opened her eyes to find the demon. The murky water made it difficult to see, but she was determined to get back her promise.

She swam downward, and her heart rate accelerated when she glimpsed her shimmering sapphire in the creature's hand as it sank to the bottom. It twisted violently as bubbles escaped its monstrous mouth. No matter how hard it kicked and flapped its arms, it kept plummeting down.

Adeline's thigh stung as she swam after the demon. It landed on the bottom, flailing its arms and claws around, attempting to save itself. Its rapid movement stirred up whatever coated the floor of the cesspool.

At first, Adeline thought it was covered in sticks. As she got closer, her chest constricted when she saw bones. She couldn't tell if they were human or animal, but she chose not to think about it as she hovered above the demon.

She kept her distance, trying to locate the sapphire. It no longer shined in the demon's empty hand. The creature must have dropped it in its attempt to save its life.

Adeline scanned the endless stacks of bones, but the demon made it difficult. It kept stirring up the bottom as it jerked around like it was fighting an invisible enemy. The creature didn't care about the crystal anymore; its only concern was making it back to the surface.

A faint glint caught Adeline's eyes. She spun toward it. *The sapphire!*

The frantic movements of the demon jolted it from its resting place, making it float upward for a moment. Its weight quickly sent it back down, where it landed next to a human skull.

Adeline wondered briefly how the skull had found its way down there, but she pushed it from her thoughts. The sapphire was close, but so was the flailing demon.

She waited, thinking for a moment until the demon's movements slowed. It kicked a few more times before giving up and floating weightlessly back onto the bed of bones. It was on the verge of death, Adeline was certain of it.

Fear rattled her insides as she dove toward the fallen demon. She scooped up the sapphire, tightening her fingers around it. Exhilaration coursed through her as she swam toward the surface, but it didn't last long.

The demon snatched Adeline's ankle, sinking its dagger-like fingers into her delicate skin. It tugged, pulling her back down.

Adeline squirmed and kicked madly, clutching the sapphire firmly in one fist. With the murky water and her blood clouding her vision, she could barely see what was in front of her. She continued to thrash, and the demon's strength seemed to diminish. It loosened its hold, allowing her to slip her ankle free. She swam hard out of the demon's reach, daring to glance over her shoulder. The creature floated lifelessly atop the pile of bones.

That's what you get.

Adeline dashed upward and didn't slow until she surfaced. She inhaled the rotten air, paddling to the swinging bridge. The movement irritated her wounds, but she kept moving.

She stuffed the sapphire in the remaining pocket on her leggings before grabbing one of the wooden planks of the bridge. Her arms shook as she tried to haul herself up, but her muscles gave out and she fell back into the water.

Adeline popped back up and swiped the water from her eyes. Her nostrils flared as she reached up and latched onto the bridge again. She grunted, using every ounce of strength she had left. Her muscles screamed in agony as she dragged herself out of the dark water.

Adeline lay back on the wooden boards, allowing herself a moment to breathe as she listened to the water droplets hit the smelly pool beneath her. Her body was tense, her wounds burned, and her mind reeled.

That was insane.

Never had she done anything so courageous or so dumb. As she sat up to check her ankle, she realized she was proud of herself—for the first time since Dad had passed.

Another surge of pain rippled up her leg when she saw how much blood she was losing. It made her queasy seeing the deep puncture wounds. She needed to go back to the healing spring immediately.

She looked over her shoulder and frowned. The door she had entered through was no longer there. The only door in the room was the one she hadn't been through yet. Henry had told her she was in the final room, but it didn't reduce her rising anxiety as she eyed the exit.

"Let's get this over with," she mumbled.

Using the rope for support, Adeline groaned as she used her good leg to stand. The bridge wobbled, but she kept her balance. It took her a while to hop along the moving boards, but she eventually made it to the crimson door.

Blowing out a final breath, Adeline swung open the door and was blinded by a bright light.

Chapter Twenty-Two

ADELINE SHADED HER EYES from the excruciating light, breathing in the fresh air that smelled of pine and mulch. It was abruptly replaced by her own repulsive stench.

She held her nose to keep herself from vomiting as she adjusted to the bright sunlight. She would have to burn her clothing and bathe for hours, if not days, to get rid of the stench from the murky water.

Once her eyes settled, she took in the quiet forest bursting with color. A warm breeze whispered through the fall leaves that went on for miles. Adeline was grateful to be outside, but her heart still pounded as if she were in danger.

Glancing back, Adeline eyed the massive boulder that towered over her head. There was no door in sight, which heightened her uneasiness as she skimmed the pretty forest once more.

Movement ahead snatched Adeline's attention to the winding path ahead of her. Footsteps crunched closer and closer against the fallen leaves. Half expecting another monster to step from behind a tree, she was relieved to see Henry sporting his button-down shirt and cap.

"Henry!"

"Hello there, Adeline." Henry waved as he strolled toward her.

Closer than before, Adeline noticed his clothes were dry. Not a single drop dripped from the hem of his trousers.

Adeline hobbled toward Henry Snow. Each step was painful, but she didn't stop until she crashed into his open arms. He smelled of tobacco and leather, and she relaxed in his embrace. He squeezed her tightly, not even caring that she was soaked and smelled like sewage.

"Well done, Adeline." Henry released her with a grand smile.

"Thanks," she said, wiping her teary eyes.

"I am so pleased that you didn't give up." He gripped her on the shoulder. "And now you can keep the promise."

Adeline grinned for the first time in hours. She had forgotten about the sapphire. Stuffing her hand into her pocket, she pulled out the solid gemstone and held it to the sun. The sunlight filtered through the flat faces of the stone, throwing geometric puddles of blue along her arms and Henry's face. There were no imperfections in its brilliance.

"What are you going to do with it?" Henry asked.

"Probably sell it," she said honestly. "I could make *a lot* of money. And then I could buy my family a better house."

"Some things are more valuable than money."

"I know that, but money would make my life a lot easier."

A tiny smile crept across his thin, wrinkly lips. "May I change your mind?"

Adeline hesitated for a moment. "What do you think I should do with it?"

"Hold it out to me, and I'll show you."

Adeline extended the sapphire to him. She raised a brow when he placed his soft hand on top of the gemstone. The stone went hot, and she backed away, almost dropping it when she felt it liquifying in her palm.

"You don't need money right now, Adeline," Henry said, looking her dead in the eye. "You need courage."

Henry removed his hand, and Adeline gasped. The sapphire had melted!

The bright blue liquid absorbed into her skin like her palm was a sponge. Warmth traveled up her arm and spread throughout her body. It invaded every nook and cranny of her being, like it been injected into her bloodstream. Her spirit and mind coursed with a powerful sense of courage and boldness.

She felt like she could do anything.

"What's happening to me?"

"You are receiving courage," Henry said, his eyes glowing.

Adeline released a surprising laugh. She couldn't grasp what was taking place within her, but she felt incredible as she looked herself over.

"What the—"

All her cuts were gone, and so was the blood that had stained her fair skin. But that wasn't the only unexplainable thing that happened.

Her entire outfit was fully repaired. She was no longer wet, and her bare feet were now covered in the exact sneakers she'd left at the fountain. Even the stench from the gross water had evaporated, along with the irritating sand.

Adeline touched the pocket that had magically been restored. "How is this possible?"

"I told you it would be worth it," Henry said, directing his honey-brown eyes to her hair.

Adeline's hand shot to her head. Her rich, auburn mane wasn't only dry, but squeaky clean with a fragrance of sweet peaches. It was still securely tied up in a high ponytail, but she could comb through the smooth waves that gently bounced down her back. It never felt that soft, and she couldn't keep herself from playing with it.

Laughter burst through her. "I don't know what is going on, Henry, but I feel great."

"I knew you would."

Adeline weaved her fingers through her ponytail as the exhilarating sensation swirled beneath her skin like it was alive. The thought of selling the sapphire no longer crossed her mind as she savored the tangible courage that now lived inside her.

"Can I still breathe and see underwater?"

"Unfortunately, no." Henry shook his head. "That was only temporary to help you enter and complete the tunnel."

"Well, that's disappointing," she said, her shoulders drooping. "Does that mean I can no longer communicate with you through my thoughts?"

Henry smirked.

"That was a gift from Godfrey, and it is yours to keep." Henry's voice entered her mind, mouth unmoving. *"You can now speak to all of us inside or outside this world."*

"Really?" Adeline perked up. "So, we can talk all the time now?"

"Yes. We are only a thought away."

"That's so cool," she said with a wide grin. "Especially since you guys don't have a phone."

Warm laughter drifted from Henry. "This is way better than a phone call."

"Seriously."

The ground began to shake and rumble beneath their feet. The thunderous noise was so loud, Adeline was certain an earthquake was heading their way.

"What's going on?"

"Look." Henry pointed his chin toward the wooded trail.

Adeline kept her eyes on the curved path as the noise got louder and louder. Leaves fluttered from the nearby trees, floating to the rumbling ground. Whatever was coming was big *and* powerful.

Two majestic horses trotted around the bend, moving with grace and in perfect unison. The white mare advanced with her head held high, her purple highlighted mane flapping with each step. She looked confident and lovely, but small compared to her companion.

It was the biggest horse Adeline had ever seen. The solid black stallion was larger than a Clydesdale, with huge hooves that confirmed he was the one making all the noise. He even made his male rider look tiny as his dark blue highlights waved through his black mane and tail.

Adeline narrowed in on the young man in the plaid, bouncing on the back of the massive animal. She would recognize his happy face anywhere.

"Great job, Adeline!" Jesse applauded, the sound muffled by the leather reins held in place by his thumb. "I knew you could do it!"

"Jesse!"

Jesse pulled on the reins, and both horses came to a stop as Adeline rushed forward. She was breathless by the time she reached the fascinating creatures. They were even prettier up close.

The different hues of purple on the white mare made it appear as if she was a unicorn without the horn, while the large stallion's navy highlights in his black mane and tail made him look fierce yet spectacular.

"Are these your horses?" Adeline asked, bouncing from foot to foot.

"Yep. This is Regal." Jesse patted the black beast on the side. "And that white beauty is Angela."

Her breath quickened as she combed the mare's soft, white coat. She gently stroked her side before moving her hand to a single, tiny braid entwined in the purple and white mane.

"She's beautiful," Adeline said, rubbing the coarse hair between her fingers.

"She sure is," Jesse said. "Want to ride her?"

"Are you serious?" Adeline asked, louder than she intended. "I would love to."

It had been over a year since Adeline had ridden a horse, but she had plenty of experience since her childhood friend from the beach owned a stable.

"But what about Henry?" Adeline glanced back at her sweet friend, who was approaching from behind.

"What about me?" Henry asked, his posture straight.

She gestured to the horses. "There's only two."

"I would prefer to walk on this beautiful day."

"Are you sure?"

"I'm quite sure, love," he said with a wink. "I will see you both at the cabin."

Henry gave Adeline's shoulder a gentle squeeze before looking up at Jesse. He stuck his tongue out playfully while Jesse made a goofy face at his old friend. They both exploded with laughter as Henry turned to leave.

Adeline giggled as Henry cut through the trees, making his own way home. She still heard him chuckling to himself even after he disappeared behind the trees.

"I'll help you get on Angela," Jesse said, about to jump from his saddle.

Adeline raised her hand to stop him. "I got it."

She gripped the reins and placed her foot in the leather stirrup. In one fluid motion, she swung her other leg up and over the horse until she was sitting on the saddle.

"I'm impressed." Jesse clapped.

"I have some experience with horses," she said, adjusting the other stirrup.

"I can tell." He took up his reins again.

Adeline smiled, gently stroking Angela's neck before sitting up straight. "Where to?"

"Let's turn around." Jesse directed Regal until he faced the way he'd come. "I want to show you something."

"Okay."

Regal waited until Adeline circled Angela around before trotting down the shaded path with his companion by his side. The sunshine shimmered through the breaks of branches and leaves; she relished the fresh air she had been deprived of in the tunnel.

"I haven't been on a horse in a long time."

"I couldn't tell," Jesse said, flashing a smile. "You're a natural rider."

"Thanks." Heat reached her cheeks.

"What did you think of the tunnel?"

"It was the hardest thing I have ever done."

"But totally worth it."

"It was," she said, rocking atop the saddle. "I knew I was out of shape, but I didn't realize how bad."

"Nothing we can't fix."

Flashbacks of Dad came to Adeline, then a rush of sadness. Her face folded into a frown as she blinked back tears. Jesse's optimism reminded her so much of Dad. She could still hear Dad's cheerful voice waking her at the crack of dawn, and his ongoing encouragement and praise that kept her from quitting when things had been tough.

Adeline desperately wanted to be healthy and strong again, but she knew what it would cost. Physically, she could handle it, but emotionally? She wasn't so sure.

If she chose that route, Dad would always be on her mind, and she would have to battle with the guilt and heartbreak that came along with it.

"Do you want my help?" Jesse asked, his long hair swaying at his waist.

Adeline hid her face from him, afraid he would see her tears. "I don't think that's a good idea."

"Why not?"

She rubbed her face in the crook of her arm, hoping she could play it off as dust from the trail. When she felt ready to look at Jesse, his expression was soft. She was certain he knew about the accident, but she wasn't ready to talk about Dad.

"You probably don't want to waste your time with me," she told him, hoping that was a good enough excuse. "I haven't done anything active in a *very* long time."

Jesse snorted. "Challenge accepted."

Adeline swallowed the lump rising in her throat. "I didn't say I wanted you to help me."

"You didn't have to."

Adeline fidgeted with the reins, pushing thoughts of Dad and the accident away. She wouldn't allow depressing thoughts to ruin her time with Jesse, so she focused on the reward of her being healthy. She needed help and motivation to get herself back to a routine, and Jesse seemed up to it.

If I could just control my emotions, then maybe this could work.

"Fine," she said after a long exhale. "I would like your help."

"I knew it," Jesse said gleefully. "I'll whip you into shape in no time."

"I don't doubt it," Adeline said, letting a laugh slip.

"But just so you know, I will not go easy on you." Jesse tossed her a glance. "This world is dangerous. If you want to stay alive, you'll have to learn how to defend yourself."

"I have no interest in fighting, Jesse. I just want to run without feeling like I'm dying."

"You're going to want to be trained in combat," Jesse said. "Ralock isn't the only thing that can harm you here."

Adeline adjusted uncomfortably in her seat. She didn't want to think about Ralock or any other deadly creatures who lived in that realm.

"Your best bet is to have a weapon," Jesse said.

She snuck a glance at the blade gently bouncing against Jesse's hip, safe in its sheath. He wasn't carrying his bow and arrows, but she was confident he was just as deadly with the longsword.

"I have no idea how to use a weapon."

"I will train you if you're willing to learn."

Adeline didn't doubt Jesse's skills. She had seen the way he'd shot his bow and only imagined what he could do with a sword. But she was an entirely different story.

"You won't regret it," Jesse spoke again.

Adeline looked at him and was captured by his bright emerald eyes. She wasn't sure why he had so much confidence in her. "I guess I can try it, but don't get your hopes up."

"My hopes are always up," he said, his smile growing. "I'll make a warrior out of you in no time."

Adeline threw him an exaggerated eye roll. She wasn't a warrior; she was just a teenage girl barely surviving life. But she would try for Jesse.

Drawing in a refreshing breath, Adeline pushed her worry aside and reveled in the surrounding forest. The air was warm, the sun was out, and the trail was clear.

The winding path continued for the next few miles until the trees cleared, revealing a scenic view. The horses stopped near a steep ledge with plenty of room to spare, allowing Adeline a front-row view of the meadow below.

Millions of poppy flowers dotted the expansive meadow, the wind making it look like currents of a red sea. Beyond the wildflowers was another patch of woods. Evergreens grew alongside strong hickory and oaks, along with maple and beech trees bursting with color. They soared atop a mighty mountain range that nearly touched the blue sky and spread out as far as the eye could see, intermingling with the forest that had no end.

"Whoa," Adeline said, her eyes expanding. "This is beautiful."

"It's quite the view, but that's not why I brought you here."

Adeline pulled her eyes from the meadow to look at him. "Then why did you bring me?"

"To tell you to stay away from that area."

Confusion danced across her face. "Why?"

"Beyond those poppy flowers is the Dark Territory," Jesse said, pointing his bearded chin toward the meadow below. "You must *never* go there, no matter what."

Adeline scanned the wide landscape. What could be so wrong with a meadow filled with flowers and that quiet bit of forest? "Why is it called that?"

"Ralock lives there. He rules that entire territory."

"Are you serious?" Her eyes widened, but she didn't look away. "I would have never guessed that."

"Its beauty fools many." Jesse grimaced.

"Where exactly is his territory?" she asked, raising a hand to the sun. "I don't see any walls or barriers."

"The boundaries of his land start at that tree line and go all the way back beyond that mountain range and spreads east and west into the forest." Jesse pointed to the borders of the land.

"Where is my world from here?"

"A little way to the west."

"So, part of Ralock's territory is near my world?"

"Correct."

Adeline shifted anxiously in the saddle while rubbing the smooth leather of her horse's reins in her hand. "How am I supposed to know if I step into it?"

"You won't."

"Well, that's terrifying."

"You won't have to worry about it if you stick with the paths to our cabin," Jesse said. "They're nowhere near his territory."

"Good to know."

"I didn't bring you here to scare you, Adeline." The smile was back on his face. "I just wanted you to be aware of Ralock's territory."

"I'm glad you did." She forced a smile.

Jesse tapped his boots into Regal, steering him away from the ledge and onto a new path.

An uneasy feeling lingered in Adeline as she gave the Dark Territory one last look before encouraging Angela to follow Regal. She couldn't believe a monster controlled such a beautiful area. She vowed to never step foot in his territory.

"Where are we heading?" she asked Jesse.

"We're going to make a quick stop in the training area to get you a weapon." He grinned over his shoulder.

"Great," she murmured.

The Dark Territory was still on Adeline's mind when the garden came into view. She didn't recognize the huge, trimmed hedge that had been made into a wall, but she enjoyed the way it looked as they rode under the tall archway wrapped in morning glories. The blue petals emitted a fresh fragrance that greeted them as the horse's hooves clapped against the stone walkway.

Adeline brightened as she soaked in the view, catching small glimpses of the hummingbirds zooming by. She didn't bother asking Jesse how far they had left to go since she easily spotted the obstacle course that towered over everything.

They were there in no time, and the next thing Adeline knew, she was dismounting Angela and heading toward the rack of weapons with Jesse. Her stomach sank to her toes, but she didn't say a word as they strolled past the wooden dummies and stood before the weapon rack that lined the back wall.

Swords of different sizes, along with axes and spears, stood in neat rows along the rack. There was no end to the sharp, lethal metal. Adeline ran her eyes down the line of weapons again. No guns.

That's weird.

In her world, guns were the weapon of choice, but clearly that wasn't the case here.

"Pick your weapon," Jesse said, nodding toward the rack.

Adeline wrapped her arms around her torso. "I don't know about this, Jesse."

"Give it a try."

Adeline didn't move. The longer she stared at the shiny weapons, the more her stomach churned. There were hundreds to choose from, and none of them appealed to her. But she appeased Jesse and stepped forward anyway.

Her shaky fingers wrapped around the handle of a battle-ax. She lifted it, but the thick blade was too heavy for her. It swung down, landing in the hard-packed dirt beside her foot.

That was close.

Adeline's arms throbbed as she placed the ax back on the rack. It clattered against the other weapons but stayed in place. She massaged her muscles to relieve some of the tension. Her body had had enough action for one day.

Taking a slow breath, Adeline observed the swords. She removed the longsword from its place and awkwardly held it in the air. The steel was too weighty for her, and she hastily put it back before she dropped it.

"None of these are going to work," she said with a frown.

Jesse scrubbed a hand through his short beard for a moment before holding up a single finger. "I know just what you need."

Pivoting, Jesse signaled for Adeline to follow. She trailed behind him, maneuvering through the various training equipment until they reached the archery range. Jesse went straight to the rack of recurve bows, tapping his chin as he studied each one.

"This one will do." He retrieved a bow and handed it to Adeline.

The smooth wood fit perfectly in Adeline's hand as she tightened her fingers around the grip. Though her muscles were sore, the bow wasn't overly heavy and felt natural in her hand, almost like it had been specially made for her. She examined the exquisite craftsmanship. "This is really nice."

"Thank you," Jesse said, resting a hand on top of his sword. "I made it myself."

"You made this?"

"Yeah, I can be pretty handy when I choose to be."

"No kidding." Adeline held up the bow like she was going to fire it.

"I want you to have it."

Adeline's head snapped up to meet his gaze. "What?"

"You heard me."

"You don't need to do that. I don't even know if I'll use it."

"Trust me, you will use it."

Adeline slid her index finger along the curvature of the bow. She liked the way it looked and felt, but she still had unsettling thoughts about using it.

"I changed my mind, Jesse," she said, offering the recurve bow back to him. "I don't want to learn to fight; I would rather focus on getting in shape."

"Are you sure?" he asked, his expressive green eyes searching hers.

"Yeah."

"No problem." Jesse's face deflated a little as he placed the bow back on the rack. "But the bow is still yours if you change your mind."

"Okay, thanks."

"I want to take you to one more place before we head back to the cabin."

CHAPTER TWENTY-THREE

Shifting in the saddle, Adeline absorbed the uniqueness of the area that looked like a Japanese garden. Bamboo and beech trees shaded serene pools, the edge of the water lapping against smooth pebbles.

The peaceful sound soothed Adeline as the horses rode by beautiful camellia bushes. Their bright red petals were so vibrant and large they could easily be mistaken for roses.

The journey through that remarkable space was short and sweet, ending sooner than Adeline wanted. The path led them to a wide, open pasture. A beautiful white barn stood tall amongst the large elm trees and rolling hills. There was also a large pond full of water lilies that looked deep enough to swim in. The field was a sight to see, but it was the stunning creatures that excited Adeline.

Horses grazed throughout the pasture, paying no mind to them. There were nearly twenty of them, uniquely colored with bright highlights, like Regal and Angela.

Adeline slid off Angela and approached a painted horse with large brown spots and red streaks in his hair. The powerful horse lifted his head. He looked her square in the eyes, his gaze pinning her in place. His deep brown eyes explored hers for a long second, making her heart beat a little faster.

"His name is Scout." Jesse hopped off Regal and walked toward Adeline.

Adeline was cemented in place as Scout went back to eating, no longer interested in her. He reminded her of the horses Native Americans used to ride. All he needed was a feather and some war paint to fit the part perfectly.

"He won't hurt you," Jesse said, caressing Scout's side.

Hearing that eased some of Adeline's concerns as she cautiously stroked Scout's thick coat. He didn't flinch, nor acknowledge her as she combed through his hair once more.

"I love his red highlights."

"Me too."

Adeline grinned, shielding her face from the sun to get another look at the other horses. Regal was undoubtedly the largest horse there, but the others were just as breathtaking, with radiant colors throughout their long, flowing hair. Each was unique and stunning in their own way. One mare had a full rainbow blended in her mane and tail, while another had streaks of aquamarine, light pink and purple, reminding Adeline of mermaids.

"Do you own all these horses?" Adeline asked.

"No, most of them are wild, but they like the company of the other horses."

"Which ones are yours?"

"Scout is one of mine," Jesse said, patting the painted horse. "Along with Regal, Angela, and Blaze."

"Which one is Blaze?"

"Take a wild guess." Jesse's mouth twitched.

Adeline looked from horse to horse. She instantly knew which one was Blaze. The champagne-colored horse had red and orange hair that looked identical to flames of a fire, especially when the wind tossed it around. It seemed so real that Adeline was certain she would get burned if she got too close.

Adeline pointed. "It has to be that horse that looks like it's on fire."

"Yep, that's her." Jesse nodded, his smile broadening. "She's the fastest horse out here, but she hates to be ridden."

Adeline wondered what it would be like to ride the fiery horse. She could envision herself flying across the pasture while holding onto the blazing mane. Her chest fluttered at the thought.

"Blaze would buck you in a heartbeat," Jesse said, laughter in his voice.

"I bet I could ride her." A smile pulled at her lips.

"You better stick with Angela. She's way nicer."

"You're probably right."

Adeline looked back at Angela, and her heart swelled. She already felt an undeniable attachment to the pretty white horse. She had ridden many horses over the years, but none were quite like Angela.

"Which one is your favorite?" Adeline asked.

"Regal," Jesse said without missing a beat. "He's not only fearless, but very loyal and smart."

"I believe it," she said. "He's the most intimidating horse I've ever seen."

"He does have an intensity about him, but it helps me when I take him on long journeys." Jesse chuckled as he gave Regal a loving pat. "No one in their right mind would mess with him."

"Is he dangerous?"

"He can be; he's a warhorse," Jesse said. "He thinks it's his job to protect me, and he will attack anyone who looks like a threat."

"I'm pretty sure you could handle anyone who tried to attack you," Adeline said, glancing at the sword on his hip.

Regal let out a loud snort, like he had been eavesdropping on their conversation. He gave his owner a sharp look before going back to chomping on the grass.

"I don't think Regal agrees with you," Jesse said lightly.

"I don't think he does either."

They burst into laughter. Regal gave them another irritated glance, which only fueled their amusement.

After their giggles subsided, Jesse patted Regal on the back. "We'll stop teasing you, Regal. Let's head to the barn so I can get that saddle off."

Regal raised his head and nodded like he understood.

"You too, Angela," Jesse called out to the white mare.

Angela stopped eating and quickly trotted to Jesse, who was already heading up the hill.

"Are you coming, Adeline?" Jesse threw a glance over his shoulder.

"Where are we going now?" Adeline asked as she caught up with him.

"The barn."

The grass shifted with the light breeze as they hiked to the barn. Adeline entered the wide-open doors and paused, inhaling the potent smell of hay. Clean, empty stalls lined the sides, with equipment and accessories lining the back wall.

"This is the cleanest barn I've ever seen," Adeline said.

"Thanks." Jesse headed to the back of the barn with the horses. "I do my best to keep it clean."

"I can tell."

Adeline admired the barn while Angela and Regal stood next to the racks along the wall. Jesse went to work, unbuckling the strap on Angela's saddle before hauling it off her back.

"Do you need help?" Adeline asked.

"I think you've used your muscles enough today," Jesse said, placing the saddle on the stand.

Jesse worked quickly and efficiently. He freed Angela from her bridle and reins, hanging them on the designated hooks before doing the same with Regal. Regal's saddle was a little more complicated since it looked like it weighed a ton, but Jesse tugged it off and easily put it away.

Once Jesse was done, the horses took off. The heaviness of Regal's hooves rattled Adeline's bones as he advanced toward her. He darted by Adeline without even a glance, heading straight into the sunshine with Angela at his heels.

Now that both horses were unrestricted, they happily roamed around the pasture. Regal went back to eating while Angela ran with a sudden burst of energy. She did circles around the other horses until she reached Blaze, who took off like she wanted to be chased.

Adeline grinned at their playfulness as they dashed through the field like they were playing tag. Angela moved quickly and gracefully as she galloped through the pasture, trying to catch the fiery horse while weaving through the others. Blaze was much faster than Angela, but that didn't discourage her from trying to catch her friend.

"This is by far the best place in the garden," Adeline said as Jesse approached.

"I agree." Sticking his hands in his pockets, Jesse leaned against the barn, watching the game of tag. "If you could have any of the horses out here, which one would it be?"

"I don't know." Adeline shrugged. "They're all beautiful."

"You can only pick one." His lips pulled up into a smirk.

Adeline matched his smile as she took her time looking at every horse. She really liked the light brown horse that had white hair above his hooves, as if he wore socks. The long silver highlights throughout his mane sparkled in the sun. She also thought the spotted stallion with a golden mane was very handsome.

Each horse was captivating, but Adeline felt a pull toward Angela. She spotted the white beauty trotting toward the pond. Adeline not only adored the purple in her hair, but she really enjoyed watching her playful personality come out.

"If I had to pick one, I would probably choose Angela," she finally said.

"Good choice," Jesse said, cracking a smile. "She's going to be very happy that you chose her."

"Why do you say that?"

"Because earlier today, I told Angela you were going to be her new owner."

"What?"

Jesse smiled wide enough to show his slightly uneven teeth. "Angela is yours."

"You can't be serious."

"I'm dead serious."

Adeline covered her mouth as tears emerged. Since she was a little girl, she had wanted a horse of her own. She never thought it would happen. "I don't know what to say."

"A simple thank you would be perfect."

"Thank you, Jesse," she said, blinking back tears. "You have no idea how much this means to me."

"You're welcome." He threw an arm over her shoulders, leading her into the meadow. "Let's tell Angela the good news."

Adeline felt like she was on the verge of exploding as she walked with Jesse to the shaded pond where Angela was getting a quick drink. Hearing their footsteps, Angela lifted her head, water dripping from her chin.

"I have exciting news for you, Angela," Jesse said. "Adeline is officially your new owner."

Adeline lost the ability to breathe when Angela looked at her with affection. Her light blue eyes searched hers. Though they couldn't communicate with words, there was an internal connection forming between them.

"I'm going to take good care of you." Adeline nuzzled her face into the horse's soft hair, inhaling the clean, floral scent.

"And she will do the same for you," Jesse said, combing Angela's side. "Isn't that right, girl?"

Releasing a loud neigh, Angela lifted her head up and down.

"She acts as if she understands you." Adeline giggled as she brushed her fingers through Angela's coat.

"That's because she does," Jesse said. "She cannot speak, but she comprehends everything we say."

"So, Angela can understand me?"

"Yep. So can the other horses, but they'll probably ignore you."

"Well, that's just rude."

"Super rude." Jesse laughed.

Adeline snickered, massaging Angela's neck. "I'm assuming I can't take Angela back to my world."

"That's correct," he said. "I think your family would have some serious questions if you came home with a horse."

"You're right about that."

"But you can ride her as much as you'd like when you're here."

"I'm glad. Will she always be in this pasture?"

"Mostly, but if you ever need her, all you have to do is call her."

"Call her?" She raised an eyebrow.

"Yep. Each of my horses has a unique whistle that I taught them."

"That's really cool."

"It's very helpful when you need them. I'll teach you Angela's."

Jesse backpedaled until he was a few yards away. He moved his fingers to his lips and whistled a quick burst of chirps. It was loud but cheery like a bird call, and Angela immediately reacted. Her head shot in his direction, and she galloped straight to him.

"Good girl," Jesse said, praising her. "Now stay here for a moment."

Angela bowed her head and stayed put as Jesse hustled back to Adeline.

"You sounded exactly like a bird," Adeline said.

"I'll take that as a compliment." He smiled while blocking the sun from his face. "Now I'll show you how to do it."

Adeline knew how to whistle, but Angela's specific call was tricky. After multiple attempts, she finally got it.

"All right." Jesse parked his hands on his hips. "Now call her to us."

Adeline inserted the tips of her fingers to her lips, as Jesse instructed, and released a noisy whistle. The chirps were a little shaky, but recognizable to Angela, who darted to her new owner.

"It worked!" Adeline threw her hands in the air as Angela stopped before her. "Great job!"

"Thanks," Adeline said joyfully. "She's so smart."

"She really is," Jesse said. "Now that that's settled, let's head to the cabin and get us some food."

"Good thinking. I'm starving." Adeline latched onto Angela, giving her a loving squeeze as Jesse made his way down the hill. "I'm so glad you're mine," she whispered into her soft neck.

Angela neighed and rested her head against Adeline like she was hugging her back.

Adeline held her for a long moment, feeling the connection deepen between them before she let go. "I'll see you later."

Angela dipped her head, releasing a vocal neigh that made Adeline laugh. She gave her fluffy chin a final rub before chasing after Jesse.

"Wait for me!"

Chapter Twenty-Four

Evening arrived, and Adeline was having a hard time keeping her eyes open lounging around the cozy fire. Her eyelids grew heavy as warmth invited her to drift to sleep. She was tempted to spend another night at the cabin, but staying away from her world for too long could cause problems. Especially in school. She already felt overwhelmed in her classes and didn't want to make it worse.

"I better head home." Adeline yawned, stretching her sore arms.

"I'll take you back." Godfrey tapped his knees before rocking out of his seat.

Adeline said her goodbyes to Henry and Jesse before heading to the front door, but Godfrey didn't follow. He went over to the dining area and stood before a small coat closet.

"Let's go this way," Godfrey said, his eyes twinkling.

Adeline scrunched her face in confusion. "You want to go into the closet?"

"It's not a closet." Godfrey grinned, showing the small gap in his teeth. "It's a shortcut."

Godfrey opened the tall wooden door and shuttled his hefty physique inside. Not a second later, the door swung itself shut.

Adeline jumped, jerking her head to Henry and Jesse for answers, but they just smiled as they reclined by the fire.

"You better get going, Miss Adeline," Henry said, raising his teacup toward her. "He's waiting for you."

Adeline crept to the coat closet. Twisting the knob, she cracked the door and paused. Her mind jumbled with questions as she stood in the doorway, staring at the endless amount of sand.

"What...?"

A cold, salty breeze nipped against Adeline as she stepped forward, her sneakers sinking into the soft sand. She hugged her arms to trap in some heat as she admired the breathtaking sunset. Pink and orange conquered the sky, reflecting against the lively ocean that crashed against the shore.

She was on a beach...but not just any beach.

Shooting a glance over her shoulder, she froze. Rolling sand dunes separated her from a row of colorful beach houses she had walked by hundreds of times.

Her chest tightened as she turned toward the boardwalk. The North Carolina flag flapped in the wind, taunting her.

The last time she'd been in that exact spot was when Dad had been alive.

She trembled, eyes welling with tears. "This can't be real."

Everything was the same as it had been that dreadful day in April that had changed her whole life: the cold weather, the deserted beach, the setting sun. The only difference was Dad wasn't there.

"I have to get out of here." Panic clawed up her neck as she turned to leave.

The door was gone.

"No!" She spun in a circle, nearly tripping over herself as the roaring ocean pounded in her ears. There was no way out.

"Do you know where we are?" Godfrey asked, his red hair tossing in the breeze.

"This isn't p-possible."

"You'll learn that anything is possible when you're with me."

Her lungs went heavy and tight, turning her breaths into short, frenzy gasps. "I can't breathe."

"It's all right, Adeline." Godfrey gently touched her shoulder. "Just take a deep breath."

"You don't understand!" She sobbed, knocking his hand away. "I can't be here!"

"I do understand," he said in a soft voice. "That's why I brought you here."

She glared at him, tears flowing down her cheeks. "To torture me? I want to leave *now!*"

"I know you do," Godfrey said, kindness beaming from his eyes, "but we are not leaving."

"Why are you doing this to me?"

"Death comes in many forms, even while alive," he said, looking out into the ocean. "And your father wasn't the only one who died that day."

Another sob tore from Adeline's throat as she collapsed onto the sand. She buried her face in her hands, screaming out her misery and frustration. She cursed the deer that ran out into the road, and the old family Jeep that failed to deploy Dad's airbag. She even cursed the oak tree that totaled the vehicle and ended Dad's life.

But as she wept, she knew the only thing she truly blamed for the tragic accident was herself.

Godfrey's warm, firm hand rested against Adeline's shoulder again. He sat in the sand with her, watching the waves lap against the shore. She wasn't sure how long he had been next to her.

"Please take me back to the cabin," she said, her eyes tired and heavy.

"I know this is hard—"

"Don't act like you know how I feel!" She launched to her feet. "You have *no* idea what I've been through!"

Godfrey's countenance remained neutral as he pulled himself up, brushing the sand from his swim trunks. "I know a lot more than you believe I do." His words were gentle. "Just like I know you blame yourself for your father's death."

Heartbreak sliced through her chest as she faced the ocean and released an ear-splitting scream. Her throat grew raw and sore as she yelled into the sunset.

When her screaming died down, Godfrey went to her once more and softly touched her arm. His enormous body blocked some of the wind. "Adeline."

"Don't touch me." She jerked her arm away from him.

Godfrey allowed his hand to fall to his side as he stood next to Adeline, watching tears drip from her face. He stayed by her side and wiped away his own tears.

They didn't speak for a while until Godfrey broke the silence.

"It's not your fault, Adeline."

Adeline balled her fists, refusing to look at him.

"Your father's death was an accident," Godfrey said, "and it's time for you to forgive yourself and move on."

Godfrey's speech was kind and full of love, but his words infuriated Adeline.

"It *is* my fault," she said, glaring at him with reddened eyes. "*I* was the one who killed him."

"No, you weren't."

"Yes, I was!" Angry tears spilled down her face. "Stop lying to me!"

Red took over Adeline's vision and the next thing she knew, she was pounding her fists into Godfrey's stomach while screaming at the top of her lungs. She hit him again and again like he was her own personal punching bag.

Godfrey didn't budge. He stayed planted in the sand, allowing her to take out her pain and rage on him.

Never in her life had she ever behaved in such a manner, but she had *no* control in that moment. Her punches grew weaker as she lost strength, and then Godfrey grasped her wrists and held them in place. Snot and tears dripped from her face as Godfrey got down to her level.

Adeline squeezed her eyes shut, expecting to be reprimanded for her horrible behavior. She shook uncontrollably as she waited for Godfrey's wrath, but it never came.

"Look at me."

Peeling her eyelids open, Adeline stared into his crystal blue eyes glossed over with tears. Her heart sank.

What have I done?

Before Adeline could apologize, Godfrey spoke in a startling tone. "It was *not* your fault."

Adeline's head blew back from the sheer force of his voice like she had taken a hit to the face. It didn't hurt, but it scared her, especially the extreme tingling that ripped throughout her body.

She was burning hot within seconds and trembling from the overwhelming feeling growing in her chest. It was almost too much to bear, and she feared the strange heat would detonate at any moment, blasting her from the inside out.

But what started as absolute terror gradually turned into unexplainable peace. The burning simmered into a comfortable warmth, invading every corner of her being. Her shoulders slackened as she exhaled a slow breath.

She couldn't explain what was happening to her, but she felt better. It was like the anger and heartbreak she had been hauling around had trickled away until it could no longer torment her. Neither could shame and guilt consume her thoughts. It was as if they'd been flushed from her soul.

Finally, something clicked. Godfrey was telling her the truth.

Dad's death hadn't been her fault.

"Is it really not my fault?" she asked, her bottom lip quivering.

Godfrey released her wrists with a gentle smile. "It was never your fault, Adeline, although you've been telling that lie to yourself for months."

"But my mom…"

"It doesn't matter what your mother told you; it isn't true," he said. "Tragedy will sometimes happen in life, but you're not to blame for your father's death."

Lowering her head, Adeline allowed the tears to fall freely. Gratitude overwhelmed her. She no longer had to carry around the guilt of Dad's sudden death. It was gone for good.

"I'm sorry I hit you," she said, staring at her sandy shoes.

"I'm not afraid of your pain, Adeline." Godfrey lifted her chin. "And besides, my big belly can handle a few punches."

Adeline choked back a sob as she rubbed her puffy eyes. "I don't deserve you, Godfrey."

"Nonsense." Godfrey wiped away a tear.

"I'm serious," she said, wiping her nose with the back of her hand. "You've been nothing but nice to me, and I treated you horribly."

"You think I'm surprised by your behavior?" Godfrey asked. "I brought you here to face your pain, not to condemn you for it."

One look at his happy, freckled face, and Adeline knew he meant it. There was no frustration or aggravation, only kindness. "I'm glad I met you."

"Likewise," Godfrey said, his body shifting with the sand as he headed down the beach. "Come now. We must go before it gets dark."

Sniffling, Adeline matched his stride. "Where are we going?"

"You'll see."

Adeline walked with Godfrey as the salty breeze picked up. It tugged a few strands from her ponytail, but she tucked them behind her ears. A smile pulled on her lips as she stared at the sea, captivated by the vibrant colors that reflected against the foamy water. She hadn't been to the beach since the accident and had forgotten how much she loved it.

"Over here!"

Godfrey was heading away from the ocean, and a surge of anxiety hit Adeline as he neared the boardwalk. The same walkway with the North Carolina flag that led to the parking lot where Adeline and Dad used to park every time they'd come to the beach.

A sickening feeling churned in her as the flag fluttered in the wind.

"We have to go this way," Godfrey said, stepping onto the wooden planks.

"I'd rather not." She didn't move.

"You'll be glad you did."

There was mischief in his smile as he waddled forward, his flip-flops slapping loudly against the boardwalk. Adeline lost sight of his bushy red hair as he disappeared behind the pampas grass that overcrowded the walkway.

Shuddering, Adeline watched the sun slowly dip down into the sea. It would be dark soon. A weight formed in her stomach as she trailed after Godfrey, hugging herself as she stepped onto the boardwalk. The weathered planks groaned with each step. She stopped abruptly, all the breath leaving her when she saw the sandy parking lot.

The old family Jeep stared back at her.

The top was down as always, and she even spotted the patches of rust that had corroded the light blue paint. Her throat went dry. It was exactly as she remembered before it had been totaled and hauled to the junkyard.

"What's happening?" she asked, inching off the boardwalk.

"It's time for you to face your fears." Godfrey placed the car key in her hand.

The key burned a hole in her palm as she glared at the Jeep Wrangler. Graphic images of the accident flashed in her mind the longer she stared at it. She could still see the cracked windshield and smell Dad's blood pouring from his head. She would never forget her ear-piercing screams blaring through the darkness as she shook Dad, begging him to wake up.

"Nope." She stumbled back a step.

"You have to do this if you want to be free."

Adeline clenched the key, blinking away fresh tears. Courage was still pulsing through her veins, but so was fear.

"Adeline, I know you're nervous—"

"Then why would you make me do it?"

"Because I'm more interested in your freedom than your comfort."

Pressing a knuckle to her mouth, Adeline stared at the Jeep with what little sunlight was left. She didn't want to drive, especially now that it was getting dark.

"You can do this." Godfrey placed his palm on her upper back, urging her forward. "I will be with you the whole time."

Tension built in her as she shuffled to the driver's side.

"It's time." Godfrey opened the squeaky door for her.

Sand covered the floor, and the rips in the worn leather seat were the same as she remembered. Everything about the vehicle was familiar and inviting, but she couldn't bring herself to move. She threw Godfrey a pleading look. "Please don't make me do this."

"Do you want to be free?"

"Yes," she said, smearing away a tear.

"Then you must drive this vehicle."

Emotion raged war in Adeline. She didn't want to sit inside the vehicle, let alone drive it. But there she was, in the middle of another tough predicament. Should she face her greatest fear or walk away from it? She had faced her fear in the cave earlier that day, and she was so proud of herself for doing so. Could she do it again?

"Okay." Her voice quieted to a whisper. "I'll do it."

A deep, sinking feeling settled into her as she slid into the driver's seat and shut herself inside. The hard splits in the leather poked into her leggings as she buckled her seatbelt with shaky hands. She inserted the key into the ignition as Godfrey hopped into the passenger side.

With one twist, the engine roared to life; so did Adeline's anxiety.

Her heart tripled in speed as she grabbed the cold steering wheel. More tears fell as she inhaled the faint smell of her father's cologne that was embedded into the interior of the car. The memory of him was too painful. For a split second, she considered jumping out of the Jeep and running back to the beach.

But she remained seated.

"Let's get going," Godfrey said, buckling himself in.

Adeline released a long breath as she wrapped her trembling fingers around the gear stick and put it in drive. Her stomach dipped violently as she pressed on the gas, rattling the Jeep as it putted through the parking lot and onto the paved road.

The cold, salty air whirled through the Jeep, sending chills through Adeline as she turned down the road that had changed her entire life. Her blood pumped faster as the streetlights blinked to life, barely illuminating the quiet street. She kept cruising, the headlights tearing through the darkness.

"Just breathe." Godfrey demonstrated breathing in through his nose, then out through his mouth. "You're doing great."

Adeline tried but couldn't bring her lungs to work as she leaned forward, focusing on the fast-moving asphalt. There was no music playing on the radio this time, only the sound of the breeze whistling in the car as they neared the site of the accident. Her body went stiff as she tapped on the brake, expecting a deer to dart across the road.

But it never came.

Clenching the steering wheel, Adeline came to a complete stop, tears pouring from her eyes. The large oak tree was in perfect condition. There were no signs of damage.

Adeline choked up, struggling to get out the words. But slowly, eventually, she whispered, "That's where it happened."

"I know," Godfrey said in a soothing voice.

Heaviness and despair consumed Adeline as she stared at the oak tree. There were no marks on the rough bark, but she could still envision the crunched hood of the Jeep spewing smoke from the hard impact. She could also hear the ambulance wailing through the night as it took Dad away, and Mom's screams as they declared him dead on arrival.

But as Adeline looked at the very thing that had taken her father's life, she felt something rise in her.

Hope.

Hope that things could get better. Hope that she could find happiness without Dad around. Hope that she could have a new beginning. Though it would take some time to fully heal, deep down, she knew she would be okay.

"Let's keep going," Godfrey said.

Adeline wiped the wetness from her cheeks and released the brake. The Jeep drove onward until they entered her old neighborhood with no unexpected incidents.

Familiar houses rolled by, but Adeline's heart didn't react until she caught sight of her old home, the blue siding still as bright as she remembered. Endless memories emerged as she approached the two-story home, parking in the empty driveway.

Cranking off the ignition, Adeline unbuckled her seatbelt. She stayed glued to her seat, looking at the front entrance lit by the porch lights. "I did it," she said in disbelief.

"You sure did." Godfrey smiled.

She blinked away the tears forming in her eyes. "I didn't think I would ever drive again."

"Things are different now."

Adeline let her tears fall as she leaned into Godfrey. She hugged him tightly, burying her face in his Hawaiian shirt. She inhaled his fresh cologne as he held her against him.

"Thank you," she whispered.

"You're welcome," he said, rubbing a hand down her back.

Peace fell over her as she clung to Godfrey. She couldn't get enough of his warm embrace; it was like hugging a huge teddy bear. Though she couldn't understand exactly who Godfrey was or why he cared so much about her, she didn't mind. She liked the way he made her feel, and that was all that mattered.

"You were right." Adeline leaned back in her seat, wiping her wet face. "I feel so much better."

"I knew you would, Adeline."

"Call me Addie." She gave a tiny grin. "My dad used to call me that."

"Addie," Godfrey said with mischief in his growing smile. "I like that."

Hearing her nickname roll from Godfrey's tongue made her chest constrict. Revelation hit her like a smack in the face, and in that instant, she knew Godfrey was the one who had called out to her the first time she entered the forest.

"It was you." Her eyes grew wide. "You were the one who said my nickname in the forest."

"You caught me," he said, his smile expanding.

"But how? And why?"

"Because you were lost...and needed a friend."

Godfrey opened his door, shuffling his heavyset body out of the Jeep, while Adeline sank deeper into her seat. Her mind was reeling with unanswered questions as Godfrey moved to the hood of the vehicle.

"Come along, Addie." Godfrey beckoned her to follow.

A ping of happiness jolted through Adeline when she heard her nickname. She hadn't allowed anyone to call her that after Dad's funeral, but it felt good to hear it again.

Adeline hopped out of the car and raced to Godfrey. He waited for her at the bottom of her old home's front steps.

"Are we going inside?" she asked, staring up at the charming house.

Godfrey grinned as he used the railing for support and climbed the many steps to the front porch. Adeline stood frozen. She was unsure if she wanted to go into her old home. She was already overwhelmed by the entire situation. But again, she pushed through and followed Godfrey.

He was waiting for her at the front door and gave her a reassuring nod before opening it. Blinding light burst through the opening, and she lifted a hand against the sudden brightness.

Godfrey went in first, quickly vanishing in the light. Adeline inched closer, her heart running ragged. Before she could chicken out, she stepped through the threshold.

The intense brightness vanished, and it took Adeline a few seconds to adjust to the drastic darkness. She blinked a few times, smelling the fresh scent of pine. It was too dark to see clearly, but there was enough light from the moon to see that she was in the forest with Godfrey.

Adeline spun around and found the rusty gate that led to her current backyard. She could see the bright sun shining on the old house. Nothing moved; it was like she was looking at a picture.

"Did you like my shortcut?" Godfrey asked, his jolly laugh ringing with delight.

"That was insane." Adeline rubbed a hand down her face. "How in the world did you do that?"

"I can do anything."

"I'm realizing that." Shaking her head, Adeline moved to the gate, latching her fingers into the chain links before pulling it to her. The gate reluctantly opened with a squeak, but before she went back into her world, she looked back at Godfrey. His large silhouette waved at her, and she could sense that he was smiling, though she couldn't see his face.

"Goodbye, Addie."

"Bye, Godfrey." She waved. "Thanks again for everything."

"You're welcome," he said. "I will see you again soon."

Joy swelled in her as she entered her backyard, lit by the afternoon sun. The harsh cold brought her to a halt; she had forgotten how cold it had been when she'd left.

Chills raced down her exposed arms as she slammed the gate shut, locked it, and removed the key. She looked at the fully lit forest through the chain-link fence, expecting to see Godfrey, but he was gone.

She had to remind herself that the other realm was concealed from her world as she ran toward the house. The wind stung her face and her achy muscles screamed for relief as she darted up the stairs and entered the warm house.

She was well aware that she'd been wearing different clothes when she left her world and rushed to her bedroom before Rebecca could see her. Once she was safe in her room, she grabbed her cellphone off the nightstand. She felt like she had been gone for days and groaned when she saw it was still Wednesday.

"Ugh, I have school tomorrow." She hurled herself onto the mattress.

Her sore body sank into the bed, and she shut her weary eyes. All she could think about was going to sleep, but that wouldn't be possible with Mom coming home from work soon. She would have to eat dinner with her family or they would suspect something was wrong, and she didn't want to deal with that. So, though Adeline had had a full, adventurous day in the other realm, it was only afternoon in her world, and she would have to stay up until bedtime.

Moaning, Adeline forced herself to rise, feeling the full effect of her strained muscles as she changed into comfy loungewear. Standing before her full-length mirror, she redid her ponytail and smiled when she caught a small whiff of sea salt that lingered in her hair. She would never forget that experience on the beach with Godfrey.

Her smile widened as she tightened her hair tie before eyeing her full reflection. She stared at her reflection, stunned by the radical difference. There was zero evidence of any sorrow and anger. Instead, her face radiated joy and confidence, something she had *never* seen before, even when Dad had been alive.

Covering her mouth with her hand, she giggled at the stunning transformation. She couldn't look away from her deep blue eyes, illuminated with hope and excitement.

It wasn't just her appearance that had changed, but how she felt. There was a newfound freedom and happiness brewing in her. It was so tangible that she couldn't deny it. Something had clearly happened while she was in the other realm with her mysterious friends.

Tears once again emerged as she reflected on the last twenty-four hours. She endured some of the toughest trials she had ever been through, but the pain was well worth the victory she was now walking in.

Chapter Twenty-Five

The next morning was rougher than Adeline had anticipated. Everything ached. Even breathing was uncomfortable. She had no strength to get out of bed. So, instead of getting up, she stared at the ceiling, contemplating if she should skip school.

A generic ringtone blared from her nightstand. Adeline reached for her phone, her arm stinging as she brought it to her face. Squinting, she saw it was Carol and groaned. Carol drove Adeline and Rebecca to school every morning since she lived nearby, and they didn't want to ride the bus more than they had to.

She rubbed her eyes and answered. "Hello?"

"Are you almost ready?"

"I'm in bed," she said, her voice groggy.

"Well, get up and get dressed," Carol said. "Rebecca and I are waiting for you in the car and don't want to be late."

"I'm going to skip today."

"No, you're not."

"I'm tired, Carol."

"I am too, but you don't see me skipping school."

"Ugh, fine." Adeline gave in. "Give me five minutes."

Hanging up the phone, Adeline threw off the covers and forced her aching body into motion. She washed her face and brushed her teeth before throwing on a pair of jeans and a warm hoodie. She shouldered her bookbag and popped a few ibuprofens to help with the pain before hustling out the door.

A burning sensation throbbed in her calves and thighs as she rushed down the stairs and hobbled to the Toyota Corolla in her driveway. She desperately hoped Carol and her sister wouldn't notice her pain as she held back a groan while entering the passenger side. Lucky for her, Carol was too busy chatting with Rebecca to notice Adeline's discomfort.

"It's about time," Carol said as she put the car in reverse. "I thought I was going to have to pull you out of bed."

Adeline laughed as she buckled her seatbelt and settled into her seat. Carol struck up another conversation with Rebecca while Adeline struggled to keep her composure. Any sudden movement fired a vibration of soreness through her muscles, especially when she steadied herself as they made turns.

Sealing her lips together, Adeline wasn't sure she would survive the school day, but there was no going back now.

Rebecca was the first one out of the car when Carol pulled into the school parking lot. She quickly adjusted her pleated skirt before slipping on her bookbag and hustling toward the old brick building.

"See you after school," Rebecca said over her shoulder, her brown hair flowing behind her.

"Someone's in a hurry." Carol closed her door.

Adeline rolled her stiff shoulders, watching her little sister race through the front door. She had obviously woken up early to perfect her outfit. Even though Rebecca always had her nose in a book, she had an eye for fashion that Adeline didn't.

"She hates being late," Adeline said, heading toward the entrance.

"I can see that."

Noisy conversations and laughter filled the cold morning air, but Adeline barely noticed. She was lost in her own thoughts as her canvas shoes tapped against the sidewalk. It hadn't even been a full day since she left the other realm, and she longed to go back. There was something special about her peculiar friends that made her life exciting and worth living.

As she contemplated the wild, mind-blowing things that had happened, she wondered if she dreamed the entire thing, but she quickly tossed that thought aside. The soreness in her muscles was enough evidence to confirm that everything she experienced had indeed been real, and so was the exhilarating level of courage and freedom she now walked with.

She felt invincible as she climbed the steps, entering through the main building. The feeling was so strong that she wanted something or someone to challenge her, which made zero sense to her. She had always been afraid of confrontation, but things were different now—and she liked it.

Carol said little as they headed to their first class, but Adeline noticed her strange glances, especially when they entered their English class. Adeline slid into her seat, watching her noisy classmates fill the room.

"Are you okay?" Carol asked, eyeing her with concern.

"Yeah." Adeline reached into her bookbag, placing her textbook on her desk. "Why do you ask?"

"You're walking funny."

"I'm just sore."

"From what?"

Adeline scrambled for an answer. No one knew about the other realm. She was close to her cousin, but she wasn't about to share her secret. It was something she wanted to keep to herself for now.

"After you left yesterday, I decided to work out."

"I knew you missed it," Carol said, her lips cracking into a smile. "You should have just come with me."

"I didn't want to slow you and your friend down."

"Whatever." Carol swatted at her. "I bet you can still outrun me."

"Not a chance." Adeline gave a quick laugh.

Giggling, Carol turned to her close friend, David, who had just dropped his skinny frame into the desk next to hers. Carol and David grew up together and their moms were long-time best friends. Adeline met him a few years prior when she visited Carol and her family for Christmas. She didn't remember much about him, but now that she lived there and saw David often, she could see herself potentially being friends with him as well.

"I heard a rumor this morning," David said loud enough for Adeline to hear. "Do you want to hear it?"

"Duh!" Carol said.

David pressed his mouth to Carol's ear and spoke quietly. Giggles erupted from her as she turned to Adeline.

Carol pulled Adeline to her and whispered, "Apparently, Patrick has a *huge* crush on you."

Adeline stirred awkwardly in her seat as she fired a look at David, who was grinning at her. He motioned his head toward the guy in the letterman jacket.

Her lips pursed in disgust, knowing exactly who he was gesturing to. Patrick was her lab partner and the main reason she *hated* chemistry class. His cocky personality and perverted mind made her very uncomfortable any time he spoke.

"Want me to give you his number?" David joked, pushing his glasses up his nose.

Adeline snorted. "I'm good."

The tardy bell rang, and the teacher dove straight into the lesson. Adeline quickly lost interest and started daydreaming about the other realm. It was way more exciting than her world, especially when she was stuck at school.

Leaning on her hand, she wondered what her friends were doing. Were they at the cabin eating delicious food or roaming around the infinite garden? Or maybe they were riding the horses through the forest.

"We are waiting for you to come back and visit."

Adeline jolted in her seat when she heard Jesse's voice. She forgot that she could now communicate with any of them whenever she wanted.

"I wish I was there now," she answered in her mind. *"School is so boring."*

"I know, but you'll be done before you know it."

"If I don't die from boredom."

Jesse's contagious laughter bounced around the walls of her mind, bringing a smile to her face. She probably looked like an idiot smiling to herself in class, but she couldn't help herself. Jesse had that effect on her. Life would be way more interesting now that she could talk to him any time.

"I have a really cool place I want to take you next time you're here," Jesse said.

"As long as it doesn't involve anything dangerous...I'm in."

"You know I can't guarantee that. But you need to pay attention to your teacher now; she's going to give a pop quiz at the end of class."

Adeline made a face. *"How do you know that?"*

"I just do. I'll talk to you later."

Still grinning, Adeline retrieved the notebook and pencil from her bookbag. She didn't understand how he knew things about her life, but she didn't bother with it and focused on the new material.

Her hand was cramping by the time she jotted down two whole pages of notes. And fifteen minutes before class ended, her teacher surprised the entire class with a pop quiz.

Adeline held back a laugh.

Jesse was right.

***

Adeline stepped out of the locker room in shorts and a T-shirt with a straight face that masked her discomfort. Her muscles were still sore, but she didn't show it as she joined her classmates on the bleachers.

One more class to go.

The cold metal seeped through Adeline's running shorts as she sat next to Carol, waiting for P.E. to begin. Little by little, students trickled into the gym as the instructor waited with a clipboard in hand. Glancing at the clock, he blew hard into his whistle, piercing through the loud chatter.

"Today we will play indoor soccer," the teacher said, rolling back his broad shoulders.

Adeline grimaced. She could barely walk, let alone run for the next hour, but she kept her mouth shut as the instructor split the students up into two teams.

Stifling a groan, Adeline rose when her name was called and moved to the left-hand side of the gym. Carol joined her shortly after, along with a few other students. Nothing captured her attention until Jonathan McThorn's name was called.

Time seemed to slow as Jonathan stood in a cotton tee that hugged his obvious muscles. He ran a hand through his thick black curls as he moved toward her team. Adeline couldn't look away.

Her heart did a sudden nosedive when his grayish-blue eyes connected with hers. There was curiosity and humor in his gaze as he walked by her. It only lasted a split second, but it was long enough to make her blush.

Carol watched their interaction and concealed a smile as another guy joined their team.

"He's never going to know you like him if you don't talk to him," Carol said, nudging Adeline with her elbow.

"I don't want him to know." Adeline shot her a pointed look. "I don't have a chance with someone like him."

"Whatever." Carol rolled her eyes. "You are way prettier and nicer than the girls he hangs out with."

"If you say so."

"I'm serious. Plus, he stares at you just as much as you stare at him, which tells me he is totally into you, too."

Adeline's abdomen stirred. She had caught him looking her way, but she figured it was just her imagination since she found out at lunch that he was in a relationship with a cheerleader named Stephanie. She was a little disappointed at first, but not surprised.

"He has a girlfriend, Carol."

"It won't last long," Carol said, waving a hand. "Most of his relationships only last about a week or so."

"Does he date a lot?"

"Oh, yeah," she said. "I'm pretty sure he has dated the entire cheerleading squad."

Adeline scoffed. "That's disappointing."

"Don't feel bad. Most of the girls in town have a huge crush on him."

"Do you?"

"Absolutely not." Carol laughed. "He's not my type."

"What's your type, then?"

"I like smart, funny guys," Carol said. "Athletes are too full of themselves."

Adeline's thoughts went directly to David. Considered a cool nerd at school, David was top of the class and well-liked by everyone. "So, someone like David?"

"No way!" Carol hit Adeline in the arm. "David is like a brother to me."

Adeline perked a brow. She viewed Jesse as a brother, but her relationship with him was way different from the friendship between Carol and David. She didn't flirt with Jesse, nor did she treat him like he was her boyfriend, but Carol and David acted as if they were already a couple, though they would never admit it.

"I think you two would be great together," Adeline said, her mouth quirking up. "He is one of the few people I like here."

"I'm glad you like him." Carol sent a smile her way. "He's a great guy."

The instructor released another obnoxious whistle blow, alerting the students that the game was about to begin. Heading toward her team's goal, Adeline glanced at Jonathan. He wasn't looking her way, but his proximity made her heart run wild as she purposely positioned herself near him.

Another whistle blew, knocking Jonathan out of her mind. The soccer ball was heading her way, and she released a slow breath.

Let's get this over with.

Chapter Twenty-Six

Cold air rushed in through the windows of the old bus as it made a sharp turn onto Pivotal Point Road. Adeline dug her nails into the seat ahead of her, holding on for dear life as she knocked against Rebecca. They were the last ones to get dropped off, as usual, and the bus driver was clearly ready to be rid of them.

"I am so sick of this," Adeline grumbled.

"Me too," Rebecca said, letting her head fall back against the seat.

Before the accident, Mom took both girls to school and picked them up, since she didn't have to work. But after they'd lost Dad's income, she was forced to get a job, which had drastically changed their lifestyles. Neither of them had ever ridden a school bus until six months ago.

"I'm going to ask Mom if I can get my driver's license when she gets home," Adeline said, frowning.

"Are you sure?" Rebecca asked, the color leaving her face.

"Yes." Adeline was firm. "I'm *not* riding this bus anymore."

Rebecca grew silent, staring into her lap as the vehicle came to a stop. She didn't say a word as she collected her things and exited the bus. Adeline followed her into the quiet house and went straight to her room. She could tell her little sister thought her plan was terrible, but she wouldn't let that stop her.

Thirty minutes passed, and Adeline was nearly finished with her homework when she heard the front door open. Her ears perked up, listening to weighty heels tapping against the hardwood.

Mom was home.

Adeline stayed put for a few minutes, wanting to give Mom a little while to unwind from her hectic day at the elementary school. When she couldn't wait any longer, she scooted into the hallway and paused at the archway leading to the living room and kitchen.

Peeking around the corner, Adeline spotted Mom picking through an array of bills that were scattered on the table. Her countenance dropped as she lifted one. She rose and went straight to the cabinet and poured herself a generous amount of wine, settling into her seat and taking a big gulp before reviewing the overdue bill.

Adeline pressed herself against the wall. Mom was clearly stressed, but that was nothing new.

It will be fine.

Adeline shook her hands to help settle the rising nerves before stepping into the living area and heading to the kitchen.

"Hey, Mom." Adeline attempted to sound chipper.

"Hi, Adeline," Mom said, placing the bill down. "How was your day?"

"Fine. I need to talk to you about something."

Worry flared across Mom's face as she sat up, her brown curls bobbing above her shoulders. "Is everything okay?"

"Yeah." Adeline took a seat across from Mom, fidgeting with the drawstrings of her hoodie. "I just have been thinking about something important today."

"Okay." Mom folded her arms on the table. "What is it?"

"Well," Adeline said, rubbing her neck, "I was thinking...maybe I could get my driver's license."

The color drained from Mom's face as she studied Adeline. She didn't speak for a long, drawn-out moment, and Adeline started to sweat.

Once Mom collected her thoughts, she leaned forward with an unreadable expression. "I thought we both agreed that it would be best if you didn't drive for a while."

"I know we did, but I want to start driving again."

Mom held her gaze. "Does this have anything to do with you riding the bus?"

"Partially."

"I understand the bus is inconvenient," Mom said calmly, "but after volleyball season, Carol will bring you home from school every day."

"I don't want to wait."

"It's only a couple months."

"That's too long," Adeline said, resisting the urge to stomp her foot. "I want to get my license now."

Mom fell silent. She stared down at her hands, twisting her wedding band around her ring finger. "I don't think you're ready."

"But I am ready, Mom."

"No, you're not," Mom said firmly, her watery eyes fixed on the table. "We can revisit this next year."

"I can't wait a whole year!" The chair scraped against the floor as Adeline stood. "I'm ready now!"

"The answer is no."

Adeline gritted her teeth while holding Mom's fiery stare. She was tempted to fire back like usual, to spew her anger on Mom, but she didn't give in to the urge. Clamping her mouth shut, she walked off.

***

Adeline paced her bedroom as another loud crack of thunder struck the quiet house. It was Saturday afternoon, and she had waited all morning for Aunt Peggy to arrive.

Where is she? Adeline went to the window. *She should be here by now.*

Earlier that week, Adeline had told Aunt Peggy about the conversation she'd had with Mom about her driving again. Aunt Peggy had fully supported Adeline and promised to help. They came up with a plan. It was a long shot, but if anyone could convince Mom, it would be Aunt Peggy.

Storm clouds were moving in. The sky was getting darker by the second, and Adeline's hope started to dwindle as raindrops tapped against the glass. She desperately hoped Aunt Peggy hadn't changed her mind.

Headlights pierced through the darkness as a car materialized from behind the thick trees.

Aunt Peggy had arrived.

Tightness fisted in Adeline's gut as she stepped away from the window and started to pace again. She heard Mom greet Aunt Peggy, and she waited a few minutes before cracking open her bedroom door.

Adeline snuck down the hallway and stopped before entering the living area. She peeked her head around the corner. Mom and Aunt Peggy were drinking coffee at the kitchen table, their voices loud and clear thanks to the hardwood floors.

Mom had little to say at first, but Aunt Peggy kept asking her questions. She got Mom talking about her new teaching job, along with the challenges and advantages of living in a small mountain town.

The conversation went dry again, and Adeline froze when Aunt Peggy glanced her way. Their eyes met, but Aunt Peggy acted like she didn't notice as she casually looked back at Mom.

"So, how are the girls adjusting to their new school?" Aunt Peggy asked.

"I think it's going well," Mom said, taking a quick sip of coffee.

"Any complaints?"

"They don't like riding the bus, but that's inevitable right now."

"Have you thought about Adeline driving?"

Mom paused, her body stiffening. "She doesn't have her license."

"I know she doesn't have her license yet," Aunt Peggy said with caution, "but Carol mentioned Adeline wants to get it."

Tension entered the room and expanded as Mom traced her pointer finger along her mug. She stared down into what was left of her coffee while Aunt Peggy waited in the silence. It was so thick, even Adeline felt it from where she stood.

"Carol also told me Adeline asked you about it the other day," Aunt Peggy said.

Mom cleared her throat. "She did, and I told her no."

"I understand your concerns about her driving again, but I think this could be a good step for her."

"How?" Mom asked sharply. "You know exactly what happened the last time she drove."

Aunt Peggy reached across the table and grabbed Mom's hand. Tears prickled her eyes and spilled over. "I miss him too, but you can't keep blaming Adeline for his death."

"It was her fault!" Mom shouted, yanking her hand away.

"It was an accident," Aunt Peggy said firmly. "It could have happened to either of us."

"That accident killed my husband!"

"And my younger brother!" Aunt Peggy said.

Mom wiped her wet cheeks with shaking hands. She wrapped her frail arms around her waist and held herself as silence stretched between them.

"We're all learning how to heal and move forward, Victoria," Aunt Peggy said, her words cracking slightly. "Adeline getting her driver's license is a step in the right direction."

Neither of them said a word. After what felt like ages, Mom lifted her head. She didn't look at or acknowledge Aunt Peggy.

"Fine. You take her," Mom said, her voice lifeless. "But if she kills someone else, you'll be to blame."

Mom rose, her chair squealing against the tiles as she left the table. She was headed straight toward Adeline.

Fear flared in Adeline as she dashed into her room. She made it just in time to hear Mom storm by. The slamming of a door made Adeline flinch, and she waited a moment before peeking her head out the doorway. The coast was clear.

Heavy footsteps came from the kitchen, and a moment later, Aunt Peggy came into view. Walking to the coatrack, Aunt Peggy sniffled as she put on her jacket and scarf to leave. She grabbed the doorknob, then paused and looked directly at Adeline. There was sadness in her eyes, but it faded as she gave a small smile.

"Thank you," Adeline mouthed.

Aunt Peggy nodded and blew her a kiss before letting herself out.

Adeline retreated into her room, locking the door behind her. A tear slipped down her cheek as she exhaled a long breath. Mom's hurtful words replayed in her mind, but she quickly dismissed them. Their plan worked, and that's what she'd focus on.

Chapter Twenty-Seven

"Keep your eyes closed." Aunt Peggy trotted down the long flight of steps ahead of them. "No peeking."

With a hand covering her eyes, Adeline laughed as she tightened her grip on Uncle Pete's arm. He took his time helping her step down and was the only reason she hadn't rolled down to the bottom.

She took another slow step, wondering what they wanted to show her. Her aunt and uncle had arrived at her house unexpectedly, claiming they had a surprise for her outside, but she had to close her eyes before exiting the house.

It had been over two weeks since Aunt Peggy's conversation with Mom. Since then, Adeline spent every day driving around with her aunt and uncle to prepare for the driving test.

It was a little rocky at first, but Adeline was a natural, and all Dad had taught her came back quickly. She was ready to drive on her own in no time. So, Aunt Peggy and Uncle Pete had pulled Adeline out of school that morning and took her to the Department of Motor Vehicles, where she walked out with a brand-new driver's license.

"Okay, you can open your eyes now!" Aunt Peggy squealed.

Steadying herself on the gravel driveway, Adeline opened her eyes. Aunt Peggy's outdated Honda Civic was parked next to Mom's Bronco. It was just as ancient as Mom's vehicle, with dings and dents on the exterior and fading paint on the roof, but overall, it was in good condition.

"It's yours," Uncle Pete said, his voice deep and kind.

Adeline slung a surprised glance at Uncle Pete and then Aunt Peggy. "You two are giving me your car?"

"We sure are," Aunt Peggy said. "I know it's not much of a looker, but it's reliable."

"And great on gas," Uncle Pete added with a chuckle.

Tears attempted to break through as Adeline stared at the generous gift. There was nothing fancy about the well-used car, but it was just what she needed. "Thank you."

"We love you, kiddo." Uncle Pete pulled her into a side hug. "And we know you'll take good care of it."

Aunt Peggy placed the key in Adeline's hand before kissing her on the cheek. "We are so proud of you."

Adeline dabbed at her eyes. "Does Mom know about this?"

"Yes. I worked everything out for you." Aunt Peggy smiled, the lines around her eyes deepening. "Now go on; I know you want to take it for a spin."

Joy split across Adeline's face as she skipped to the driver's side and jumped in. Excitement swelled inside her as she cranked the car and secured the seatbelt. Heat blasted through the vents as she gave her aunt and uncle a final wave before backing out of the driveway.

Her spirit soared as she headed down Pivotal Point Road, blowing past the trees that had no end. Victory was in the air, and she could taste the newfound freedom that she had been desperate for. Her life was still messy, but things were falling into place.

Chapter Twenty-Eight

Driving became another piece of freedom Adeline hadn't known she need-ed. It had been a couple of days since she had gotten her license, and she was loving every second of it. So was Rebecca.

Mom was still uneasy about it, though she tried to hide it. She drilled Adeline about safety, especially in the mornings before Adeline drove Rebecca to school. Mom didn't voice her deepest fears, but Adeline could see them in her worried eyes every time she left the house.

But she wouldn't let that steal her happiness.

The school day flew by for Adeline, and she was thrilled that Carol could come home with her since her practice had been pushed back to a later time. They spent their time watching a couple episodes of their favorite television show before hiding out in Adeline's room, chatting about the latest gossip.

"So, don't get mad at me." Carol rested against the headboard. "But I may have talked to my volleyball coach about you joining the team."

"You may have?" Adeline raised a brow.

"Okay, I did."

"It's the middle of the season, Carol."

"I know, but we could really use your help," Carol said. "My team *sucks.*"

"I don't think that's a good idea." Adeline twirled a strand of hair around her finger.

"Please," Carol begged.

The rhythm of Adeline's heart quickened at the thought of her picking up a volleyball again. Dad had been her high school coach. After he died, she vowed she would never play again, and she had meant it. She thought about Dad enough and didn't want another reason to bring up the pain of losing him.

"Will you at least try it?" Carol asked.

"What makes you think I'll be an asset to your team?" Adeline hoped Carol would drop it. "I haven't played in forever."

"Pshh, whatever." Carol flailed a hand in the air. "You're the most athletic person I know."

Adeline shook her head. "I'll pass."

"Too bad," Carol said, mischief coating her hazel eyes. "I thought for sure you would want another excuse to see Jonathan McThorn."

Adeline sat up straighter. "What do you mean by that?"

"He goes to *all* of our home games." Carol reclined with a mischievous smile. "And so do all the hot guys on his baseball team."

"Why?"

"Guys can't resist girls in spandex," Carol said with a laugh. "I'm sure it was the same way at your old school."

Adeline giggled as she recalled the football players who'd gone to her home games. She could still see them crowding the bleachers and hear their obnoxious hollers when the referee made a bad call.

Thinking about it made her smile, but it vanished as quickly as it appeared. She missed her old life and the great friends she left behind. It pained her to think about all the friendships she had sabotaged. After the accident, she isolated herself from everyone, including her close friends who tried to support her. After a while, they had all given up on her.

It had been her fault, but it still hurt.

"I'll think about it," Adeline finally said.

"I kind of need to know now." Carol chewed her bottom lip. "My coach needs to pull some strings if you decide to join."

"Carol, you can't just throw something like this at me. Joining your team is a big deal, and I don't know if I'm ready."

"You and I both know you are."

"I don't think so."

Carol went quiet as she rearranged herself to a more comfortable position. "If your dad was still alive, he would want you to play because he knew it made you happy."

Tears welled in Adeline's eyes and spilled over in silence as she looked away. Sliding off the bed, she moved to the window and stared out into the dreary evening. It was overcast and gloomy, matching the way she felt.

"I just want you to be happy again." Carol bounced off the mattress and moved to Adeline. "And I really think this will help."

Adeline sniffled. Her cousin was only trying to help, but she didn't know if she wanted to take that big of a step yet. She forgave herself for the accident, but that didn't take away the grief and sadness she was still battling. Plus, she was afraid volleyball would be a big trigger for her.

"I miss him so much," Adeline whispered, her voice cracking.

"I know you do." Carol shed her own tears as she hugged Adeline. "I miss him too."

Carol held Adeline briefly before giving her a tight squeeze. She took a step back and mustered up a smile while smearing away her tears. "You don't have to join my team, but I just wanted to give you an opportunity to play again."

Wiping her wet cheeks, Adeline looked back outside while contemplating what to do. Should she join the team or decline the offer?

She couldn't deny the flicker of excitement she felt. Her passion for the sport was still there. She just wasn't sure she could handle playing again.

What if I have a mental breakdown during a game? Or what if my teammates don't like me? What would I do then? Or what if I embarrass myself in front of Jonathan McThorn and the entire school?

Believable doubts came pouring in, dominating her thoughts. It didn't take long for them to frighten her out of joining the team. Before she could inform Carol, a jolly voice thundered in her mind.

"You can do it!"

Adeline jerked, surprised by Godfrey's unexpected statement. She still wasn't used to her friends popping into her thoughts at any given moment.

"What if I fail?"

"What if you don't and love every second of it?"

Focusing on the gloomy weather, Adeline pulled in a deep breath before slowly releasing it.

"You'll never know until you try," Godfrey said.

"Give it a try, love!" Henry's charming accent chimed in.

Jesse chanted in the background. *"Do it! Do it!"*

Adeline bit back a grin. Their joy and encouragement engulfed the nagging doubts she had been entertaining. Now that her head was clear, she thought about some of the positive things that could happen if she took a leap of faith.

"I can't believe I'm saying this," Adeline said, rubbing her tear-stained cheeks with her sleeve, "but I'll do it."

"Really?" Carol's eyes brightened.

"Yeah."

"Yay!" Carol squeezed her again. "You won't regret it."

Carol rushed back to the bed and grabbed her cellphone. "I'm going to call my coach right now. She's going to be so excited."

Adeline pasted on a smile, hiding the sudden sickness that arose.

Carol's coach answered on the first ring, and Adeline felt sick as she listened to the conversation. It was less than a minute, and Carol was beaming when she hung up the phone.

"She wants me to bring you to practice tonight!"

Heat crept up Adeline's neck. "Tonight?"

"Yeah!" Carol said. "There was some kind of event in the gym after school, so we have a late practice."

"I don't even know where my volleyball stuff is." Adeline panicked.

"You can borrow mine," Carol said, collecting her belongings. "We have enough time to go to my house."

Carol bolted out of the room before Adeline could refuse. Nauseous, she slipped on her sneakers and snatched her cellphone before racing after her.

Adeline caught up with her cousin in the living room, where Mom and Rebecca were curled up on the couch, reading. Rebecca was enthralled with a non-fiction book about space while Mom enjoyed a predictable romance novel. Their peace was abruptly disturbed by Carol's excitement.

"I convinced Adeline to join my volleyball team!" Carol's voice rang with enthusiasm. "Isn't that great?"

Mom and Rebecca exchanged looks.

"Is that true?" Mom asked, closing the book and placing it on her lap.

Adeline shifted her weight, avoiding Mom's stare. "Yes."

"Are you sure you want to do that?"

Adeline shrugged. "Yeah, I want to try it."

Mom gave a quick smile, but it didn't reach her eyes. Though she had never been an athlete, she fully supported Adeline in the past. But things were different now. Her concern had more to do with Adeline's mental state than anything else.

"My coach wants Adeline to come to practice tonight," Carol said, interrupting the awkward silence.

"All right." Mom exhaled, moving her weak gaze to Adeline. "But I don't want you driving at night."

"I'll drive us," Carol said with a charming smile. "And don't worry, I'll be super careful."

Nodding, Mom kept her eye on Adeline as she slipped on her jacket. "Text me as soon as you get to the gym."

"Okay," Adeline said, following Carol out the door.

"And make sure you both wear your seatbelts," Mom added in a rush.

"We will," Carol said as they exited the house.

The girls raced to the car, and Carol slammed it into reverse and sped home. It was only a five-minute drive, and they were in and out of the brick house in a matter of minutes and on their way to practice.

Adeline was already sweating bullets as they pulled into the quiet parking lot and stepped out into the cold. She prayed the team would accept her as she followed Carol into the old gym.

Volleyballs bouncing along the floor pounded in Adeline's ears as she breathed in the stale air. The room full of girls looked to be younger than her.

There wasn't a tall person in sight, which was likely one reason the varsity team had lost every game that season. She kept her assumptions to herself, trailing behind Carol to the bleachers where some players laced up their shoes.

"This is my cousin that I told you guys about," Carol said loud enough for the entire gym to hear.

The space fell silent before erupting in a cheerful shout. Each player dropped what they were doing and ran to greet Adeline.

Stiffening, Adeline was crushed by a wave of girls dying to meet her. Cheerful voices spoke over each other, making it next to impossible for Adeline to catch any of their names, but they didn't seem to mind. They were just happy to make a new friend.

She thought she recognized a couple of their friendly faces but couldn't be sure as introductions were cut short.

The coach blew the whistle, informing the girls that practice was beginning. "Everyone on the court!"

The team moved as one toward their coach, and Adeline relaxed her shoulders and took a quick breath. She pulled her kneepads up over her high socks and adjusted her spandex shorts before heading onto the court with Carol.

It only took Adeline a few minutes into practice to confirm that Carol hadn't been kidding about the varsity team. They were awful. Even so, Adeline felt herself coming alive with every drill they did.

Everything came back like clockwork, and the entire team, including the coach, watched with wide eyes as she dominated every position she played. She could not only set and pass the ball easily to her teammates, but she could also spike it with tremendous force, placing it wherever she wanted to.

Adeline was soaked with sweat by the time practice ended. Her body ached, but her heart was full as she exchanged goodbyes with her teammates. Their kindness and acceptance blew her away.

"I'm so glad you decided to join our team." The coach approached Adeline with a smile. "Our next game is Friday. I'll get you a uniform before then."

"Oh." Adeline froze, her heart beating in an unsteady rhythm. "That's in two days."

"I know, but there's no sense in wasting any time," the coach said, shouldering her gym bag. "You clearly know what you're doing."

Patting her shoulder, the coach laughed before parting ways with Adeline. Nagging thoughts surfaced as Adeline headed to the exit where Carol waited for her, but she refused to let them ruin her evening.

Adeline stepped out into the cold with Carol, inhaling the crisp air as she replayed all that had taken place in practice. Though it had been easier and more laid back than she anticipated, she enjoyed every minute. They wouldn't be region champs like her old team that Dad coached, but that didn't matter to her.

She was part of a team again, and it felt good.

"Dude, you killed it." Carol bumped shoulders with Adeline. "I knew you were good, but I had no idea you were *that* good."

"Thanks," Adeline said, her warm breath forming a cloud. "I forgot how much I missed it."

"We are going to dominate now that you're on the team!"

Adeline grinned as she hopped into the passenger seat. Staring out the foggy window, she leaned against her hand as she thought about Dad. He had been in her thoughts all throughout practice, but it didn't hurt as bad as she assumed it would. She had expected it to be unbearable, but it had been soothing imagining his smooth, rich voice instructing her.

The pain of losing him was still there; she would never deny that. But down in the deepest depths of her being, she knew he was proud of her.

And that made her smile.

Chapter Twenty-Nine

"Are you ready?" Carol whispered to Adeline as they headed toward the away bench.

"I think so," Adeline said, her voice shaky.

Adeline's first official volleyball match hadn't even started, and she was already battling nausea. It began when she watched the junior varsity team get slaughtered by their opponents. One look at the opposing varsity team made Adeline believe the same thing was about to happen to them. Carol mentioned they were one of the top teams in their division, and Adeline could see why.

"Good thing Jonathan isn't here." Adeline tossed a glance at the packed bleachers.

"I told you he doesn't come to away games," Carol said.

Adeline spotted Aunt Peggy and Uncle Pete, but there was no sign of Mom or Rebecca. Her heart sank. They told her that morning they couldn't make it because of other plans, but she secretly hoped they would surprise her.

They never missed a game when Dad was her coach, but that was probably why they weren't there. They weren't ready to step back into a gym. Adeline couldn't blame them for that, but her feelings were still hurt.

The referee blew the whistle, announcing that the first set was about to begin. The coach swiftly directed each player to their starting position, but Adeline couldn't hear her. Breathing became difficult as the gym shrank in size. She was about to make a run for it, but Carol gripped her arm.

"Breathe, Addie. You're going to do great."

"I'm not ready for this." Adeline shuddered.

"Yes, you are."

"What if I mess up?"

"We all mess up," Carol said. "And besides, you have nothing to prove to anyone here; you showed up today, and that's all that matters."

Adeline closed her eyes and freed a slow, steady breath. "You're right."

"Of course I am," Carol said, tugging her toward the court.

Adeline's heart was still beating roughly as she positioned herself in the only vacant spot next to the net. The coach had chosen her to be the setter. She had more experience being an outside hitter, but she didn't argue.

She rubbed her sweaty hands down her jersey as the ref blew the whistle, notifying her teammate to serve the ball. Mary tossed the ball in the air, but she didn't toss it high enough. The ball went straight into the net, giving the other team a point along with the ball.

Things went downhill from there.

For the next twenty minutes, Adeline watched as her teammates failed to pass the ball. The other team had powerhouse servers who not only hit the ball hard but placed it in open areas where her teammates couldn't reach. The few times they could get the ball, it went flying into the stands or soaring behind them. It was the worst game Adeline had ever participated in.

It ended, and they had only scored two points.

The next set wasn't any better.

Adeline's team got defeated once again, amping up the hopelessness the players were already feeling.

With heads hung low, the team shuffled to their coach.

"We can do this!" The coach attempted to uplift the players. "It's not over yet!"

"We've already lost two sets," a junior named Lauren said. "There's no way we can win the next three."

"She's right," another teammate said. "We might as well forfeit."

Adeline frowned as the complaints came piling in. Never had she witnessed such nonsense from teammates. The one time it happened on her old team, the player who whined sat on the bench for the rest of the match. This coach was clearly not as strict as Dad had been and had no plans of stopping the whining.

So, Adeline ended it.

"Cut it out," Adeline said, firing looks at her teammates. "This is *not* how winners act."

A hush fell, and everyone's eyes went to Adeline as she turned to address the coach. "Put me in the back row."

The coach pursed her lips, running a hand through her short blonde hair. "We need you to be the setter."

"There's no point in me being the setter if no one can return any of their serves," Adeline told her.

Silence lingered as the girls looked at one another.

"She's right," Carol said. "I'll be the setter."

The coach's jaw flexed as she snatched her clipboard from the bench and glanced over it. "Fine, let's give it a try," she said, scribbling something down. "Carol and Adeline will switch positions, and everyone else will start in the same spot as before."

The team agreed, and they put their hands in, stacking them on top of one another. Carol caught Adeline's eye, trying her hardest to conceal a smile, as the team did a quick cheer before stepping onto the court.

The third set began, and another powerful server stepped up to the serving line. The stocky girl squared up with Adeline, an arrogant smirk splitting her plain face. As soon as the referee blew the whistle, she served the ball.

The volleyball soared right over the top of the net, heading straight toward Adeline.

"Got it!" Adeline said. She positioned herself under the ball and popped it into the air, giving Carol the perfect pass. Carol set the ball to the outside hitter, who smashed it over the net. The other team dove to get the ball but failed to retrieve it before it slammed into the back corner of the court.

"We scored!" the spiker said, her arms raised high.

Celebration broke out, and Adeline giggled as she moved to the next position. It was a good start, but they would need a lot more points if they wanted to win the set.

But that one point sparked something in her teammates. The hopelessness of the previous sets vanished, and the girls played better. They worked together as a team, and though there were a lot of messy plays, they kept scoring.

Before too long, the set was over, and Adeline's team had somehow won. It was the sloppiest game Adeline had ever played, but it was still a win. Her team was thrilled. They started the next set with the same spirit, and after another messy game, they won it as well.

The final set arrived; whoever won it won the entire match.

Adeline started out in the back row once again and passed every single serve that came her way. So did her teammates. They played even better now that they had a streak of confidence and a sliver of hope that they could win.

That little bit of hope made all the difference.

The entire set was neck-and-neck and got more exciting as the game progressed. Even the fans were getting into it by hooting and hollering during every play. The other team had better players, but they kept making silly errors.

Adeline and her teammates took full advantage of it.

Adeline dripped with sweat by the time she rotated around the entire court. It was her turn to serve. She glanced at the scoreboard, and her throat went tight. If she missed the serve, it would give the other team a chance to come back. But if she got the ball over the net, her team had the potential to win.

"You can do this," Godfrey whispered internally.

Adeline paused, drawing in a swift breath before stepping behind the serving line. Silence struck the gymnasium, and she felt all eyes on her as she got ready.

Once she decided where she wanted to place the ball, she gave it a quick bounce before tossing it into the air and smashing her palm against it.

The ball zoomed over the net. The opposing team dove for it, but they weren't fast enough. It smashed into the gym floor, exactly where Adeline planned for it to go.

She got an ace, and the game was over.

"We won!" Carol threw her arms in the air.

The entire team shouted as they rushed to Adeline, nearly tackling her to the ground. The gym rumbled in celebration as Adeline jumped and laughed with her teammates as if they had just won the state championship. Even the parents and dedicated fans were going wild in the stands, clapping and stomping their boots against the metal bleachers.

It was only a small victory, but Adeline felt like she had conquered the world. She held back tears as she hugged her teammates, rejoicing with them.

In that moment, Adeline felt her hardened heart begin to thaw. She had faced another one of her fears, and she couldn't have been happier as she celebrated with her team.

Chapter Thirty

News about the big win spread throughout Black Mountain High School. Adeline was no longer viewed as the new girl from the beach. She was now in the spotlight as one of the school's star athletes.

It had been a full week since the extraordinary victory, and Adeline was slowly making friends. At first, opening up to others had felt awkward and forced, but it had become easier with each passing day. She genuinely enjoyed the new friendships she was creating with the girls on her team.

"Are you sure you don't want to spend the night?" Carol asked, tossing her gym bag into the back seat of her car. "We can order pizza."

It was Friday night and their practice just ended. Though Adeline was tempted to go over to her cousin's house, she had other plans. She missed her friends at the cabin. She kept in touch with them through her thoughts, but she wanted to see them face to face.

"Maybe another time," Adeline said, rubbing her sore neck. "I want to relax at my place tonight."

"Suit yourself." Carol slid into the driver's seat. "Let me know if you change your mind."

"I will."

Adeline waved as Carol drove off before heading home herself. It was dark by the time she pulled into the empty driveway. All the lights were off, and Mom's vehicle wasn't there.

"They probably went out to eat without me...again," Adeline said, her hands bunching into fists.

It was the second time that week she hadn't been invited. Her schedule was busier now, but it irked her that her family hadn't even tried to include her.

"They could have at least texted me or something." Adeline grabbed her gym bag.

Slamming her car door, Adeline entered the quiet house, trying to tame her rising irritation. Mom and Rebecca always had a close relationship, while Adeline and Dad had been inseparable. Now that Dad was gone, Adeline felt like the odd one out, and neither Mom nor Rebecca seemed to care.

Adeline stomped into her room and threw her bag on the bed. A quick glance in the mirror showed that her messy French braid needed to be redone, but she didn't bother fixing it as she retrieved the key from her nightstand. She thought about changing her black spandex shorts and tall matching socks, but she could change at the cabin if she wanted to.

Instead of wasting any more time, she rushed out the door.

Zipping her winter jacket up to her neck, she jogged across the backyard in an all-black outfit that hid her well. She didn't stop until she reached the entrance to the other realm. The forest was pitch black beyond the chain-link fence as she grabbed the lock and inserted the key.

"Please don't be dark," she said under her breath as she removed the constricting chains.

Adeline wouldn't travel through the forest at night. It would be next to impossible to find the star pins without light; plus, Ralock could show up again. She couldn't take that chance. So, if the forest was dark, she would come back at another time.

Adeline pushed on the rusty gate, and it opened with a loud screech. It took a few seconds before she gained the confidence to step into the dim forest.

Everything changed in a flash. The darkness vanished, replaced by the rising sun filtering through the tree branches.

"Thank goodness," she said, letting out a sigh.

Warmth filled her lungs and her skin flushed with heat as she closed the gate, purposely keeping the key in the lock. She quickly peeled off her heavy jacket and tossed it against the fence.

Inhaling the pleasant scent of pine, Adeline smiled as she adjusted her black T-shirt before moving along the well-worn path. She located the first star pin and continued her search as the pleasant chirps of the morning birds greeted her.

She only ventured a few steps before stopping dead in her tracks. The loud snap of a dry limb caught her attention. Whatever it was, it was close.

Adeline held her breath as she searched the heavily wooded area.

"Probably just a squirrel." She let out a nervous laugh. She went to move again, but the uneasy feeling intensified. Someone was watching her; she could feel it in her gut. Ralock came to mind, and she didn't waste any time. She whipped around and took off toward the entrance to her world.

A tall figure jumped out from behind a tree onto the path.

"BOO!"

Adeline launched herself backward, her heart rocketing against her ribcage. She felt like her soul left her body as she stopped and stared at a young man, who was laughing hysterically.

"I got you," Jesse said, slapping his hand against his knee.

"That wasn't funny!" Adeline punched his arm. "I almost had a heart attack."

"It was kind of funny."

Adeline attempted to keep an angry face, but one look at Jesse and the giggles broke through. There was no stopping them when Jesse joined in.

"Just so you know," Adeline said between chuckles, "I'm still mad at you."

"I'm sure you are."

"I'm serious," she said, placing a hand on her hip. "I thought you were Ralock."

"I'm sorry I scared you, and I apologize in advance for doing it again."

"Jesse!" She shoved him in the chest.

"What?" he asked, regaining his balance. "I like to prank my friends; just ask Henry."

"Oh, I've heard."

"Yeah, I've gotten him good over the years." Jesse puffed out his chest. "He's my usual victim."

"You should probably keep it that way."

"I'll think about it." Jesse winked. "But on a serious note, you won't normally have to worry about Ralock coming this close to your world."

"Why not?" she asked, remembering how soon he had found her after crossing through the gate before.

"Ralock can't go through the barrier, so he stays away from it for the most part."

"Barrier?" she asked. "Are you talking about that old fence?"

"No." He shook his head. "There is an invisible barrier that separates our worlds, and it happens to be exactly where the fence is. The Wilder family built that fence years ago so they would know exactly where the barrier was."

"Oh, I didn't know that," Adeline said, tucking back a strand of hair that had escaped her braid. "So, Ralock can't go into my world?"

"Correct."

"Why?"

"It has always been that way. Anyone from your world can come and go as they please, but that isn't the case for the people and creatures here."

"I had no idea that no one from this realm could go into my world."

"Well, not everyone," Jesse said, smiling as he scratched his short beard.

Adeline lifted an eyebrow. "What about you?"

"What about me?"

"Are you stuck here as well?"

"Nope. I can go wherever I want," he said with a devious smile. "So can Henry and my dad, but we choose to stay here."

Adeline was certain Jesse could easily blend into her world. His long brown hair may get him a few odd looks from the older folks, but his jeans and T-shirt wouldn't draw any unwanted attention. The sword strapped to his side would have to go. He couldn't walk around the small mountain town with a weapon like that.

"Why are you guys allowed to come into my world and others can't?"

"That's just the way it is, Adeline."

"That doesn't seem fair to the others here."

"The only one who really wants to come into your world is Ralock," he said, "and you don't want that."

"Not going to argue with that. And by the way, I'm sure you already know this, but you can call me Addie now."

"And you can call me Jesse."

Adeline giggled and swatted at his arm. "You're the goofiest person I know."

"Thank you." He grinned, his uneven teeth gleaming in the sunlight.

Adeline kept smiling as she glanced around the peaceful forest. "So, what do you want to do today?"

"It's a surprise."

"What kind of surprise?"

"A really good one, but we'll need to catch a ride."

Jesse inhaled a huge breath before whistling a loud burst of chirps that had Adeline's ears ringing. The forest erupted in song as the birds mimicked the unique tune.

"What's going on?" Adeline swiveled in a circle, listening to the noisy melody echoing through the forest.

"The birds are carrying my whistle to Angela and Regal," Jesse said as the birds continued their game of telephone.

"How did you teach them that?"

"I didn't." Jesse laughed. "Anytime they hear a pleasant sound, they'll copy it and spread it throughout the forest and into the garden where the horses are."

"That's awesome!"

"It really is," he said as the melody fizzled out. "So, if you ever decide you don't want to walk to the cabin, just do the whistle I taught you and Angela will come running once she hears it."

"But how does she know where I am?"

"She just does," Jesse said with a simple shrug. "Once a horse in this realm bonds with you, it will always know where you are."

"That's impossible."

"It's also impossible for you to hear me in your thoughts." Jesse's voice entered her mind. *"But you can."*

"Touché," Adeline said, her lips curling into a smile. "This world is so weird."

"You love it." Jesse knocked his shoulder into hers.

"I do," she said. "I'm just not used to all the strange things here."

"You'll get used to it the more you visit."

Adeline spent the next few minutes telling Jesse all about her life in Black Mountain. From getting her driver's license to joining the volleyball team, there was a lot to catch up on. And though she understood he knew everything that happened in her world, she enjoyed talking to him about it and getting his positive feedback.

"That's great, Addie." Jesse gave her an energetic high-five. "Look at you, making new friends."

"I know. Who would have thought I would like living in that tiny mountain town?"

"I did." A grin appeared on his face. "You'll like it even more as time goes on."

The ground rumbled. Within seconds, Regal and Angela stormed onto the scene, running in unison without a saddle or bridle in sight.

"Hey, pretty girl!" Adeline waved as Angela slowed her pace and trotted toward her. "Did you miss me?"

Neighing loudly, Angela dipped her head as Adeline latched onto her furry neck. The soft, white coat tickled against her nose as she breathed in the mare's clean scent.

"I missed you too."

"I took good care of her while you were gone," Jesse said as Regal approached him, demanding to be rubbed.

"Thanks." Adeline released Angela's neck and began running her fingers down her bare side. "How are we going to ride them without saddles or reins?"

"Bareback."

Adeline turned to him, one eyebrow raised. "Are you serious?"

"Yep. I do it all the time."

"How are you going to get up on Regal?" she asked. "He's *huge*."

"Like this."

Regal stood like a statue as Jesse gripped a hunk of his black mane. In one swift motion, Jesse pulled himself up and swung his long leg over Regal.

"And that's how you do it," Jesse said, adjusting himself on Regal's back.

"Impressive." Adeline did a quick clap.

"Now you do the same with Angela," Jesse said. "It won't hurt her."

Adeline had ridden bareback once before and had found it very challenging, but she was willing to try again.

After a few failed attempts, she hauled herself onto Angela. Tangling her fingers in the mare's mane, Adeline kept a tight grip as she glanced down at her dangling legs. Nothing was holding her in place. "I hope I don't fall off."

"You won't." Jesse smiled her way. "Just hold on to her mane and let her run; she will follow Regal."

"All right," Adeline said, maintaining a firm grasp of Angela's mane. "Do I need to stop by the cabin and change before we go to this unknown place?"

"Nope. You look great."

Jesse flashed a cheesy grin before kicking the heels of his boots into Regal. A loud snort blew from his nostrils as he took off down the path. Angela hastily followed.

Adeline yelped at the fast takeoff. Leaning forward, she closed her eyes as she held on. Her long braid swung against her back as Angela stormed behind Regal, their heavy hooves smashing into the dry dirt.

Adeline felt like she was on a rough rollercoaster ride as the horses bolted from path to path, weaving around the vast forest trees.

"Isn't this great?" Jesse shouted over his shoulder.

Still holding onto Angela with a death grip, Adeline opened her eyes and gasped. Jesse was riding Regal like a stuntman. He was no longer holding onto the horse, but had his arms lifted to the sky as Regal continued to sprint. His tucked legs were the only thing keeping him on his horse's back.

"You're crazy!" Adeline yelled back.

Jesse smiled back at her, his brown hair flapping with the wind. He went back to gripping Regal's mane right as the stallion shot out of the woods and entered the garden.

"Slow!" Jesse said.

Regal obeyed, slowing his pace. Angela did the same.

Now that they were at a slower speed, Adeline could breathe properly. She smoothed down her braid. "That was wild."

"It sure was." Jesse chuckled.

Adeline loosened her grip slightly as she looked around the pretty garden. She had no idea where they were. "How many entrances are there?"

"Forty-seven."

"Forty-seven? That's a lot!"

"I told you this garden is big."

Adeline bounced along on Angela's back underneath the wisteria that hung along the branches of the monstrous maple trees. Their sugary fragrance mixed well with the rich perfume of the sweet peas growing along the sides of the path.

Smiling, Adeline took in the spectacular sight that kept getting better the farther they went. Cardinals and meadowlarks darted from the flowering trees, chirping a delightful tune as the bees buzzed from flower to flower.

A small pond overrun with tiny, colorful fish appeared, but soon vanished as they moved along. Just as she was about to ask if they could go back to look at the fish, something unusual came into view.

Two large walls made of thick stones surrounded the dirt trail, and they were headed right for it. Once enclosed between the fortified barriers, Adeline sat up straight, taking in the old stones covered in vibrant green vines.

The path turned narrow, forcing Angela to travel behind Regal. Adeline brushed her fingers along the thick vines that overtook the stones. They were stronger and sturdier than they appeared. She wondered if they could hold her weight. For a split second, she thought about climbing to the top, but she stayed seated.

"Where are we going?" Adeline asked, her voice echoing off the stone walls.

"You'll see."

"Why can't you just tell me?"

"Because it's more fun to show you." Jesse turned around, throwing her a playful grin.

Adeline rolled her eyes. "If you say so."

The sun warmed Adeline's fair skin as she swayed atop Angela, hoping they were close to their destination. Her legs were cramping and her back was aching, but she held back her complaints as she trailed behind Jesse.

The walls receded, making the path more breathable, but they were headed straight toward a dead end.

A massive wall, identical to the ones around them, ended the trail with nowhere to go. By the looks of it, they would have to turn around and go back the way they came.

"Looks like a dead end," Adeline said, disappointment ringing in her tone.

Jesse ignored her comment as he parked Regal right in front of the massive roadblock and slid to the ground. He moved with confidence to the wall and pushed aside a group of overflowing vines. They moved out of his way like a curtain, revealing an opening as wide as a door.

"Doesn't look like a dead end to me," Jesse said before disappearing behind the dangling vines.

Adeline leaped off Angela, landing hard on the dusty floor. She darted to the wall, shoving the vines out of her way, and entered the unknown.

Blackness engulfed her as soon as the thick vines fell back into place. A chill came over her as she blinked rapidly, hoping her eyes would adjust to the darkness.

"Jesse?"

"I'm right here."

Adeline jerked when a warm, callused hand touched her arm. She couldn't see Jesse well, but she could see his tall silhouette. She shivered from the dramatic temperature drop. "Where are we?"

"We're in a tunnel," he said, his boots tapping against the rocky floor as he moved ahead, "but it's super short."

Following his footsteps, Adeline hugged her chilly arms as they moved toward a dim light that was about forty paces ahead. "Where does this tunnel lead to?"

"You're about to find out."

Adeline kept up with Jesse's long strides and paused when they reached the end. Blinding sunlight poured into the tunnel as Jesse swept aside the thick vines concealing the opening.

Adeline squinted and stepped outside. Warmth made her skin tingle as she adjusted to the brightness. It only took a moment, but once she could see clearly, she gasped at the view.

Spread out before her was an ancient kingdom that nature had completely reclaimed. Lush greenery devoured the massive ruins tucked inside a damaged wall that went as far as she could see. Fern moss crept along the partially intact stone structures, intertwined with pesky vines that twisted along the rocks.

Adeline ran to the ledge. "What is this place?"

"It's nothing more than ruins now," Jesse said, glancing down at the forgotten city, "but it used to be a powerful kingdom called Loydaya."

"So cool," she said. "Let's explore it."

Jesse grinned. "You got it."

Adeline searched for a way down. They were a long way from the bottom, but she was determined to find a pathway into the ruins. She took her time searching high and low through the thick vegetation, but there didn't seem to be a safe passageway. There were sections of broken stairways throughout the ruins, but nowhere nearby.

She turned to Jesse. "How can we get down there?"

"We will have to go this way," Jesse said, ripping out a wild shrub and throwing it aside.

Adeline peeked around Jesse, and her stomach bottomed out. The long section of boulders formed a makeshift pathway into the ruins, but they were covered with vines and shrubs that would make them difficult to descend. "Is it safe?"

"It's our only option," Jesse said.

"That doesn't answer my question."

"I'll go first."

Jesse lowered himself to the ground, shifting his sword as he scooted to the ledge. His long legs dangled over the edge before he dropped to the first rock. He landed upright with a thud and maneuvered around the plants until he could lower himself to the next boulder.

"Come on, Addie!"

Adeline gulped as she sat on the edge and climbed down the unusual stairway. Each step caused her heart to slam against her ribs, but she took her time.

The rocks came in different shapes with various obstacles, so she had to adjust to each one. She was on her hands and knees, sliding down the huge rocks that were double her size. Her knees were a bloody mess from the merciless stones, but she kept going until she was standing on solid ground.

"You did it!" Jesse cheered.

"Barely," Adeline said, her breathing rough.

Wiping her filthy hands on her shorts, Adeline straightened and took in the vast ruins. The tall structures were wrapped in thick vegetation, and the ancient roadways were overgrown with plants. Various trees and weeds ripped through the stone streets that had once been accessible, but that wouldn't keep her from exploring.

Adeline took off, stumbling through the undergrowth and rubble that stood in her way. She entered various entryways, finding them occupied by a whole lot of dirt and weeds. Each one was fascinating and only heightened her excitement.

Swiping the sweat from her forehead, Adeline grinned as she traveled toward an enormous structure that dominated the surrounding buildings in size and height.

Thorns picked at her knee-high socks as she burst through the thick vegetation before running up a flight of broken steps and disappearing through the wide doorway.

Light poured through the many cutouts along the walls, revealing an open space devoured by old, brittle vines. The potent smell of earth permeated the air as Adeline scanned the floor, gawking at the broken pieces of corroded metal half eaten by the hungry weeds. A fragment of a face stared up at her from the debris. It had likely once been a statue, but it was merely rubble now.

Adeline stepped outside, smiling as Jesse climbed the stone stairway to meet her. "This place is amazing!"

"I knew you'd like it." Jesse mounted the top step with sweat seeping through his white T-shirt.

"Do you know what turned this huge place into a wasteland?"

A smile broke across his face. "I sure do."

"Tell me."

Jesse squinted at the sunlight while surveying the area. "Corruption took over the heart of the leader of Loydaya, which caused this place to fall apart."

"What did the leader do?"

"He made a grave decision that cost him his life and the lives of his people."

"That's sad," Adeline said as a much-needed breeze swept past them. "I can only imagine how extraordinary this place once was."

"It was the most astounding and exciting kingdom around," Jesse said. "People from all over would come to see its beauty and trade goods. They would also visit to be a part of their memorable festivals and parties."

"You describe it as if you were there."

"That's because I was."

"There's no way you could've been here." Adeline stared at him. "This place is like a hundred years old."

"That's what you think," he said, directing a smile her way.

"You confuse me, Jesse."

"Nothing new." He playfully jabbed his elbow into her side.

A small laugh slipped out as Adeline went back to scouting out the old ruins. She was deciding where she wanted to explore next when Jesse spoke again.

"Would you like to see this place as it was?"

"Well, duh," she said, "but that isn't possible."

"Nothing is impossible, Addie," he said, his words laced in mystery. "You should know this by now. Take my hand."

Adeline stared at his rough palm. "Why?"

"Because it's the only way."

"The only way to what?"

"Just trust me," he said, inching his hand closer to her.

Adeline went silent, her mind running wild.

"You'll be glad you did. I promise."

Adeline sighed and grabbed his hand.

Chapter Thirty-One

A sudden gust of wind pounded against them, nearly knocking Adeline off balance. She tightened her grip and pressed herself against Jesse as the ruins changed before her eyes. Her breathing came to a halt as everything began to repair itself, as if they had pressed a rewind button on time.

The aggressive vines and weeds melted away, along with the fern moss and dirt that had conquered the ruins. Crumbling stones connected back to their original foundation while roadways became clear as trees and shrubs shrank into the ground, vanishing from sight. Even the massive wall surrounding the city was fully restored, with guard towers along the top.

But that wasn't all.

Farm animals appeared throughout the kingdom, followed by a strong stench that made Adeline gag. Horses and cows grazed in outdoor stalls connected to stone homes while chickens roamed free, pecking along the ground. They multiplied as the city morphed back into its original state.

Laughter and chatter buzzed around Adeline, and within seconds, hundreds of people emerged right in front of her.

Standing at the entrance of the temple, Adeline had the perfect view of the busy marketplace packed with the citizens of Loydaya. Elegant men and women of all ages crowded the popular streets, suddenly full of local vendors selling their goods under colorful booths. Delicate fabrics were on display, along with fresh fruits and bold spices that wafted through the air.

There were tons of interesting items for sale; however, it was the people that fascinated Adeline the most. Adorned in gold jewelry, the women strolled through the marketplace in white, silky toga dresses that brushed the ground. Their long, dark hair was perfectly styled atop their heads and heavy, black eyeliner exaggerated their brown eyes.

Some were accompanied by children dressed similarly, while others walked the market street alone. They carried themselves with poise and grace that didn't seem conceited, but confident in their own skin.

The men were no different.

Dark eyeliner circled their eyes as they strolled through the bustling market with chunky gold jewelry hanging from their ears and wrists. The only difference from the women was their long togas were not white but varied in color. Navy and red seemed to be the most popular shades, as far as Adeline could tell.

The powerful breeze ended abruptly, and before Adeline lay a fabulous kingdom, fully alive.

"Welcome to Loydaya!" Jesse said.

"This is incredible!" Adeline dropped his hand and spun in a circle. "Are we really back in the past?"

"We sure are."

The lively city was whirling with life as Adeline took it all in. Men and women with flawless brown skin mounted the steps and skirted by her and Jesse without a glance before disappearing into the temple behind them. Adeline stared at them as they passed, but no one looked her way.

Adeline's brows stitched together as she glanced down at her gym attire. Her black T-shirt and spandex shorts stood out amongst the stylish togas, and surely her pale skin would attract some attention.

So why did no one notice her?

A middle-aged gentleman hustling through the crowd caught Adeline's eye. Worry shadowed his sharp features as he bumped into his peers while running up the steps, heading straight toward her. She jumped out of his way only to get in the path of a young man exiting the temple.

Bracing for impact, Adeline stood frozen as the short male rushed forward as if he didn't see her.

But the collision never happened.

Heat whizzed through Adeline as the man walked through her like she was a phantom. The strange sensation quickly faded as he tore down the stairs, vanishing into the crowd.

"What just happened?" Adeline asked, wide-eyed.

"They can't see or feel us, Addie."

"Are we ghosts?"

"No, we're not ghosts." Jesse laughed. "We're in the past to observe it, not to change it."

"This is so weird."

Trumpets cut through the noise of the market, rattling Adeline. It didn't take her long to find where the loud noise was coming from. A little way ahead, a group of stout men marched in a square formation through the market.

These muscular men were obviously guards. Their brass plates, armored skirts, and weapons in hand were a dead giveaway. So were their heavily muscled arms covered in tattoos.

As they advanced, Adeline saw they were protecting someone, but she was too far away to see who it was. The trumpets continued to blow, grabbing the attention of all the citizens, who bowed as the soldiers passed by.

A small figure walked in the middle of the guards. It was a teenage boy clothed in a golden toga and an excessive amount of jewelry. His long black ponytail swayed as he moved with cruelty in his painted brown eyes, ignoring the people who were paying him honor.

"Who's that guy?" Adeline asked.

"His name is Cora," Jesse said. "He's the king of Loydaya."

Adeline's mouth dropped open. "The king?"

"Yep."

"He looks like he's my age!"

"That's because he is," Jesse said as the soldiers walked past the temple. "He just turned sixteen."

"Why would they let a teenager be their king?"

"They didn't have a choice. He was next in line," he said. "Cora was the prince and took the throne right after his father mysteriously died three months prior."

"What happened?"

"Cora wanted to be king more than anything and didn't want to wait, so he took matters into his own hands," he said. "One evening during dinner when no one was looking, Cora poisoned his father's drink. Later that night, his father became ill and died."

"That's horrible."

"It really was." His expression dimmed. "The entire kingdom was shocked by the king's unexpected death, but no one dared voice their concerns because they were afraid to become the next victim."

"What about the queen?" Adeline asked. "Did she try to stop him?"

Jesse frowned. "Cora executed his mother before she could do anything."

"What an evil person." Adeline slammed her hands on her hips. "I cannot believe he murdered his parents and got away with it!"

"No one ever gets away with evil, though they may think they do," Jesse said. "It'll eventually come back at them in full force."

"Well, it looks like he did because he's the king." Adeline beckoned to King Cora, who was still strolling through the crowd.

"He won't be the king for long."

"Good."

Folding her arms, Adeline sneered down at the wicked king as he walked the length of the road while the people of Loydaya cheered for him. Their shouts of praise roared throughout the marketplace as they threw daisies and other wildflowers at him. It seemed like genuine praise, but Adeline was convinced it was all an act to preserve their own lives.

King Cora mounted a flight of steps and turned to address the crowd. With his chin lifted high, he acted like he was a god and gave a slow, smooth wave. The citizens went berserk when he flaunted a wide smile and continued to climb the steps.

The celebration didn't die down until the young king and his guards entered a beautiful palace made of stone. And just like that, everyone dispersed and continued with their day like nothing had happened.

Chatter broke out once more, but Adeline was too focused on the palace to notice. Armed soldiers were posted next to the large doors that were wide open for anyone to enter.

"Can we go in there?" Adeline asked.

"Of course," Jesse said. "We can go wherever you want."

Adeline raced down the temple steps and entered the crowd. Warmth pulsed through her as she scurried through the people like they were holograms and scaled the steps two at a time.

She slowed when she reached the top, eyeing the guards' sharp spears.

The men were tall and stout, looking like statues as they stared straight ahead. They couldn't harm Adeline, but her heart still beat faster as she slipped by them and entered the palace.

The intimidating guards flew from her mind as she stood in awe, taking in the extravagant room with high ceilings held up by pillars. Sunlight poured through various openings, glistening against the fountains made of gold.

Soldiers stood along the walls, but King Cora was nowhere in sight. Instead, the room was full of busy servants rushing about.

A small group of young, dark-skinned women passed by Adeline in silky white togas, carrying large baskets of fresh vegetables and fruits. They hurried across the space, making sure they didn't run into their fellow servants who were on their hands and knees scrubbing the stone floor.

Adeline felt sorry for the hardworking women cleaning the endless floor as she stepped around them. They were stuck with the most grueling job she could see. She would much rather dust the golden statues like some of the other girls or feed the koi fish that occupied the fountains, but they likely didn't have a choice in what tasks they'd been assigned.

Tossing the servants from her thoughts, Adeline progressed into the room until she stood before a massive pillar. Detailed carvings of people, plants, and animals covered the stone from top to bottom like the artist was trying to tell a story.

Adeline stared at the rough indentions, mesmerized by the ancient art that had been chiseled by hand. "I wonder how long this took to complete."

"A long time," Jesse said, arriving at her side.

"They did a great job."

"They sure did."

Moving along, Adeline was about to make her way up the stairway that led to the second level, but something else snagged her interest. In the center of the back wall, was a set of double doors that nearly reached the ceiling. They were suspiciously large, and she had to check them out.

Adeline moved with haste, her sneakers tapping along the rocky floor. She was there in an instant, standing before the wooden doors that swallowed her whole. Ancient writing was carved into the thick wood in large, unrecognizable letters. She had never seen anything quite like it as she wondered what it said.

"A united kingdom will flourish like a bud in spring, but a nation divided shall surely fall," Jesse said, standing beside her.

"What?"

"That's what it says." He gestured to the double doors.

"Oh." Adeline scanned the unfamiliar markings once more. "I'm positive King Cora didn't come up with that."

"Those words were written by Loydaya's very first king; he was a man of great integrity and wisdom."

"Too bad he's no longer around."

Adeline took a few more moments to admire the exquisite door before reaching for the doorknob. Her hand went through it.

She shot Jesse a concerned look.

"We can walk through doors." Jesse snickered. "Follow me."

Jesse stepped through the door like a ghost, and Adeline hastily followed.

Chapter Thirty-Two

Loud, angry voices stopped Adeline in her tracks. She was on high alert as she skimmed the large throne room. Bright red banners inscribed in gold decorated the walls, and pleasant pools lined the wide walkway to a raised platform with a single golden chair. It was occupied by King Cora, and there were two older men arguing before him.

The king looked like a child compared to the white-haired gentleman in the navy robe and the middle-aged guard who argued with him. The guard's tattooed biceps were on display as he pointed an angry finger at the old man.

"What are they saying?" Adeline asked quietly.

Jesse placed both hands over Adeline's ears. When he removed them, Adeline could somehow understand the ancient language they spoke. She heard foreign words, but her mind translated them to her native tongue.

"Better?" Jesse asked.

"Much better." Adeline nodded. "Who are those men?"

"That's the general of the army," Jesse whispered, pointing to the man in the military uniform. "And the older one is the king's advisor."

The arguing continued, and King Cora sat impatiently, drumming his fingers along the arm of his chair. His lips flattened, and without warning, he exploded.

"That's not good enough!" King Cora slammed his fist into the armrest and stood.

Silence struck the room. The only thing Adeline could hear was the beating of her own heart as she kept her eyes on the general and advisor. Neither said a word for a long second until the old man gained the courage to face the king. His hunched back and deep wrinkles showed his age. He looked frail, but his voice was strong and prudent.

"Your Majesty, please consider what I am advising. We have plenty of gold and resources in our land. So, would it be wise to attack our allies just to take possession of something we do not need?"

"Do not tell me what we need!" King Cora shouted, spit spewing from his mouth.

Again, the room went stone silent as the advisor and general trembled. Though they were respected leaders in Loydaya, they clearly understood what the king was capable of.

Adeline was so engrossed with the drama that she flinched when someone walked through her from behind. Heat rushed through her like a hot flash and swiftly disappeared as a tall, black-haired man strutted toward the throne.

Moving with confidence and poise, the man adjusted the collar of his three-piece suit as his leather Oxfords echoed in the hushed room. Horror gripped Adeline when she noticed the thin gold streaks moving along the black fabric like a current.

The only person she had ever seen in that bizarre formal attire was Ralock, but how could it be him?

Just as the thought crossed her mind, the young man glanced back. Dark, lifeless eyes peered through her, confirming that it was indeed Ralock.

Staggering back, Adeline struggled to breathe. She didn't understand how he was there. When she first met him, in her time, he appeared to be in his late twenties, but there was no denying it was him.

Chills prickled down her skin as she watched Ralock walk leisurely toward the king like he owned the place.

"Greetings, King Cora," Ralock said in a smooth voice as he planted himself between the other men. "You look well, my friend."

"You as well, Ralock." King Cora took his seat once again.

"Thank you, Your Majesty." Ralock bowed slightly. "Please pardon my intrusion, but I wanted to stop by and see if you have thought about my proposition."

King Cora cut a disapproving look toward his advisor. His eyes were as dark as his skin, and the advisor stilled, shuddering even after King Cora shifted his attention over to Ralock.

"Funny you should say that, since my men were just advising me on what I should do," King Cora said, slouching in his chair. "The military is on our side, but there seems to be some hesitation with my advisor, who believes we should be content with what we already have."

A mocking laugh thundered from Ralock as he combed through his short black hair. He directed a devilish smile to the wise man, who hastily took a step back. "Loydaya will never reach its fullest potential without conquering all the nearby kingdoms."

"Our allies keep us prosperous," the aged advisor said, his voice steady though his hands shook. "We need to continue to uphold our relationships with them so we can peacefully trade goods and fight alongside them if war were to arise."

"Nonsense; they make this kingdom weak." Ralock scoffed and pivoted toward the teenage king. "Your Majesty, take my advice and destroy your allies and plunder their cities. It is the only way to gain full power."

"I agree," the general said. "We have the best military around and could easily take down our allies."

"But what about the thousands of women and children?" the advisor asked, directing his stern words to the military leader. "Are you planning on slaughtering them as well?"

"They will be considered collateral damage," Ralock answered for him with a condescending sneer. "Greatness always comes at a price."

"Very well." King Cora nodded in agreement. "We will attack Elebeck in the morning. After it is destroyed, we will attack the others."

"Your Majesty, please reconsider," the advisor said, pleading with folded hands. "Once Elebeck is attacked, the others will turn on us."

"Silence!" King Cora shouted.

The room went deathly still, and Adeline inched closer to Jesse, a troubling feeling expanding in her. She wasn't sure if it was from King Cora's shouting or the possibility that she may have just witnessed Loydaya's death sentence.

"Let it be that this time tomorrow, Elebeck will be nothing but ashes," King Cora said. "Assemble the soldiers; we attack at dawn."

"Yes, Your Majesty." The general pounded his fist against his breastplate. "Let us kill all in Elebeck and take what rightfully belongs to us."

King Cora dismissed the general with a swift wave, who then folded into a quick bow before turning to leave. His haughty face spread into a smirk as he marched past Adeline and Jesse, smelling of dirt and sweat.

The unpleasant odor lingered even after the general exited the throne room, but Adeline was too captivated with the frail old man to care. Worry consumed his tired eyes as he slowly bowed and slipped out of the room without saying a word.

"You are making a wise decision, King Cora," Ralock said in a velvet tongue. "I will assemble my warriors and meet you at Elebeck at dawn."

King Cora dipped his chin slightly. "I look forward to hearing about the victory."

Smirking, Ralock bowed before turning on his heels and heading back the way he came. Adeline hustled out of his way, her lungs refusing to draw air.

I'm in the past, she reminded herself. *He can't hurt me.*

The tense atmosphere lightened once Ralock left, allowing Adeline to breathe with ease. She spun to Jesse. "How is Ralock here?"

"He has been around for a long time, tricking and destroying whomever he can," Jesse said. "Sadly, King Cora was another one of his victims."

"But how is that possible? He looks like he's in his twenties."

"Ralock is not a human."

Her brows bunched. "Then what is he?"

"A very evil creature."

Adeline studied his face, hoping for clarification. All she got in return was a simple smile.

"Not everything will make sense to you, Addie."

"Obviously." Adeline huffed, looking back at King Cora.

The king was sulking on his throne, massaging his forehead in slow strokes, until a squeaky door hinge startled him. He sat up straight when a young servant entered from a side door with a platter full of grapes. His face hardened, and he shooed her off with a nasty tone, demanding her to leave him alone.

"King Cora has no idea that his decision is going to destroy Loydaya," Jesse said, his words somber. "If he had listened to his advisor, this kingdom wouldn't have fallen so tragically."

"What made him want to destroy his allies?"

"Pride and greed are a deadly combination. Nothing good comes out of them."

"I'll say."

Jesse slung an arm around her shoulders. "Let's get out of here."

Adeline gave King Cora a final glare before allowing Jesse to escort her out of the palace. The warm sun welcomed them as they paused at the top of the stairs, taking in the magnificent view of the city.

Adeline wanted to be thrilled that she was experiencing the past, but she couldn't shake the growing sadness. Her heart broke for the people; they had no idea that destruction was on the way.

"It's not fair," she said, staring at the lively kingdom. "Why do they have to die because of one person's decision?"

"Not all of them perish," he told her. "Some will escape, but only with their lives."

"When do they get attacked?"

"Right after they attack Elebeck," Jesse said, and offered his hand to her. "I'll show you."

Adeline didn't hesitate and grabbed Jesse's hand. His grip was warm and tight as a mighty wind whipped around them, the same as before.

But this time, everything moved forward at a greater speed.

People seemed to run in every direction before clearing the streets as darkness came. Bright stars flickered across the heavens before the sun rose high above the city.

Again, citizens flooded the streets and rapidly departed before the moon and stars took over the dark sky. When the bright sun appeared again, the strong wind stopped, and they were now in the heart of a huge celebration.

Live music electrified the crowded streets that were full of Loydayians. Chatter and merry laughter mingled together as they flooded the vendors offering tasty treats, beverages, and festive attire such as beads and colorful masks. There were even booths offering unique games and other activities.

"Wow!" Adeline squealed. "This is unreal!"

"You haven't seen anything yet."

A ripple of laughter rumbled out of Jesse as he pulled Adeline down the long flight of steps and into the crowd. Dropping his hand, Adeline broke into a smile as she did a slow turn. Heat zapped in her as citizens passed through her while she observed the epic party.

"Let's go this way," she said above the noise, motioning toward the row of colorful stands.

Jesse nodded, and off they went.

Breathing in the appetizing smells, Adeline couldn't calm her rapid heartbeats as she walked the long street with Jesse. There were multiple fruit and dessert stands lined with buyers, along with drink stations that were just as popular. Most of them offered fruit juices, but a few sold alcoholic beverages for those who wanted something stronger.

Walking onward, Adeline stared at the wild hog cooking over an open flame, but the rowdy stand next to it distracted her. She went to get a closer look and gagged when she saw what the vendor was selling.

Countless buyers stood in line to purchase a skewer stacked with roasted insects. Cicadas, beetles, and other creepy crawlies were selling like hot cakes.

Wrinkling her nose, Adeline couldn't stop her stomach from rolling, especially when a little girl bit into a cooked cockroach right in front of her. The girl beamed with joy as she skipped past Adeline and vanished into the crowd.

"It's not as bad as you think." Jesse stood next to her.

"I'll take your word for it," she said as she moved along.

The number of activities overwhelmed Adeline. Children laughed as they hopped along the stone road painted with symbols similar to hopscotch, while other kids threw darts at a board, hoping to win a prize. There were craft stations for those who wanted to make beaded jewelry. There was even a kissing booth lined with teenagers who wanted to pay for a quick smooch.

When they reached a drum circle, Adeline stopped to view the elegant men in robes pounding their palms against ancient drums. She swayed with the rhythm of the beat, enthralled by the large group of Loydayians dancing as one.

Laughter bubbled from Jesse as he joined in. He inserted himself into the crowd and danced along. He stomped, clapped, and spun on cue, as if he was familiar with the dance.

"Come join me, Addie!" Jesse signaled to her.

"I don't know how to do that."

"Who cares?" Jesse said, followed by deep laughter. "No one can see us."

Adeline giggled, but before she could decline, Jesse broke away from the crowd and pulled her onto the dance floor. He showed her the basic steps, but it was way outside of her skill set.

"Follow my lead," Jesse said over the drums.

Laughter spilled out of Adeline as Jesse took her by the hand and twirled her through the people unaware of their presence. He led her into quick steps and fast spins that matched the beat of the drums. He even lifted her above his head and spun her in the air like a ballerina before placing her back on her feet.

Adeline was having the time of her life, and all too soon, the drumming ended and the crowd dispersed for a quick break.

"That was fun," Adeline said, her throat raw from laughing so hard.

"Yeah, it was." Jesse used his shirt to wipe his sweaty face. "I love dancing."

"Me too."

Adeline glanced around the massive party, attempting to calm her hectic breathing. She had only seen a small section of it and could only imagine what else was there.

"What are they celebrating?" she asked.

"The fall of Elebeck," he said, his face turning into a frown. "Yesterday evening, they received word that their military destroyed the city, and shortly after the report, King Cora declared a day of celebration."

Guilt and disgust hit Adeline. She had blindly joined in with the celebration, having no idea they were rejoicing over the death of their once-allies.

"But what they don't know is that the report they got earlier was false and sent by Ralock, who betrayed them," Jesse said. "His warriors, along with Elebeck's military, killed all the Loydayian soldiers when they tried to attack the city. Now, all the allies have banned together with Ralock and are on their way to destroy this place."

"But I thought Ralock was King Cora's friend."

"Ralock does not have friends," Jesse said flatly. "He only cares about himself."

"But why would he want to destroy this place?"

"Because it was growing in power, and once a kingdom becomes powerful, he destroys it."

A cloud of gloom settled over Adeline as she looked into the beautiful faces of the Loydayians. They strolled past her with happy children bouncing at their sides, having no idea disaster was on the way.

"Follow me." Jesse turned from the crowd. "I don't want you to be down here when the fighting starts."

Adeline felt queasy at the thought, but she kept it at bay as she trailed behind Jesse, away from the rejoicing crowds and toward the towering wall. They scaled a long flight of steps until they reached the top, where the guard towers stood. Adeline looked one way and then the other, but she didn't see any soldiers patrolling.

They're probably all dead, she told herself, meeting Jesse at the railing.

Scanning every which way, Adeline took in the entire kingdom. It stretched farther than her eyes could see. She could still hear the festive music, blending with the people celebrating in the streets.

"This place is beautiful." Adeline sighed. "I hate that it gets destroyed."

"I do too," he said, grimacing.

A terrifying war cry pierced the air, followed by the sound of galloping horses.

Adeline whipped around, her heart hammering as she searched the open field sprinkled with purple wildflowers. She saw no one.

The booming noise continued to rise and the bordering forest quaked. The branches of the trees bounced with the uproar, and within seconds, an army spilled out of the tree line. Dressed in black armor, the warriors were mounted on armored steeds that showed no fear. They looked like a deadly plague riding at full speed toward the main entrance to the city.

"We need to help them!" Adeline cried.

"We can't, Addie," Jesse said with sorrow.

Adeline watched helplessly as the approaching army poured from the forest. They advanced with a black stallion leading the charge. One look at the lean frame and short black hair and she knew it was Ralock. He rode like a madman with his sword raised high, shouting obscenities as he crashed through the front gate that had been raised for the celebration.

All hell broke loose.

Bloodcurdling screams ripped from below as the army barreled through the oblivious city. Slamming her hands over her ears, Adeline sealed her eyes shut and screamed until she could no longer hear the torturous cries.

Tears dripped down her cheeks, and she jerked in surprise when a comforting hand touched her shoulder. She knew it was Jesse, but it took her a minute to find the courage to unplug her ears and open her eyes.

The tension drained from her posture when she saw they were back in the present. The horrendous cries of the Loydayians had been replaced with pleasant chirps from the songbirds that fluttered by.

Wiping her wet cheeks with shaky hands, Adeline studied the forgotten ruins. It was a jungle now, eaten alive by the wilderness.

An unexpected boom had Adeline leaping from the ground and latching onto Jesse like her life depended on it.

"It's just thunder," Jesse said, reassuring her.

"Sorry." She released his arm.

"It's okay." He smiled. "We better go before it rains."

Adeline still trembled as dark clouds swirled above her. The wind picked up, pulling pieces loose from her braid as another crack of thunder rumbled across the sky.

A big storm was rolling in. They were going to get soaked if they didn't act soon.

"Let's get moving," Jesse said.

Jesse brushed past Adeline to their only exit and carefully descended the broken steps that led to the bottom. It was the same flight of stairs they had climbed a few minutes prior, but it looked nothing like before. Plants and moss covered the chipped stones that had been beaten down by nature. It looked sketchy, but Adeline followed. Each step had her holding her breath, especially on the sections where the steps were missing altogether, but she made it to solid ground in one piece.

"This way, Addie," Jesse said over his shoulder. "The entrance we came from isn't far from here."

Lightning cracked across the blackening sky as Adeline took off after Jesse, pushing through the thick vegetation that tried to hold her back. She leaped over rocks and slapped away briars, stumbling through the bothersome weeds that attempted to trip her up.

Raindrops fell as Adeline raced behind Jesse.

Looking ahead, she glimpsed the staggered boulders that would take her to the tunnel they had entered from—

WHOOSH!

The dirt ground crumbled beneath her, causing her to tumble downward.

"JESSE!" she screamed as she plummeted into the dark unknown.

Chapter Thirty-Three

ADELINE LANDED HARD ON her back, pain shooting up her spine. The sharp sting turned into a throbbing sensation as she lay on the pile of dirt that broke her fall.

Twisting her head, Adeline tried to see where she was. Her sight was limited by the vast darkness. The only source of light came from the small hole she had fallen into, but the approaching storm barely put a dent in the suffocating blackness around her.

"Are you okay?" Jesse's face appeared as he leaned over the opening.

She couldn't see the alarm in his expression, but she certainly heard it in his voice. Seeing how tiny he was from her viewpoint didn't help her rising fear. If she had to guess, he was at least fifteen feet above her.

Adeline grunted, slowly propping herself up with her elbows. "I think so."

She struggled to her feet and brushed the filth from her gym clothes. Her body ached from the fall, but she was grateful none of her bones were broken.

"How do I get out of here?" she asked, using her hands to amplify her voice.

"Looks like you're in the secret tunnel system," he said, his voice bouncing along the walls. "If you follow the tunnel, it will bring you back to the surface where the old palace used to be."

"Great," Adeline grumbled. "Another tunnel."

A shiver charged across her shoulders as she hugged herself. The darkness was too thick to see anything that wasn't directly under the small opening of light.

"How do you expect me to do that?" she yelled up to him. "I can't see anything!"

"Use this." Jesse fumbled through his pocket and dropped something through the hole.

Adeline went toward the flat noise, swiping her palms along the cold floor until she found a small box. It rattled. She held it up to the weak light—a pack of matches.

"There should be old torches along the walls," Jesse said. "Light one of them."

Adeline forced her hands out and took a tiny step forward. She didn't feel anything, so she shuffled onward until her palms touched an icy, hard surface.

Withholding her breath, Adeline roamed her jerky fingers along the rough, uneven rocks. She quivered, her hands inching along the rough wall until she felt something metal.

She probed it bit by bit, her heart picking up speed with each touch. A thick cobweb latched onto her skin, and she leaped back. She slapped her hand against her spandex shorts until she couldn't feel the sticky web.

"The spiders are long gone," Jesse said. "No need to worry."

It took Adeline a full minute to regain her composure as she shook out her quivering hands. Once she calmed down, she patted the hard piece of metal again and felt along the chilly iron until she touched a solid piece of wood.

Finally.

Now that she knew where it was, she struck a match and moved the tiny flame toward the top of the torch. It ignited, casting a glowing orange light into the darkness.

"It worked!"

"Awesome," he said. "Now take it from the holder."

Adeline gripped the handle, cringing as the spider webs brushed her hand. She tugged upwards, but the stubborn torch stayed put. After another hard tug, it jolted from its resting place.

Adeline stumbled back but kept her balance with the flaming torch in hand. Doing a cautious turn, she shivered as the warm glow illuminated the tunnel. It looked like a pathway leading into a dungeon.

"What do I do now?" Adeline asked nervously.

"Follow the tunnel to the right," Jesse said from above. "I will meet you at the end."

Adeline lifted the torch. The passageway was too long to see where it led. She stiffened with terror as she stood in the middle of the space, glancing at the rough markings in the stone. It looked like it had been dug by hand.

"And one more thing before you go," Jesse said.

"What's that?"

"Don't be afraid."

Dread pooled in her stomach as flashbacks of the courage tunnel came to mind.

"Too late for that," she muttered.

"I'll see you soon."

Jesse disappeared from view, while Adeline stayed glued to the floor. Fear crept into her bones as the flickering flame cast eerie shadows along the lengthy passageway.

"Here we go again." She exhaled and took her first step.

Shivers raked across her exposed skin as she moved with caution, using the bright torch to light the way. She dodged the spider webs coating the ceiling and the mice that scurried past as she crept forward.

She hadn't gone far when a small doorway came into view. The tunnel continued onward, but Adeline stopped when she was about five paces from the opening.

A sudden coldness shuttled down her back as she tiptoed to the opening and stuck her torch inside. It was a small space, no bigger than a study room, but it was a complete mess.

Raising her torch high, Adeline stood in the doorway. The room looked like a tornado had whipped through it. A wooden table and chair were tipped over, and there were mounds of dust mixed with broken pottery and ancient remnants that littered the floor.

Wanting a better look, Adeline stepped inside, but stopped when her sneakers crunched on something hard.

A skeleton.

Adeline shot backward with a scream, fear firing down her spine.

The skeleton was sprawled on the floor with a sharp arrow lodged between its ribs. One arm stretched out like it had been trying to grab something right before it died. And since the room was a complete disaster, Adeline assumed whoever the person was had put up a fight before dying on the stone floor.

It probably happened when Ralock and their allies attacked Loydaya, she thought as her breathing leveled out. `

Her blood ran cold as she stepped over the dry bones and picked up a broken piece of pottery. It crumbled in her hand, as did everything else she touched.

After a few minutes of probing around, Adeline found nothing interesting and turned to leave. She lingered at the skeleton once more. It looked odd with its arm extended, pointing toward the corner of the room like a compass.

"What were you trying to reach?"

Adeline looked across the space, searching the floor for anything out of the ordinary.

One of the large stones that made up the floor was a little higher than the rest. It was the size of a textbook, and though it was only raised about a half an inch above the others, it looked suspicious.

Placing her torch in an empty holder, Adeline went to the elevated stone and dropped to her knees. The scrapes on her kneecaps stung as she prodded and probed the suspicious-looking rock that wobbled like a loose tooth.

Adeline dug her fingers between the cracks and wiggled the stone upward. Inch by inch, the rock lifted until it completely gave way. Dust billowed from the hole, making her cough as she placed the stone aside. Fanning the filth from the stale air, Adeline peered into the hole and gasped.

Inside the secret compartment was a big black book. It was the size of an encyclopedia and solid as Adeline plucked it out. It didn't crumble in her hand like the other artifacts and seemed to be in good condition as she blew the dust from the cover.

Adeline placed the book in front of her and gently wiped away the remaining grime. She took a second to admire the unique markings on the cover. It was the same foreign language she had seen on the palace door.

She slowly opened the book, expecting it to be an old manuscript she wouldn't be able to read, but as she flipped open the thick cover, her mouth fell open.

The middle pages had been cut out. Inside the gap was something wrapped in a delicate fabric with a note placed on top of it.

Adeline went straight for the unknown object, working cautiously to unwind the cloth. The fabric unraveled until an extravagant dagger dropped onto the open book.

The small knife was protected in a golden sheath and looked like it had been made for a king. Tiny emeralds, rubies, and diamonds decorated the protective case and the handle of the knife, along with strange letters embedded into the grip hilt.

Adeline picked up the majestic dagger with eager fingers; it was almost as weightless as a feather. The flawless jewels sparkled against the bright flame as she gripped the handle and pulled it from its cover.

"Whoa."

The pointed blade was completely transparent like glass and filled with tiny little specks of light swirling inside it. It reminded her of glitter, but she didn't have to move the weapon to make the sparkles move. They swirled on their own.

The sparkling flakes flowing within the sharp blade made Adeline's smile grow wider. As she continued thoroughly inspecting the twelve-inch dagger, she studied the pretty jewels that decorated the golden handle and the words inscribed on it. The letters were in a language she didn't understand. She assumed it was written in Loydayian.

Adeline set the knife on her lap and gently grabbed the folded note still resting in the secret book. She tried her best not to tear the delicate paper, but her trembling hands made it difficult. Once it was completely open, she frowned when she saw it was in the same language. She ran the pad of her finger along the unfamiliar letters when Henry Snow's voice whisked through her brain.

"I will read it to you."

Adeline flinched. *"You scared me, Henry!"*

"My apologies. I didn't mean to startle you."

"It's okay." Adeline blew out a long breath. *"What does the letter say?"*

Adeline held the note out and tried to follow along with Henry's pleasant accent.

"Happy birthday, my love. I know I said I was going to give this very special dagger to our son, but I have decided to give it to you instead. It saddens my heart, but I do not believe our foolish boy will ever be ready to possess such a valuable treasure. I am so grateful that I have you and cannot wait to see what good you'll do with such a priceless gift.

"As you already know, this weapon has been passed down in my family in secret for decades and is unlike any weapon ever created. It holds special powers that are unlike anything in this world. I know you'll use it wisely, for we do not want it to fall into the wrong hands.

"We need to continue to keep this secret between us. Do not show this dagger to anyone. I have a feeling there are traitors among us, so you must be careful and use wisdom as I know you will. Here's to many more birthdays with you. Love, your devoted husband."

"Who wrote this note?" she asked aloud, knowing Henry could hear her.

"King Cora's father."

Adeline cringed. She could still picture the teenage king sitting on the throne he stole from his father. His parents had clearly not trusted him, making her wonder if they knew he was planning on taking their lives. As Adeline thought about his unfortunate parents, she was reminded of the unknown remains in the room.

"Whose skeleton is that?" she asked, pointing to the skeleton.

"The queen."

"King Cora's mom," she whispered.

"Yes," Henry said. *"After Cora crowned himself king, he commanded the soldiers to kill her. They searched the palace and followed her into this tunnel. She tried her hardest to reach this secret room to retrieve the dagger...but she wasn't fast enough."*

"That's so sad." She stared at what was left of the queen. "Did she know her son killed her husband?"

"She was uncertain but had a feeling that he did."

"He was so wicked; I'm glad he's dead," Adeline said as she glimpsed at the dagger. "So he had no idea about this?"

"No one knew about it but his parents," he said. *"And when they died, their secret died with them."*

"Until now."

Dropping the note, Adeline retrieved the precious weapon and stood. It felt good in her hand as she did a swift swipe. She would keep it. There was no point in leaving it behind in a forgotten tunnel.

Adeline sheathed the blade and tucked it into the tight elastic band of her shorts. It was a little uncomfortable as it pressed against her stomach, but it was the only place for it.

Broken fragments crunched underneath Adeline as she moved across the room and grasped her burning torch. The firelight danced along the skeleton as she went to leave. She paused, a sudden sadness washing over her.

"I will take good care of it," Adeline said, as if the dead queen could hear her.

Adeline carefully avoided the bones and exited the room until she was back in the quiet tunnel. With an extra skip in her step, Adeline continued her journey to the surface.

Chapter Thirty-Four

The tunnel didn't seem as scary now that Adeline had a new weapon. All she could think about was showing it to Jesse as she ventured onward, rubbing her thumb along the little jewels in the handle.

Adeline traveled through the dingy passageway, skidding to a stop when she thought she heard something. She listened to what sounded like a howling windstorm.

"What is that?"

A blast of wind whipped down the long tunnel, plowing straight into her. It distorted her vision and nearly extinguished her torch, but it vanished as fast as it had appeared.

It was probably just a draft of wind coming from the exit.

Adeline lifted her torch, but she didn't see an end in sight. Shrugging, she resumed, but stopped cold in her tracks when someone stepped into view. The person stood a little farther than the light could reach, but she could see a silhouette of a tall, slim man.

At first, Adeline assumed it was Jesse, but the suffocating fear spreading through her veins told her she was wrong. She stopped breathing as the man stepped forward just enough for her to see his leather Oxfords and black three-piece suit.

Ralock.

Adeline stood rigid, her arm clenched at her side as she stared at him.

"Well, well, well. What do we have here?"

Ralock's jeering tone pinned her in place, and all she could do was watch him take a step toward her.

Crossing his arms, Ralock kept his distance, sizing her up with a wicked smile that drained the color from her face. He was undoubtedly handsome, but the evil spewing from him made her physically sick.

"Where are your little friends, Bigsby?" Ralock asked with mockery. "Surely, they wouldn't have left you all alone down here."

Adeline's breathing turned ragged. She had gained courage from the mysterious sapphire she obtained in the courage tunnel, but it was nowhere near the amount of courage she needed to face someone as vile and dangerous as Ralock.

"Ralock is here!" Adeline yelled internally.

"Stay calm, Addie," Jesse said. *"I will be there soon."*

"How far away are you?"

"Fifteen minutes."

"Fifteen minutes!" Panic ripped at her throat. *"I'll be dead before then!"*

"No, you won't."

She teared up. *"What do I do until you get here?"*

"Make him leave."

"Are you crazy! He will kill me!"

"No, he won't," Jesse said, his voice sharp. *"Use the dagger you found until I get there."*

"I don't know how to use it!"

"What do you have there?" Ralock cocked his head to the side.

Adeline stepped away from him, chills traveling through her. He was talking about the weapon pressed against her stomach; she was sure of it. Her black T-shirt was tucked behind it, giving him a full view of the golden handle embedded with jewels.

"I'll make a deal with you," Ralock said, adjusting his sleeve cuffs. "Give me that dagger, and I will leave you alone."

Adeline took another step back, considering his offer. She desperately wanted to keep the fascinating weapon, but she would hand it over to save her life.

"Do not give it to him!" Jesse said.

"But he said he will leave if I do."

"He's lying. If you give it to him, he will kill you with it."

She blinked back the rush of emotion that filled her eyes. *"I don't want to die."*

"You're not going to die, Addie," Jesse said firmly. *"You have a very mighty weapon in your hand."*

Tears slid down her face as she looked at Ralock. She didn't have an ounce of confidence in her ability to protect herself, but she trusted Jesse and wouldn't hand over her only line of defense.

"Do we have a deal?" Ralock asked.

"No." Her voice shook as their eyes connected.

"Fine." Ralock's face darkened as he straightened to his full height. "I guess I'll just have to take it from you."

Sucking in a sharp breath, Adeline was rooted in place as Ralock raised his hand to his mouth. He blew on his empty palm, and a thick puff of black smoke emitted from his hand. It hung in the air like a cloud, shifting and forming until it turned into a horde of bats.

The suffocating smell of sulfur filled the tunnel as the bats let out a piercing squeal and raced toward Adeline.

"Bring me that dagger!" Ralock yelled.

Adeline dashed down the tunnel, her heart pounding as hard as her sneakers as she tried to outrun the bats, but they were gaining on her.

"Turn around and kill them!" Jesse said.

"I can't!" Adeline cried aloud.

"You must! You cannot outrun them!"

Adeline forced herself to do the unthinkable.

Stopping dead in her tracks, she faced the bats swarming toward her.

Her breaths came in short, tight gasps as she tugged the dagger from its sheath and pointed it at the enemy. Her ears rang with their horrifying cries as she tightened her grip, silently praying she wouldn't die.

When the first wave of them was close enough, Adeline swung with all her strength. The dagger sliced through the leading bats like paper, dropping them to the ground, but the remaining bats showed no fear and kept coming.

Wave after wave, Adeline cut through the horde. It was almost too easy. Before she knew it, she was surrounded by a pool of dead, bloody bats.

They lingered there for a moment before vanishing like they were never there. It was like the combat simulator Jesse had shown her in the training area.

Adeline breathed heavily, glancing at the glass blade that should have been coated in blood. Instead, it shimmered in the bright torchlight. There was no logical explanation for how the dagger was suddenly clean or how she had killed that many bats.

Looking ahead, Adeline caught sight of Ralock's expression and could tell he was just as shocked as she was. She hoped to use it to her advantage.

"Go away!" Her voice rose, high and trembling.

Ralock's angry exterior snapped back into place as he cracked his knuckles. "I'm just getting warmed up, Bigsby."

"Stab your dagger into the wall on your left." Jesse's voice slid into Adeline's mind without warning. *"It used to be a doorway."*

At a quick glance, Adeline could see the slight change in color. The darker rocks made an arch like a door. It was barely noticeable. Someone had worked hard to conceal the entryway that was now solid rock.

"There's no way my knife can break into that," Adeline said.

"Do it now!"

Jesse's command alarmed her, magnifying the fear she was already drowning in.

Adeline reared back her arm and drove the tip of the dagger straight into the wall. The discolored rocks crumbled, creating a dust cloud that swept through the tunnel.

Coughing profusely, Adeline climbed over the rubble and ducked through the small opening until she could stand. Her lungs burned as she sucked in the cold, stale air, searching for a way out.

She raised her torch as the dust started to settle and saw what appeared to be a long row of rectangular boxes. They looked like containers made of stone.

Goosebumps pebbled her skin as more of the dust cleared.

They weren't containers; they were coffins.

The long, dusty caskets were adorned with old trinkets, jewelry, and vases cracked with age and coated in a thick layer of dust.

She searched the room, but her torch could only illuminate so far. Desperate to find an exit, she bolted forward. She ran past the rows of stone coffins, searching high and low for a doorway.

Fatigue prickled her sides as she raced on, but the end came sooner than anticipated. She slammed to a sudden stop, nearly colliding with a large stone fountain connected to the back wall.

It was filled with an unknown liquid. At first glance, Adeline thought it was water, but the strong smell told her it was oil.

An idea came to her mind, and she lowered the tip of her torch to the oil.

SWISH!

The oil caught fire, and Adeline launched backward. Heat blasted against her as the hungry flames entered the connecting channels and spread throughout the room like a wildfire.

The fire scorched the tiny canals that hugged every wall in the room. Flames illuminated the tomb, allowing Adeline to have a clear view of the layout.

There was only one way out, and it was the way she had come in.

"It's a dead end!" she said aloud, panicking.

"Stand your ground until I get there."

"What?" Another round of tears emerged. "Ralock will murder me!"

"Trust me." Jesse's voice was calm. *"Strike him with your dagger, and he will leave."*

Panic spread through Adeline as she blinked away salty tears. She couldn't fathom getting close enough to Ralock to hit him.

Footsteps echoed in the outside passageway.

Adeline tossed her torch into the pool of fire and ducked behind a nearby coffin. Every breath was a battle as she peeked around the casket, focusing on the battered doorway.

A moment later, she saw movement.

Ralock crawled through the opening. A thick, evil presence swept through the room so heavily it nearly choked Adeline where she hid.

Once inside, Ralock brushed the dirt from his expensive suit and skimmed the ancient grave.

"The royal Loydaya tomb," Ralock said in a loud voice. "How appropriate."

Wicked laughter ricocheted inside the tomb as Ralock reached behind his head and retrieved a longsword from the holster on his back. The solid black blade was jagged like a chainsaw and looked like death.

"No one will ever find your body here."

Smashing a hand over her mouth, Adeline ducked out of sight and pressed her back against the cold stone coffin. Spider webs tickled her neck and dust caked her sneakers, but she dared not move.

"Come out, come out, wherever you are." Ralock stepped forward, smashing a pot with his sword.

Adeline jolted against the casket. *"He's going to find me, Jesse!"*

"You must attack him, Addie," Jesse said. *"You can do this!"*

"Have you seen his sword?"

"Have you seen yours?"

The twelve-inch dagger shimmered against the flames as Adeline took a quick look at the glass blade she was still holding. It was sharp and stronger than she expected, but all she could focus on was its size. It wasn't even close to being as long as the black, rugged sword in Ralock's hand. He would chop off her head before she even had time to swing the dagger.

She tried to think of a solution that didn't require her to get close to Ralock as he made a ruckus. He continued to destroy the place, shattering old relics atop the coffins and kicking decorative vases that got in his way. His heavy footsteps grew louder, and Adeline stiffened as another artifact crashed nearby.

She was running out of time.

Maybe she could sneak around Ralock and sprint through the tunnel until she reached Jesse. Lucky for her, there were over fifty coffins to conceal her. That gave her the assurance she could successfully escape without him noticing.

Adeline stayed crouched and quietly eased forward until she was at the corner of the stone coffin. She peeked around it and caught sight of Ralock. He was on the far side of the room, disrupting another sarcophagus.

"You can't hide from me, Bigsby!" Ralock slashed his blade into a frail bowl.

Adeline shuddered as broken stoneware littered the floor. Ralock turned his back to her, and she darted behind the next coffin and pressed herself against it.

It took a long moment before she found the courage to peer over the dusty coffin. When she did, she spotted Ralock glancing behind another grave. He wasn't looking her way, so she rushed to the next stone coffin.

Again and again, Adeline used the large graves to hide her as she rushed toward the only exit. Her thighs ached from squatting, but she refused to stand and kept moving in the opposite direction.

When she was halfway across the room, she glanced behind her before rushing to the next hiding spot.

CRACK!

Adeline slammed to a halt, staring down at the broken urn under her foot. Thick spider webs had concealed it from her view.

Ralock lifted his head and shot a dark look in her direction. His cruel mouth curled into a smile as he strutted toward the noise.

Fear cemented Adeline's feet to the floor. She'd been caught.

Without thinking, Adeline scrambled from her hiding spot and dashed toward the front of the tomb in a full sprint.

"There you are!"

Adeline's long legs propelled her forward. Short, quick breaths filled her lungs while her heartbeat thumped in her temples. She was going to make it.

Before she reached the entryway, Jesse roared in her mind.

"Take cover!"

Adeline dove behind a nearby coffin as a small object whizzed by her ear. She thought Ralock had thrown an old trinket at her, but she went white when she realized it wasn't a trinket at all. It was a knife.

She panted, eyes widening with horror as Ralock wound back his arm.

Adeline ducked, and another knife zoomed past her and shattered the vase on the coffin above her. Shards of pottery skittered down, scraping and stabbing her vulnerable skin. Covering her head, Adeline attempted to protect her face from the sharp pieces of stoneware that continued to explode around her like bombs.

The barrage of knives kept coming, but the large stone grave she was tucked behind took the hits for her. After what felt like an eternity...they stopped.

Maybe he's out of knives.

Adeline looked toward the exit. It was close. She could make it; she was certain of it.

But as soon as she stood, she realized she made a terrible mistake.

WHACK!

A piercing cry ripped from Adeline as a knife buried itself into her thigh. She stumbled back into a stone coffin, knocking a delicate bowl of jewelry to the ground.

Using the large stone grave to support herself, Adeline screamed again when she glanced down at her leg. The knife was lodged deep into her thigh, right above her knee. Warm, crimson liquid poured over her kneecap, soaking into her knee-high socks.

Adeline fought through the pain as lightheadedness and nausea hit her like a sudden blow, and she had to look away.

"Help me," Adeline whispered, tears streaming down her cheeks.

"I'm almost there," Jesse said, his voice loud and clear.

Tears clogged her throat as she leaned against the grave, trying her best not to put any pressure on her injured leg, but it didn't help with the searing pain pulsing up and down her limb.

"My apologies, Bigsby," Ralock said. "I was aiming for your heart, not your leg."

Adeline lifted her head and was met with Ralock's cocky smile. He was enjoying her pain, and he wanted her to see it.

"Don't worry. I'll end your misery."

Wickedness spewed from his arrogant laughter as he strode toward her, scraping the tip of his blade along the floor. The sound was worse than nails on a chalkboard, and Adeline went still.

Her mind begged for her to escape, but she couldn't move. Her leg was useless.

"He's coming toward me!"

"Fight him, Addie!"

Tears dashed down Adeline's cheeks as Ralock advanced. He was close to closing the gap between them, and she had to make a choice. She could either give up and die by his sword or she could fight back.

In those long, drawn-out seconds, Adeline felt something come over her. She wasn't sure if it was adrenaline kicking in or her will to live, but a surge of anger ignited in her. She would not die without putting up a fight.

The pain in her leg subsided as she darted her hand along the top of the coffin until her fingers latched onto a sharp piece of pottery. It dug into her skin as she aimed it at Ralock. She threw it but missed him by a mile.

Ralock paused, resting his sword against his shoulder. "I expected you to have better aim than that, Bigsby."

"Leave me alone!" Adeline launched a heavy cup at his head.

Ralock laughed, ducking out of the way. The golden cup flew by him and clanged loudly against the floor.

Adeline grabbed another relic within reach and hurled it at him. It hit him square in the chest, but the heavy artifact might as well have been a pebble.

"You've got spirit, girl; I'll give you that." Ralock started toward her again. "But you might as well give up."

Adeline held her dagger out in front of her with both hands, her heart beating hard. The glass blade was pointed at Ralock, who stopped when he was almost an arm's length away.

His stony gaze traveled to her injury before snapping up to her tear-stained face. Terror raced through her as she looked up at him. His features were sharp and striking, but his eyes were empty and lifeless.

"I'm going to take that dagger from you." Ralock broke eye contact and focused on the sharp weapon aimed at him. "Do you want to do this the easy way, or the hard way?"

Adeline shook violently. His calm, calculated voice sent shivers up her spine. Ralock wasn't close enough, but she swung her dagger anyway, hoping it would scare him off.

Ralock laughed through his nose, mocking her as the blade caught nothing but air. "Very well," he said, unhurried. "I see you want to do this the hard way."

In one quick motion, Ralock drew back his sword and lunged forward. Adeline froze, her eyes locked on the tip of his sword.

Before it penetrated her heart, her dagger swung itself.

Sparks erupted as the weapons collided. Ralock staggered back like he had been shoved, but Adeline kept her balance against the stone coffin. Her brows drew together as she glanced at her weapon.

She didn't have time to comprehend what was happening. Ralock pounced back, his lethal sword coming at her once more. Again, Adeline's dagger surged forward just in time to block his blow, like her weapon was alive and had a mind of its own.

Snarling, Ralock quickly regained his balance. He coiled to strike again, but Adeline slashed down the front of his suit. The glass blade burned through the fabric like it was made of acid. The clothing shriveled away, revealing a nasty cut across his chest.

A horrid snarl tore from Ralock's throat as he sprang back, patting his ruined shirt like he was putting out a flame. He pulled his hand away, blood dripping from his fingertips. The veins in his neck bulged and his nostrils flared as his black eyes bore into Adeline.

"Now you've done it," Ralock growled through clenched teeth.

Ralock charged at her and swung his sword. The black blade made a straight path for her neck, and time slowed. She could hear the pounding of her heart and the low snarl coming from Ralock.

Before the sharp edge cut into her, she ducked.

The deadly sword swished over her head. She sprung back up and swung her dagger upward at Ralock's unprotected face.

Ralock shrieked as the glass blade tore through his cheek just below his left eye. A flash of electricity zipped through the four-inch gash, followed by a steady stream of blood.

Dropping his weapon, Ralock covered his face. He screamed into his hands, twisting in anguish as his blood dripped to the floor.

"This isn't over, Bigsby!"

With one swipe of his hand, Ralock disappeared.

The oppressive atmosphere vanished with Ralock, and Adeline was able to breathe again. She fell back against the coffin, a hand on her chest. She had no idea how he left, but she didn't care.

She was alive.

A sharp jolt spiked up her leg, reminding her of the knife still in her thigh. She felt light-headed; a wave of dizziness passed over her as she stared at the bloody mess.

Adeline dropped her weapon as the agonizing pain increased. A hot sweat broke out across her body as she lay flat on the cold stone coffin, staring up at the ceiling. She shivered and felt feverish as the soft flames flickered in the quiet tomb. She needed help and needed it quickly.

"Where are you, Jesse?"

There was no response.

Tears leaked from the corner of her eyes as she lay there, drowning in agony.

"Please, Jesse," she whimpered. "I need your help."

Adeline closed her eyes and slowly gave into the overwhelming fatigue inching along every fiber in her body. She could feel herself drifting away.

"I'm here!" a familiar voice thundered inside the burial chamber, jolting her out of her stupor.

Relief settled over Adeline as Jesse rushed to her side.

She fought to hold back further tears. "I thought you were going to leave me here."

"Never," Jesse said. "I'm going to get you out of here."

Jesse quickly evaluated her injury and went to work like a trained doctor. Grabbing the hem of his T-shirt, he ripped off a long strip and gently wrapped it around the knife. Though he was gentle, Adeline squirmed in pain, biting down hard on her bottom lip to keep herself from screaming.

Once the knife was stabilized, Jesse grabbed her abandoned dagger and tucked it into his belt.

"This will do until we get to the cabin."

A strange fogginess came over Adeline as she nodded. She felt herself beginning to slacken into the coffin. Jesse's voice became muffled, and she no longer had the strength to keep her eyes open.

She didn't flinch when Jesse lifted her, cradling her against his chest. Her body jarred with every step, intensifying the horrific ache in her thigh, but his warmth and woody cologne brought her comfort as she slipped into oblivion.

Chapter Thirty-Five

A soft breeze whistled through the garden as gentle raindrops fell against Adeline's cheeks. She felt like she was floating as she wrestled to open her eyes. She blinked up at the heavy clouds, the light rain distorting her vision.

"We're almost there," Jesse said, his expression tense as he focused ahead.

"Why are you carrying me?"

His face softened. "You're injured."

"Injured?"

Then she saw the bloody knife sticking out of her thigh. The blood drained from her face as a bomb of pain burst through her leg. She remembered everything all at once and felt a rush of nausea charge through her.

"I'm going to be sick."

Jesse rushed through the cherry blossoms and onto the back porch of the cabin where Godfrey and Henry Snow were waiting for them. A clean towel was spread along the wooden planks for her, along with a comfy pillow they retrieved from the patio furniture. There wasn't a first-aid kit in sight, but Adeline was in too much agony to care.

Jesse did his best not to jostle Adeline's leg while placing her on the towel. It didn't matter how careful he was, the pain intensified.

"You are going to be okay, my dear." Henry crouched at Adeline's side.

"It hurts." A sob swelled in her throat.

"I know," Henry said, wiping her tears away, "but it will be over soon."

Adeline sealed her eyes shut, tears spilling over as Godfrey quietly inspected the wound. His touch was gentle, but Adeline tried to pull away as he unwound the bloody cloth.

"I need you to be brave, Addie." Godfrey gripped the knife. "This is going to hurt."

Godfrey jerked the knife out before Adeline could brace herself.

A scream ripped from her throat as an explosion of pain tore through her thigh. She wheezed for air while her leg pulsed violently. The pain was way worse than the snake bites had been.

"Do I need stitches?" she asked, her chest heaving while tears slowed.

"No. I have a better idea," Godfrey said.

"What?" Adeline sat up, her stomach churning as blood oozed from the open gash. "It looks really deep."

Godfrey didn't answer her; he turned to Jesse and extended his hand. "The dagger, please."

Jesse reached into his belt loop and placed the exquisite weapon in his father's open palm.

"You brought it," Adeline said in relief.

"Of course I did." Jesse smiled.

Adeline cracked a tiny smile while wiping her puffy eyes. She wasn't sure why Godfrey wanted it, but she was glad Jesse hadn't left it behind.

"This isn't just a weapon." Godfrey rotated the unique dagger. "It holds a lot of power that has not been revealed to you yet."

Turning it to the side, Godfrey lowered the transparent blade to her thigh. As it inched toward her open wound, panic struck.

She tensed. "What are you doing?"

"Just watch."

The sparkling blade hovered above the gash, heating her skin like it was made of fire.

"This will sting a little," Godfrey said, "but I need you to trust me."

Godfrey didn't wait for a reply and firmly pressed the blade against the bloody wound.

Adeline yelped at the startling shock that traveled through her leg like an electrical current. The strange sensation pulsed through her veins. Within seconds, the discomfort faded, along with the pain.

Godfrey removed the dagger, and Adeline's jaw dropped. The gash on her thigh was completely healed.

"How did you do that?" Adeline touched the two-inch scar that no longer hurt.

"I told you this dagger was powerful," Godfrey said, a smile breaking through.

"It can heal wounds?"

"Yes. That's one of the many things it can do."

"This is unbelievable," she said, smearing the blood away from the fresh scar on her thigh.

"It's quite remarkable." Godfrey brought the dagger close to his face so he could inspect the golden handle. "But wait until I show you what's on it."

Godfrey scanned the foreign letters on the precious handle. He took his time gliding his thick finger along the grooves of the ancient language like he was searching for something.

After a quick moment, Godfrey's face brightened. He pressed his index finger to one of the engraved markings and moved the dagger to Adeline.

"Whose name is that?" His smile matched the happiness in his tone.

Squinting, Adeline brought the blade closer to her. The letters Godfrey was pointing to were small, and it took a second for her eyes to adjust to the tiny carvings.

She gasped when she saw the name.

Adeline Bigsby was perfectly engraved between the foreign words.

"No way." Adeline snatched the dagger from Godfrey and marveled at her name engraved into the handle made of gold.

"How?" She looked at Godfrey for answers. "My name wasn't on there when I first found it."

"The dagger needed some time to test you."

"What?" she asked, her brows furrowed.

"Whenever someone new holds this dagger, it will immediately test the heart to see if the person can handle its power," Godfrey said. "If that person is found worthy, the dagger will engrave their name on the handle and will help them all the days of their life."

Adeline blinked at him before looking back at her name on the dagger. "So, let me get this straight; this knife liked me and magically carved my name into it?"

"Yes."

"That makes no sense," she said. "A dagger can't know my name."

"It clearly does." Godfrey released a hearty laugh.

Henry and Jesse laughed along with him while Adeline stared at the dagger in disbelief. Her name was there; she couldn't deny it as she ran her fingers along the letters.

"What would have happened if Ralock had found it?" Adeline asked.

"Since Ralock is a rotten being, the dagger wouldn't have let him use its power and would have acted like a normal weapon," Godfrey said.

"Then why did he want it so bad?"

"So he could destroy it. He knows how powerful it is and planned on destroying it before it could be used against him."

"This is so wild." Adeline ran her dirty thumb across the inscribed letters of her name again. It looked as if it had been there for centuries, which only added to her confusion. The entire situation was so beyond reason she didn't know what to think. "What else can this dagger do?"

"That is for you to find out," Godfrey said, his lips lifting into a smile. "There will be many more adventures that will give you the opportunity to discover the power that lies within this weapon."

Grinning to herself, Adeline gave the shiny weapon a slow turn, hypnotized by its beauty. She was clueless about what Godfrey was telling her, but one thing she knew was that the ancient dagger was special. From the priceless jewels embedded on the handle to the tiny flickers of light dancing within the glass blade, everything about the dagger was perfect.

And it was hers.

"I changed my mind, Jesse." Adeline looked at him. "I want you to teach me how to fight."

Jesse lit up with a smile. "I thought you would never ask."

Thank You For Reading!

If you enjoyed this story, please consider leaving a quick review. Whether it's on Amazon, Goodreads, or wherever you picked up this book, your honest review makes a big difference. It doesn't have to be long—just a few words can help other readers discover this book. Thank you for being a part of this adventure. I can't wait to share more with you soon! If you'd like to be the first to hear about new releases and special offers, visit www.elizabethmowery.com to sign up for my newsletter.

Acknowledgements

First of all, I want to give a massive thanks to God for giving me the idea of creating this book. I had no idea I could write until You suggested it to me. You not only gave me the pieces I needed to string this story together, but the perseverance to push through until it was finished. I couldn't have done this without You.

My amazing husband, Adam. This book would've never been published if it wasn't for your encouragement. You were the first person who told me I needed to share this story with the world, and I'm so glad I listened! Thank you for loving me so well during this wild journey. It has meant the world to me.

Mom and Dad—thank you so much for all your love and support! Y'all were with me throughout this whole process, encouraging me every step of the way. I'm so grateful for you both and couldn't have asked for better parents.

A huge thank you to all my editors, beta readers, and friends. Your suggestions, honesty, and skills helped make my first book shine. Each of you played a special role in crafting this book, and I cannot express how thankful I am. Y'all are truly the best!

Lastly, I want to give a special thanks to you, dear reader. I had you in mind since the very beginning, and I'm so thrilled that you took the time to read this book. I hope this story has sparked your curiosity because this is just the beginning. There's way more to come, so stay tuned!

About the Author

Elizabeth Mowery is an avid writer who has a passion for creating exciting stories that capture the imagination of her readers. She lives in the foothills of North Carolina, where she loves spending time with her family and friends. When she isn't writing, she can be found enjoying the simple pleasures in life—a hot cup of coffee, the fresh air of the outdoors, and a good book. Connect with her at www.elizabethmowery.com